THE FRENCH WINEMAKER'S DAUGHTER

ALSO BY LORETTA ELLSWORTH

The Shrouding Woman

In Search of Mockingbird

In a Heartbeat

Unforgettable

Stars Over Clear Lake

Tangle-Knot

THE FRENCH WINEMAKER'S DAUGHTER

A Novel

LORETTA ELLSWORTH

HARPER

NEW YORK • LONDON • TORONTO • SYDNEY

HARPER

This is a work of fiction. Names, characters, places, and incidents are products of the author's imagination or are used fictitiously and are not to be construed as real. Any resemblance to actual events, locales, organizations, or persons, living or dead, is entirely coincidental.

HarperCollins books may be purchased for educational, business, or sales promotional use. For information, please email the Special Markets Department at SPsales@harpercollins.com.

FIRST EDITION

Designed by Jamie Lynn Kerner

Library of Congress Cataloging-in-Publication Data

Names: Ellsworth, Loretta, author.
Title: The French winemaker's daughter : a novel / Loretta Ellsworth.
Description: First U.S. edition. | New York : Harper Paperbacks, 2024.
Identifiers: LCCN 2023058552 | ISBN 9780063371811 (trade paperback) | ISBN 9780063371828 (ebook)
Subjects: GSAFD: Novels.
Classification: LCC PS3605.L476 F73 2024 | DDC 813/.6--dc23/eng/20240315
LC record available at https://lccn.loc.gov/2023058552

ISBN 978-0-06-337181-1 (pbk.)

24 25 26 27 28 LBC 5 4 3 2 1

To my sister Monica, whose beautiful poetry unveils a sensitive soul.

THE FRENCH WINEMAKER'S DAUGHTER

CHAPTER ONE

THE ARMOIRE

MARTINE

JUNE 1942

BURGUNDY REGION NEAR ALBERTINE, FRANCE

MARTINE PEEKED AROUND A TALL VINE AT HER PAPA when she heard her name being called. A gentle breeze fluttered her dress and tickled her bare feet as her knees sunk into the loamy soil. She had been pretending to make wine, crushing a few green grapes between her fingers in an old bowl and adding her spit, then twirling it with a stick until it was a liquid consistency. She'd been so focused on her task that she'd forgotten about the time.

"Martine!" Papa cupped his hands around his mouth. The little girl was hesitant to show herself; she had sneaked away from her schoolwork again, and she wasn't supposed to be playing alone in the vineyard.

Papa called again. He sounded irritated, frantic, even. Martine finally stood up from between the rows of vines and brushed the dirt from the back of her dress before she ran to him.

"Je suis désolée, Papa," she began, worried that she had annoyed him and that he would be furious, but instead he grabbed her and hugged her tightly.

"Are you angry?" she asked. He often scolded her for disobeying, although he rarely punished her. Making her attend school was punishment enough; Madame Reza was horrible.

The letters did not make meanings she could figure out. And she'd heard Madame Reza tell Papa the same.

"Her mother, Élisabeth, died shortly after she was born, no?" she'd heard Madame Reza tell Papa. "Perhaps deficiencies resulted from the stress of her birth."

Papa had defended her. "Martine can tell the difference in grape skins that even adult men cannot taste—when it is prone to fungus, and when it is peak ripeness. She can select the best grapes and tell just how much water the plants need. She notices the invisible; the air and light among the vines; and she can nurture a sickly plant back to health when others give it up as a lost cause. No one who is stupid could do such things."

"These are not things taught in a classroom," Madame had replied.

"But they are important things," Papa had said.

Every inch of the vineyard was mapped upon her heart: the low stone wall that enclosed their property from the dirt road, the pale stone house they lived in, and behind it the dark cellar where Papa made the wine. And beyond that, a barn that held their horse, Cédric, who pulled the carts to and from the rows of vines that dipped over sloping hills. Bordering the vineyard was a small forest of oak and beech trees. This was her entire world, and she loved it here.

But Martine could not read, and soon she would turn eight. Madame Reza tapped the back of her hands with a long stick each time she made a mistake, calling her lazy. One day Martine sneaked inside after lessons and took the stick, which she broke in two and threw in a ditch. Madame Reza accused her of stealing her stick, but she couldn't prove it. Even so, she hated Martine even more after that and called her an imbecile.

Now, Martine hugged Papa, feeling bad for disobeying him once again. "I'm sorry," she repeated.

"I love you, Martine." Papa's voice was thick and hoarse. This was different than Papa's usual hugs. It was one that hinted at sadness, tight and clutching, as if he was afraid to let go.

"What's wrong, Papa?"

He looked around, as if she'd been followed, then ushered her into the house. "We have little time," he said as he opened the armoire in her bedroom. "You must get inside and stay hidden."

Martine was small for her age, and she fit easily inside the white armoire decorated with pink swirls that Papa had painted for her.

Papa gathered loose clothing around her, covering her whole body, as if it was a game of hide-and-seek.

She giggled. "Are we playing cache-cache, Papa? But you already know where I am!"

Papa cupped her chin in his hand. "I'm afraid this is not a game, ma choue. But you can think of it as one if you'd like. Just promise me you will do as I ask and not open this door until it is safe."

She could hear the fear in his voice. She took Papa's hand in her own small one. "I am afraid, Papa. Don't leave me here."

Papa flashed a worried smile. He had some gray hairs in his black, stubby beard that she hadn't noticed before. "Remember how you say that you can find your way in the vineyard, even when it is dark? How you are never worried because you know where you are? Pretend you are hiding in the vineyard."

"But this is different. It doesn't smell like grapes. It smells musty in here. And where is Annabella? I can't stay in here without her."

Papa hurried to get her small stuffed rabbit, which could fit into her pocket if she pushed it down enough. "Now you have Annabella. Hug your little rabbit. Everything will be fine."

There was pounding on the door. Papa gasped.

"Is it the Germans?" Martine asked. She had heard Papa speak to Damien, who oversaw the vineyard, when he thought she was asleep. He had said that the Germans were taking Jews away. She wondered where they were taking them.

Ignoring her, Papa handed her a bottle of wine and fastened a piece of paper onto her dress, even as the pounding continued.

"Do not remove this until you are told," he said. "And let no one drink the wine. It is your birthright. It will provide for you until I get back."

"Where are you going, Papa?"

"To speak to the authorities. It is a misunderstanding, one I will clear up," he said in response. Then he hugged her and warned her, "Don't make a sound, no matter what you hear."

"I won't, Papa," Martine promised. She clutched her stuffed rabbit, whose black nose was crooked and hung loose, and whose color had faded to a dirty white. "How long must I stay here?"

"Until you no longer hear the Germans. Then you must find Damien and have him read the note.

"Be brave, ma choue." That was the last thing Papa said as he closed the door, before the shouting and screaming followed, much of which Martine did not understand.

She only understood Papa, who insisted he was innocent, who asked for mercy, and who wailed like a child when they took him away. If only she could reach out and grab Papa's hand, she would hold tight and wouldn't let him go. Tears streamed down her face as his screams grew fainter.

But she remained frozen like Papa had told her until she heard the click of boots on the wooden floor. The sound was coming closer.

The Germans! She did as Papa had said and made herself smaller under the pile of clothing. The armoire door opened. She held her breath.

A glove swiped through the clothing, inches from her head. She put one hand on her mouth, afraid she would scream. Her other hand clutched her rabbit. She smelled liquor, but not the sweet aroma of wine. She felt nauseated and swallowed back vomit rising in her throat. The door closed again, and she heard them leave, but still she stayed frozen, unsure how long she was supposed to remain there.

The slit of light that shone through a crack grew fainter. Martine's stomach growled. There had been no time to put a biscuit in the pocket of her dress. She hadn't moved for such a long time, and her legs ached, and her back was stiff. Her father's cries still hung in the air even after all this time, and she sniffed back a loud sob.

Finally, when the light turned soft and pale, Martine and her faded rabbit sneaked out of the armoire. It was almost night, and every shadow on the wall peeked at her. Martine remembered to put on her shoes before she ran outside into the quiet darkness, still hearing her father's screams in her mind.

There was no sign of Papa or the soldiers. Where was Damien, who oversaw the vineyards? He came every morning when the church bells rang and was often here late, after the sun had disappeared. There were no set hours when you made wine. It was a way of life, one that Papa promised would always be there for Martine.

Now she held on to the wine bottle and her rabbit and searched for Damien.

She sought solace among the vines, row after row of tall plants that dipped with the rolling landscape. She was short enough that she couldn't be seen, even in the light of a full moon. The grape clusters were greenish nubs awaiting the transformation into sweet fruit. The vineyard smelled of wet earth, as it had rained that morning, and still had a faint odor of copper from the sulfate Papa had put on the vines. Papa said only Martine could detect the subtle odors that permeated the plants and attributed it to the fact that his wife had gone into sudden labor and gave birth to their only child right in the middle of the vineyard.

Perhaps Damien was in the cellar checking on the barrels. She loved the huge casks, each carved with intricate swirls and the only letter Martine knew by heart: *V*, for her last name, Viner.

She inched her way there, the heavy wine bottle braced against her chest while her other hand clutched the ear of her stuffed animal. The cellar was behind the house, and as she got closer, she heard voices. Damien! She rushed toward the door, then hesitated. The people inside were not speaking French.

The Germans were in her father's cellar! The sound was growing louder. They were coming out.

Martine turned, almost tripping as the wine bottle slipped from her hand onto the soft ground in front of the cellar door. She stopped, trying to decide if she had time to rescue it, then let out a small cry as she left the bottle behind and headed toward the forest.

CHAPTER TWO

HÔTEL DROUOT

CHARLOTTE

1990

PARIS, FRANCE

"YOU KNOW ABOUT WINE, YES?" HENRI ASKED AS HE ACCELerated the black Renault convertible down a crowded Parisian street.

I hugged the armrest. I'd never get used to the aggressive way Frenchmen drove. "My grandfather owned a small vineyard in California. I spent summers there when I was young."

"And he passed this knowledge to you?"

"He taught me a bit about growing grapes, although I was always disappointed when he gave me a sip of his wine. It didn't taste a bit like red Kool-Aid."

Henri didn't laugh, but he did flash a smile. "You are too funny, Charlotte. You do like the taste now, though?"

"Yes, I'm doing my best to replace that Kool-Aid habit of my youth," I assured him. Images of my grandfather flashed through my mind: his gravelly voice from smoking cigars all his life, his leathery face, wrinkled and tanned from so much time in the hot sun. But mostly I remembered him bent over the vines, the tender care and attention he gave to each plant, and the way he always looked at the sky, assessing every cloud that passed overhead as a possible threat, or a welcome rainfall. He drank one glass of wine daily, as he said it gave strength to those who tasted it but ruined those who drank without restraint. He was a man of few words, but when he spoke, it was always something worth listening to.

Grandpa had died two years ago, and now his vineyard was up for sale, a fact I didn't want to dwell on. "I'm not much of a wine expert, Henri. My grandfather didn't make wine. He just grew the grapes. I won't be of much use at an auction."

The truth was that Grandpa's vineyard was always facing one disaster after another, making it a constant battle to survive: heat, lack of rain, smoke from wildfires. Dad hated the uncertainty and rejected the family business to become an airline pilot. I heard that it had caused a lot of friction in the family, and that's why I usually spent my summers there alone with my grandparents, riding on Grandpa's lap on his miniature John Deere tractor that turned up the weeds between the rows of vines, helping him fix the wooden post of a broken trellis, and bringing Grandma's homemade lemonade out to him on hot, windy days.

"You will enjoy it nevertheless," Henri said, and reached over to squeeze my hand.

I squeezed back. We'd been dating for a year, our schedules permitting.

I fluffed my red hair, hoping to add some Cindy Crawford vibe, and tugged at the striped blazer covering my low-cut white shirt. I wasn't sure how to dress for an auction and had settled for a black miniskirt and boots that I'd bought in New York at Saks Fifth Avenue. As Coco Chanel said, "Dress shabbily and they remember the dress; dress impeccably and they remember the woman." French women knew fashion, and I wasn't about to be outdone.

I was tired, coming off an all-nighter, piloting a Boeing 777 to Paris while threading our way through a dangerous storm front over the middle of the ocean. But our relationship was worth the extra under-eye concealer.

Henri wore a polo shirt and khaki pants, his leather jacket draped across the back seat. He hated wearing suits unless necessary because his job as a manager at Versace required it during the week. I had to admit he looked good in whatever he wore. His dark hair was slicked back, and his lean frame fit perfectly behind the wheel as he turned the corner onto Rue Drouot. He wore Cartier sunglasses, and he seemed to have a permanent smirk on his face. I never knew if he was actually smiling or not.

I'd met Henri at the Musée Rodin in Paris. We were both alone, standing in front of the sculpture *The Kiss*. I'd felt awkward staring at the entwined naked man and woman but couldn't bring myself to leave.

"I feel like I'm intruding on them," I'd said, thinking he didn't understand English and wouldn't get the joke.

"I do not think they would even notice," he replied, and I'd burst out laughing.

We'd spent the rest of the hour touring the museum together, although neither of us considered ourselves art buffs, and by the time we'd entered the sculpture garden, we were sharing kisses next to the pink viburnum. Then I'd invited him to coffee. He'd kissed me again when we parted, and he'd winked as he said, "Perhaps next time we mimic the sculpture? The one where we met?"

I'd felt my face flush, but replied, "Let's hope not. They ended up stabbed to death."

Henri had nodded. "Perhaps just dinner then?"

We'd clicked after that. There was passion between us. I'd felt it that first moment, and every time we met since then.

Of course, the dinners were few and far between due to our busy schedules. I'd followed in my father's footsteps and was a pilot for a commercial airline. I had recently made captain, something

I'd worked hard to attain, even when the men in flight school joked it was a waste to have a good-looking woman in the cockpit. But I preferred the challenge of understanding aerodynamics and flight navigation.

No two flights were ever the same. Unfortunately, women pilots were still rare. More than a few men pilots had called me a "token" behind my back. And forming any kind of a romantic relationship was difficult.

Henri didn't demand much from me other than the few times he wanted to show me off to his influential friends. I'd liked it that way at first.

But now . . . things had changed. My biological clock was ticking. I wanted more out of a relationship.

Henri lit up a cigarette, and I reached over and pulled it from his lips.

"Must you, Charlotte?" he complained.

"I just spent the last ten hours on a flying ashtray. I've inhaled enough smoke today." If I had one objection to France, it was that everyone smoked here.

"You are lucky I like independent women," Henri said.

I flashed him a flirty grin. "I'll take that as a compliment."

Henri parked in a public garage and led us down a sidewalk past drab, old buildings. Stamp and coin shops intermingled with art sellers and apartment complexes. At the corner the Hôtel Drouot occupied a square block.

Henri's annoyance with me was short-lived. He couldn't hide his enthusiasm as we approached his favorite haunt. "It is the oldest auction house in Paris," Henri said. "It was torn down and rebuilt fourteen years ago."

The glass-and-steel modern building stood out among the centuries-old structures that lined the rest of the street. But once inside the place, it was as if it still held the years in its many rooms; so many that I was reminded of a corn maze I had once gotten lost in.

Disarray. That was the only word to describe it. We passed a roomful of people bidding on rugs, as a crowd pushed into a different room filled with clothing, and another room was filled with guns and rifles of all kinds.

"You never know what you may find here," he said, his voice rising. "Just last month a man bought a red leather Moroccan portfolio for $500. Inside was the original bill of sale for the Louisiana Purchase."

"Can you imagine misplacing that? It's never where you last left it, is it?"

"What?" Henri looked confused.

"Never mind," I said. "What room are we looking for? And how many rooms *are* there? How will we ever find our way out?"

"Do not inquiet yourself."

"You mean *don't worry*?" I smiled at his misuse of English. He prided himself on his fluency.

He scowled at my correction. "*Don't worry*. There are sixteen rooms. Salle eight is this way."

We ascended an escalator to the next floor. Room eight was a hall full of boxes and paintings and statues, a hodgepodge of items that reminded me of a garage sale more than an auction house, aside from the plush red upholstered walls. An older man with hair the color of linen approached us and shook Henri's hand. He was dressed in an elegant navy suit and white tie.

"Bonjour." He took my hand and kissed it. "Is this your American pilot?"

Henri nodded. "Charlotte Montgomery, meet Max Barcombe. He is my old friend who turned me into a wine collector."

So, Henri had mentioned me to his friend? That was a good sign.

"You are not a serious collector until you have a wine cellar," Max said, shaking a finger at Henri.

"Perhaps someday I will," Henri said.

"But you live in an apartment," I said, with a laugh. "Might be hard to put a wine cellar on the eighth floor."

Henri tipped his head. "Actually, there are solutions to incorporating such a thing in an apartment," he said. "But first I must find noteworthy bottles."

"Today promises some rare finds," Max said, pointing at a dusty box in the corner. "That crate of wine was supposedly owned by a Nazi officer. They were known for confiscating the finest wines in France during the war."

"Let us hope you're right," Henri said. "And let us hope I can get it for a reasonable price. I am prepared to go up to five hundred francs, but I prefer not to go higher . . ."

"I do not think you will find a great deal of resistance," Max said. He motioned me to a front-row chair. "Have a seat, mademoiselle. You will find this very entertaining, I promise."

"Do you think it's true about the Nazi officer?" I asked Henri as I sat down. "How would a box of fine wine end up here after all these years?"

"There are many ways. It could have been kept in someone's cellar and discovered only recently. Or a cave. They are still discovering treasures that were hidden by the Nazis: expensive paintings, fine jewelry. Then again, it could be cheap wine that is worthless. It's what you Americans call a *crapshoot*. That is the excitement of it. But Max keeps me informed, and he says this is worth bidding on."

"If the Nazis stole things, shouldn't they have been returned to the owners?"

Henri shook his head. "Many of them were Jews, and they . . . never returned. I know it may sound a bit, what is the word? Bizarre?"

"How about immoral?"

"No. Not at all. If it is a famous work of art whose provenance can be determined, then that should be returned. But wine is impossible to trace. Besides, how would you begin to return so many items?"

I didn't know, but it seemed unethical to bid on items that had been stolen from people who were then murdered. What about their descendants? How did one rationalize selling off people's belongings simply because it was difficult to locate them? And Henri was perfectly okay with this?

The clientele of the auction house was a cross section of Paris society. Some were well dressed, others in jeans and T-shirts. Henri pointed out dealers and other collectors he knew, and the Savoyards, the red collars, men who were in charge of transporting and handling the merchandise. Each one wore a black suit with a red collar, on which their official number was embroidered in gold thread.

At the front of the room stood the commissaire-priseur, or auctioneer. Beside him another man read aloud a description of each item as it was being sold. And behind that man was the cashier.

"Be careful not to raise your hand," Henri whispered. "Or you will end up paying for an overpriced lamp."

Of course, that's when my nose started to itch. I kept my hands folded in my lap, however, not wanting to risk an embarrassing misunderstanding. The bidding was in French, and I didn't understand it all, but I enjoyed watching as each item, from posters to framed mirrors, made its way to the front. And I felt the excitement of the bidding, of seeing how a simple gesture signified a bid, such as a pointed finger, or a nod of the head. And the bidding went so fast. If a person hesitated, he was often too late, and the bidding was closed.

Finally, a dusty wooden crate was placed on a table at the front.

"This box of wine was found in an old manor house of a German aristocrat in Munich. The box contains five bottles of wine that have been authenticated to have come from the Burgundy region. The bidding will start at trois cents francs."

Three hundred. The auctioneer looked at Henri, apparently knowing he was interested. Henri gave a slight nod and raised two fingers.

"We have a bid of three hundred. Three hundred and fifty. There is a bid of three hundred fifty."

I glanced behind. The bidder was a dark-haired man, a dealer Henri had pointed out before. How high would he go?

"Four hundred," the auctioneer said, and Henri raised his hand higher this time.

"Four hundred and fifty." He nodded toward the back and confirmed the bid. "We have four hundred fifty.

"Cinq cents," the auctioneer said. Instantly, Henri raised his hand again. Five hundred. That was Henri's limit.

"Six hundred."

I held my breath. "Six hundred," he said again, and I glanced back but the man was shaking his head no.

"Five hundred is the bid. How about five fifty? Who will bid five hundred and fifty?"

I put a hand over my thrumming heart, the same way I felt every time the plane touched the ground after a flight.

"We have a bid of five hundred and fifty."

Henri pushed my hand down. "You just overbid me," he hissed.

I gasped. "I did?"

"Five hundred and seventy-five," Henri yelled.

The auctioneer nodded.

"Any more bids?"

I didn't dare move.

"Going once, twice, sold for five hundred seventy-five francs."

I screamed, "You got it!"

Henri stiffened, and I felt a flush of embarrassment at my outburst.

"Sorry," I said, speaking more quietly. "I didn't mean to bid."

Henri patted my arm. "I know. It worked out in the end. Please try not to act like a novice."

"I am a novice. This was my first auction."

"And you are refreshingly unexperienced."

That definitely wasn't a compliment. "It's just that I was so nervous for you, Henri."

Henri smiled, this time a genuine one. "I thought if I was quick to bid, he would see that I was committed to any price and give up. And thanks to your additional bid, it appears that it worked. Although I did go over my limit."

Henri hadn't seen the man shake his head. His additional bid was unnecessary, but I wasn't about to tell him.

He stood up. "Let us go get our prize."

Max met us at the side of the room. He smiled at me. "What did you think?"

"That was so exciting!"

"As I noticed. Your reaction was so . . . lively. But that, my dear, is how you should feel at an auction."

He shook Henri's hand. "Well done, Henri."

Henri reached for my hand. "I owe it to my American good-luck charm, Charlotte. I think your grandfather would approve, no?"

I doubted my grandfather would approve of buying the wine of victims who died during the war.

"He'd certainly be intrigued by Hôtel Drouot," I said, avoiding the question.

"Not as intrigued as I am with you," he said, and winked at me.

CHAPTER THREE

L'AMOUR

MAX HELPED HENRI DETERMINE THAT TWO OF THE FIVE bottles were worth something, both of them from 1948 and from the distinguished estate of Maison Drouhin.

"You could sell them today for fifteen thousand francs for both. Not a bad profit for one day. But the other bottles are from 1940. They are supposedly from small villages, so not as noteworthy," Max concluded. "And that year did not produce any special vintages for obvious reasons."

"Why not?" I asked.

Max stared at me for a moment. "The Germans invaded France that year."

I tapped my forehead, feeling like a stupid American. "Of course. So, what will you do with these other bottles?" I asked Henri.

He smiled. "We will drink them. Let us go back to your flat and celebrate."

I returned the smile. "That makes the whole day worth it."

We stopped on the way for baguettes and cheese before reaching the tiny two-bedroom apartment I'd bought a couple of years ago that I shared with two flight attendants. Neither of my roommates was there, which wasn't unusual as I often didn't see them for months at a time due to our conflicting schedules.

I carried the food and Henri lugged the box of wine as we

walked up the stairway. Like most old apartment buildings in Paris, there was no elevator. But I loved the Baroque architecture and the smell of old wood, and the steps forced me to pack lightly on trips.

I'd only been to Henri's apartment once, not far from his office in La Défense, to the west of Paris. Henri was a cadre, a manager for the French retailer Versace. He often compared his position in the company to me making captain status as a pilot, an elite title that carried social prestige to a group of highly qualified people. Men, mostly.

His apartment was modern and had an elevator. And it was more stylish, which Henri said was not his doing, but that of an interior decorator he'd hired. Now I worried whether I'd remembered to clean up before I went out today.

"Maybe we should have gone to your place," I said as we stood in front of the door.

"We can't," he said.

"Why not?"

"It is being painted," he said. "And the aroma is nauseating."

"Well, then perhaps you should spend the night?" As I got out my key, Henri leaned over and kissed me.

"What a wonderful idea! Thank you for bringing good luck today."

"My pleasure," I said, opening the door.

We'd had sex many times, always rushed affairs that we managed to fit into our schedules, usually accompanied by one or the other of us rushing out the door half-dressed. But neither of us had ever slept over.

He placed the box on the floor near the counter that separated the kitchen from the living area. He brought out one of the bottles and blew on it, scattering dust particles into the air.

"Let us drink this one."

"Is it safe to drink wine that old?" I asked, trying to forget where it had come from, that it represented the wine of murdered families.

"It won't hurt us, but it may have lost much of its taste. Old wines tend to be ephemeral, losing flavor within an hour. So, we must drink the whole bottle quickly."

"I think we can accomplish that. Just make sure it's not one of the expensive bottles," I said, as I brought out two wineglasses.

The apartment was sparsely furnished, the kitchen even more so. But I had a dozen wineglasses in the cupboard, even if there were only six plates.

"I couldn't imagine drinking a thirteen-hundred-dollar bottle of wine." I'd estimated the fifteen thousand francs converted roughly into twenty-six hundred US dollars for both bottles. I tore off pieces of baguette and set out a plate with grapes and cheese. "How long will you keep them?"

"I am a collector. I will not sell until they go up significantly in price. If they're worth twenty-six hundred dollars now, think of how much they will be worth in fifteen years."

"But won't they be even less drinkable by then?"

Henri laughed. "It depends on the vintage. But even if they aren't fit to drink, they're still worth collecting for their age and name."

"That's a good investment. But if Max knew these were good wines, why didn't he bid on them himself?"

"He is trying to refrain from buying more bottles for the time being. He already has more than four thousand bottles in his cellar, and he says he has no more room. He is also a friend, so he alerts me when there is something worth bidding on."

"And how many bottles do you have?"

"Only about fifty, but today's finds are the most notable."

He opened the bottle slowly, then nodded as he sniffed the bouquet. "It has a hint of fruit and oak. I think it will taste very good." He poured two glasses. "Let us drink to our luck today. And to l'amour."

My heart fluttered. I had reservations about Henri. But he was so damn sexy. I accepted the glass and swirled it around, then sniffed, taking in the earthy aroma. "It's a lighter red than I thought it would be," I said. "My grandfather's grapes produced Cabernet, which was much darker." I remembered its woodsy flavor and bold scent.

He stepped closer. "This is a Burgundy wine. They are known for being made from smaller properties, perhaps a family farm, where there is one grape variety and one vineyard."

I could feel his breath on my face, see the intensity of his gaze.

He continued. "Burgundy wines are more sensual than other wines. We are drinking Pinot Noir, which are the silkiest, most seductive wines on the planet."

Henri took a sip of his wine. He closed his eyes, and a twist of his mouth belied his enjoyment. "Not bad at all for a fifty-year-old bottle of wine."

I followed suit. It tasted bitter to me. Maybe this was what stolen wine was supposed to taste like? But I smiled at him and took another sip.

"Cabernet is bolder," he added, running a hand through my hair, his fingers lingering at the ends. "Like you, Charlotte. You have beautiful eyes, you know."

My scalp tingled. He tucked a strand of hair behind my ear and trailed his finger down my neck. I closed my eyes, feeling my body lean into his.

"How am I bold?"

"You were the only one screaming at an auction," he said, chuckling.

"I was just caught up in the moment," I said. "Henri, I know how you always complain about me being too forward."

"And too punctual," he added.

"I admit to being both of those." I had to be, as a pilot. Surely Henri understood that. "Will this complicate our relationship?"

"This?"

"Yes. This. Sleeping over."

"This is not a complication. And don't be so American. Now is not the time for conversation, Charlotte. It will ruin the mood," he said, as he nibbled my earlobe.

I let out a soft moan. He kissed me, and I tasted the wine on his lips, and the desire they promised. Still, I couldn't let go of my train of thought.

"Henri," I said—and then stopped. Why ruin the moment? A serious talk could come later, after we'd made love. "I could drink this all night as long as it was on your lips."

"And so we shall," he announced, and I touched his smooth cheek while holding my wine in the other hand, feeling a shiver as he trailed his hand down my side.

We finished the entire bottle plus most of the next one, when Henri ventured his hand under my shirt.

I almost spilled my wine as his fingers explored my breast. He took my wineglass from me and set it on the counter. Then put down his wineglass as both his hands began to massage my breasts.

I started to pull off my shirt, but he pushed my arms down. "No. I will do it."

His fingers lingered on each piece of clothing as he undressed me slowly, as if it was a striptease, caressing every inch of my body as he did so. He unzipped my skirt and pulled it down, his hands drifting over my panties, which I desperately wanted to kick off. This man knew what he was doing.

"I'm in good hands," I said, trying to make a joke, but my voice was husky.

Finally, he slipped off my panties and took a step back. "Every time I see you undressed, I think of when I first met you at the statue of *The Kiss*," he said. "And every time you are just as beautiful as I thought you would be that first moment."

"Merci." The thought of him undressing me in his mind at the museum thrilled me. It's not that I didn't think I had a good body. But it was nice to hear someone else say it out loud, to be appreciated as a woman when I spent so much time trying to hide my femininity at work.

He led me to the bedroom. I helped him undress, folding his clothes and neatly placing them on a chair, my arousal intensifying with each article of clothing. But neither of us was in a hurry tonight.

He kissed my neck and moved his mouth gently down my body, pausing at my breasts.

"This isn't your first rodeo," I said breathily.

"I am not certain what you mean," he responded in a low whisper between kisses.

"Never mind," I said, my voice thick. I let the sensation consume me as we slid into bed, where I knew I'd have the best sex of my life.

HENRI GOT UP AT SIX THE NEXT MORNING, DRESSING MORE quickly than he'd undressed the night before.

I threw on a shirt and sweats as he used the bathroom, running my fingers through my tangled hair.

The door opened, and he walked right past me.

"Henri," I called after him.

"I am late. I promise to ring you before you fly out," he said, barely meeting my eyes. He stopped in the kitchen. We had finished two of the three bottles, drinking thirstily followed by sex, barely talking at all. He handed me the one left unopened, then picked up the box. "You can have that one," he said, hurrying out the door.

"Don't you want me to save it for us to drink together?" I asked, hoping he'd say yes. We'd both fallen asleep soon after making love last night; perhaps we'd drunk too much wine? Henri had turned away from me on the bed. There were no reaches for each other during the night, no intermingling of legs or limbs, no resting my head on his chest or whispered promises. No intimate discussions. And yet, the scent of him still lingered on me, and my body ached for him.

"Not necessary," he replied, as he left. "Enjoy it on your own. Bon voyage," he called over his shoulder.

He took the steps two at a time. He hadn't even kissed me before he left.

Pilots look for warning signs. Had his rushing off without a kiss been such a sign? He was often self-absorbed, but let's face it: not even a kiss in the morning was crossing into jerk territory.

Was what we had just lust, and nothing more?

I PICKED UP THE DUSTY BOTTLE AS A FLUSH OF ANGER WASHED over me, wishing I could drink it all right then, but of course, I was a professional and I had a flight to Chicago in six hours. Then I thought of smashing it on the floor. But on second thought, how much satisfaction would it give me to have to clean up broken glass and spilled wine?

"Thank you for flying Charlotte airlines, Henri," I said, feeling the sting of sudden tears. I pushed them away with my finger.

I set the bottle on the counter. Rubbing my hand across the label, my fingers came away smudged in dirt, which made sense, the bottle having been in a cellar for so long.

Using a damp tea towel, I moistened the label to remove the dirt. I noticed the writing on the label boasted a large black curlicue *V* followed by smaller letters: *i-n-e-r*. Viner. The French word for wine was *vin*. Perhaps this was meant to be a nondescript label. Not an impressive one, according to Max. Not even worthy of an amateur's collection, even though Henri liked to pass himself off as a connoisseur. The label started peeling up on one corner, perhaps due to age, or perhaps from getting it wet. But what did it matter? It was a cheap, old bottle of wine. I picked at it, loosening the edges.

As I pulled off the label, I realized there was another one underneath. I carefully removed the top piece and noticed dark writing on the back of it. The faded writing was in French, and a bit damp now from the soaking. A few of the words were familiar: *vigneron*, a grower of grapes; *enfant,* which was *child*. And a scribbly signature at the bottom that I couldn't quite make out, except that the first name started with a *Z* and the last name was Viner. The same name as the label. Perhaps the vintner had written this note? Why write a note no one would see? And why would someone cover up a label with another one?

I got out my French dictionary and found the word *revenir*, which meant *return*. It had something to do with returning a child, but I couldn't make sense of it.

> *Cette bouteille de vin* [bottle of wine] *est l'héritage de mon enfant* [child]. *C'est un millésime rare et le produit de sa vente fournira à ma fille* [daughter] *jusqu'à ce que je puisse revenir* [return?]. *C'est une véritable artisane, vigneronne dans l'âme.*

The smaller white label had a different name—Château Roberge, written in an antique script above a faded yellow crown and blue coat of arms with curves and stars, and a date of 1920 beneath it. The label looked fancy. I patted it dry with a towel.

"What *is* this?"

I thought of calling Henri to ask about it but stopped myself from picking up the phone. He wouldn't be at the office yet. And why should I tell him? He'd given me the bottle, after all. Told me to drink it myself, as if he had no interest in sharing it with me.

Still, as I examined the bottle a chill worked its way up my back. I felt that this was more than just a regular bottle of wine. I remembered how Max had said that the Nazis stole the best wine, and how some had built fake walls in their cellars to conceal their best bottles. The fake front could be concealing a better bottle of wine underneath.

But why? To hide it from the Nazis? But what about the handwritten note underneath? It was a mystery, and the only person I wanted to share it with was Henri.

Had I been too hard on him? He *was* in a rush this morning. And I knew he never liked to be late to the office.

Despite the clenched feeling in my gut, I decided to give him the benefit of the doubt. If he called me before my flight, then I would tell him about the bottle with the mysterious note under the label.

If he didn't call? Well, I'd find someone else to translate the note.

CHAPTER FOUR

MADAME MOREAU

MARTINE

1942

MARTINE CREPT BEHIND THE LINE OF CYPRESS TREES bordering the vineyard. She didn't approach the village for fear of seeing the German soldiers. She knew it was late, perhaps after eight o'clock, which was curfew, and businesses would be closed. She was cold, hungry, and afraid. She slowly made her way to the nearest neighbor, who lived a kilometer away, stopping often to hide as the menacing trees made monstrous shadows that frightened her.

She almost wet herself, but the thought of wee running down her leg made her stop, pull down her underwear, and squat before the stream that she'd been suppressing all those hours in the armoire flowed out.

She remembered, before the Germans arrived, how a parade of people, animals, and wagons congested the roads as they fled their small village. Martine had waved at them, watching the bikes, pushcarts, and wheelbarrows full of luggage that crowded the streets, thinking it was a merry sight to go on such a trip, not realizing how dangerous it was to stay.

Papa said he would never leave. Wine was more important during the war, and his French countrymen needed it to keep up their morale. Why would they take him away from such important work?

When she finally knocked on Madame Moreau's door, she could barely stand. But when the door opened, she was not invited inside. She knew Madame didn't like her, that whenever she addressed Martine, there was an ugly look on her face as though she had tasted something bitter. She had heard Madame refer to her as "dirty Jew" once, and she had never forgotten it. Papa had said Madame was coldhearted. Her scrawny barn cats often had mangled limbs and looked to be full of disease. Martine was told never to go near them, but they were too feral and skittery to pet anyway.

Madame put a hand on her chest as though surprised to see Martine. "You should not be here," she said. "I heard your father was taken by the Germans."

"Yes," Martine replied in a small voice. "I was supposed to find Damien, but he was gone."

She could feel her body sway, as if a slight breeze might cause her to keel over. She didn't want to fall down right on the doorstep. Madame Moreau just stood there with an alarmed look on her face. She had a round face with a short, stubby nose and narrow eyes. She wiped her hands on a dirty apron and pursed her lips together.

"May I come in?" Martine finally asked.

Madame Moreau stuck her head out the door and looked around. It appeared as though she would not let Martine enter. But then her husband approached from behind and said, "Let the child in, for God's sake."

She stepped aside to let the girl in but shook her head. "You are a fool. She will be the ruin of us."

Her husband had a long gray beard and mustache, and his kindly smile invited Martine into the room. "Woman, have you not read the Bible?" he asked his wife. "You shall love your neighbor as yourself."

"The Germans do not care about the Bible," she spat. "Would you sacrifice yourself?"

"I would do what is right. The French do not turn on their own people. We shall help this child. Are you hungry?" he asked Martine, who nodded.

"Get her some food," he instructed his wife. She scowled but did as she was told. Ten minutes later Martine was slurping thin soup and eating stale bread. Throughout the meal, she struggled to keep her eyes open.

Madame's husband noticed the note pinned to Martine's dress. He took it off and read it. "It is an address in Paris," he told his wife. "For an aunt of hers."

"And how does that concern us?" his wife answered. "We cannot keep her here. And you're not driving our old wagon all the way to Paris."

"I was supposed to find Damien," Martine repeated. "But he was gone."

"He was taken as well," Madame declared. "Because he was la Résistance and the Germans found out. That is why you must leave. They will suspect us of being part of the Resistance too."

Martine didn't really know what *the resistance* meant, but her heart dropped. Who would help her now?

"We will put her on the train tomorrow," Monsieur said, turning to his wife. "And then you will be rid of your tarnished conscience."

Madame slammed a cupboard door and stomped away, her arms swinging wildly, causing Martine to duck her head.

"Do not worry," Monsieur Moreau said. "I will speak to her."

Martine slept on a pallet of soft bedding at the foot of their bed. Despite the snoring and mumbling above her, she fell sound asleep and was awakened early the next morning by a short kick in her side, courtesy of Madame.

"Get up. The train leaves in an hour."

After Martine used the outhouse to relieve herself, Madame gave her three hard biscuits rolled up in a kerchief. "Don't eat it all at once," she barked, as though she begrudged Martine any food. "It must last you until you get to Paris."

Martine held the kerchief close, along with her stuffed rabbit. She remembered how she'd dropped the wine bottle that Papa had made her promise to take with her. She would not be so careless this time.

"You will ride in the back of the wagon under the straw to the train station. Do not make any noise at all. Do you understand?"

Martine nodded. "Merci," she said, because she was taught to be polite, and because she hadn't had to sleep outside in the scary darkness. Although, if Monsieur Moreau hadn't said anything, Madame might have turned her away. She knew her papa would never turn anyone away.

Monsieur Moreau lifted her into the back of the horse-drawn wagon and made sure the paper pinned to her dress was secure.

"Do you know where you are going?"

"To see Tante Anna?" she guessed. She was the only aunt Martine had.

"Your aunt, yes. Do you know where she lives?"

She shook her head.

"In Paris. It is written on the paper in case you need to look at it," he said.

Martine's eyes scrunched up. She felt the wetness squeeze out.

"Do you know how to read, child?"

Martine shook her head, feeling ashamed.

"Can you remember the address if I tell you it?"

"Yes," Martine said. She would say it over and over in her head and memorize it all the way to Paris.

"It is on Rue Chauchat in the ninth arrondissement. Near the Opéra district. Number fifteen. Now repeat it for me."

Martine repeated it exactly as he said it. She looked at Madame Moreau as if to say, *See, I am not an imbecile.*

"She will be caught before she arrives there," Madame Moreau said. "And she will cost us our lives as well." Madame stroked one of the cats who swarmed around her legs looking for food.

Her husband replied, "If she makes it onto the train, she only has to ask for directions once she is there."

"She looks like a Jew. They will turn her in before she steps onto the train."

Monsieur Moreau frowned at his wife. He took two francs and placed them in Martine's hand. She put them in the pocket of her plaid dress, which now was wrinkled and dirty and smelled a bit of wee. "This is all we can give you."

Madame Moreau spat at the ground and went inside, leaving the mewling cats behind.

"Do not mind her," Monsieur Moreau said. "Just remember to stay hidden and quiet until I tell you it's safe to come out."

Martine did as she was told. The wagon bounced and bucked and battered her little body as she slammed against the wood. But she kept repeating the address over and over in her mind. It helped calm her fears. She had only ridden the train once, and that was with Papa. And if she thought of Papa she would cry. So, she focused all her attention on that address.

The train didn't stop regularly at the small station in their village. Usually, the church bells rang each day, calling Martine to school, and again they rang at the end of the day, signaling men to quit work and go home. Today no bells rang out; it was eerily quiet. But as they neared the station, Martine could hear vehicles and voices. Then the wagon slowed down.

A German voice commanded Monsieur to stop.

"Papers," he demanded.

A moment later, the same voice barked, "What are you carrying in the back?"

Monsieur Moreau replied, "Nothing. I am on my way to pick up medicine for my wife. She is sick."

Martine heard a loud thump as the officer got into the wagon.

She heard him jab at the hay with something hard. The sound kept getting closer. She made herself as small as she could, just like she did in the armoire. Something sharp brushed against her hair and she almost cried out, but cupped her hand over her mouth so the sound would not escape.

What would happen to her if she screamed or moved? What would happen to Monsieur Moreau? Would he be taken away like Papa?

Monsieur Moreau jumped off the wagon. "I am bringing my wife's tomato and mustard tart to the doctor. Would you like a piece?"

The soldier stopped jabbing at the straw. "Yes." He got back down.

A moment later the wagon was moving again. Five minutes later, it stopped. "Do not move, but tell me if you are all right," Monsieur said.

"I am all right," Martine said.

Monsieur let out a loud breath. "I was afraid his bayonet would stab you. We should be safe from here on out. But stay hidden."

Martine shivered. She did not feel safe. She hadn't felt safe ever since Papa put her in the armoire. Was that just yesterday? It seemed so long ago already.

Her stomach ached, and she repeated the address again, over and over, until it became a prayer lodged in her heart.

CHAPTER FIVE

ESCAPE

WHEN MONSIEUR MOREAU FINALLY CALLED MARTINE out of the wagon, she rubbed her tired eyes. The clacking of the wheels on the cobblestone streets of their village had been a lullaby that put her to sleep. She stood wearily as he lifted her out.

They were on the edge of their small town, past the train station, but she could see the tracks running next to the road.

Monsieur plucked straw from her hair and dress. He handed her a ticket.

"This ticket will take you to Paris. There is just one thing," he continued. "I could not use your real name. So, your name on this trip will be Élise Moreau."

"You made up a name for me?"

"Not a made-up name. Élise was my little girl. She died years ago. I do not think she would mind you using her name. Just remember to answer to Élise when they speak to you." Another thing to remember. She tucked it away in her mind with the address.

He gave her a small squeeze of her shoulders. "You must be brave now. And you must walk to the station alone. When you are there, ask someone to help you find your train. Can you do that?"

Martine nodded. She had no choice but to be brave, even if she didn't feel that way.

"If anyone asks why you are traveling alone, just say that your mother died and your father is fighting in the war."

Martine nodded again.

"Be off with you. You don't want to miss the train."

Monsieur Moreau got back into his wagon and shook the reins and made a clicking sound, which prompted the horses to trot down the dirt road. He left without looking back.

Martine watched him leave, realizing she hadn't properly thanked him. It was too late now. She started walking, but felt too nervous, as though she was being watched, so she broke into a run, not stopping until she had reached the station. She was sweaty and out of breath, but she felt a powerful sensation well up in her chest. Maybe she could be brave as Monsieur said. She knew she would have to be, for Papa's sake. She hoped Tante Anna would know how to find Papa.

The small station was merely a window where people purchased tickets and a platform with wooden benches covered by a tall overhang. She had her ticket, but she approached the window, barely tall enough to reach the ledge. There were no trains on the empty track.

She summoned her biggest voice. "When is the train to Paris?"

The man behind the window strained to see her. "Are you traveling by yourself?"

"Oui," she said.

"You are very young to be traveling alone."

"I am very brave," Martine replied, tightly hugging her rabbit.

"I see," he said, and then chuckled. "The train will arrive in ten minutes if it is on time. Do you have luggage?"

"No," she said and realized that might sound odd. Who traveled without luggage? She needed a reason why she wouldn't have any. "My clothes are at my tante's apartment in Paris," she finally said, thinking this would make him less suspicious.

He pointed toward the benches. "You may sit over there and wait for the train."

"Merci." She wandered over near the benches, where a few people were waiting: an old woman wearing a heavy coat on this warm day, a man in a French military uniform, and two other men. No children were waiting. She didn't see any German soldiers, which made her feel safer.

She stayed standing until she saw a woman approach the bench and sit down. The woman wore a nice dress, the kind her tante Anna would wear, and her pretty brown hair was pinned up. Martine sat next to her on the bench. Perhaps people would think she was Martine's mother.

She moved closer to the woman, to make sure they looked like they were together.

The woman turned, as if she suddenly noticed her.

"Hello, little one. Are you waiting for the train?"

"Oui."

"Is someone you know arriving?"

Martine shook her head. "No. I am going to Paris to visit my aunt."

The woman frowned, and lines appeared on her otherwise smooth forehead. "But you are very young to ride the train by yourself. It's not safe, especially now." She nodded at three German soldiers who had entered the platform.

Martine drew in a sharp breath. Were they the ones who took Papa? The ticket felt soft and doughy in her sweaty palm. She remembered how Monsieur Moreau told her to be brave.

"I am not afraid," she said, even though she could not take her eyes off the German soldiers. "My mama died and my papa is fighting in the war. I must go to Paris to live with my aunt."

"And there is no one who can take you?"

"No," she answered. "I am alone."

"Well, you may sit next to me. What is your name?"

"Mar . . . Élise," she replied, remembering at the last minute that she must use a different name.

"Élise, I will make sure you get to Paris. Oui?" She smiled at Martine, and for the first time in two days, Martine felt her chest expand and her breathing ease. Her aunt would help her find Papa and then they would return to their home and the grapes that needed Papa's tender care. She hoped Papa wouldn't be too angry at her for dropping the wine bottle. Maybe the German soldiers hadn't noticed and it would still be there when they returned.

CHAPTER SIX

THE RIGHT FREQUENCY

CHARLOTTE

1990

"AMERICAN 755, TURN LEFT HEADING 320."

I repeated the communication. "Turn left heading 320, American 755."

My copilot adjusted his headset in the seat next to mine after I had performed a smooth left turn. "We got a lot of crumb crunchers on this flight."

"I thought you liked kids. You have a couple of them, don't you?"

"Yeah, but they were Louise's idea."

"I'm sure you had some part in it."

"I told her we could have kids, but I refuse to change diapers."

"Louise is a lucky woman," I said, rolling my eyes, which Drake couldn't see because both of us focused our attention on the instruments; checking cabin altitude and fuel tanks and the sky, noting the cumulus clouds that drifted around us. I'd found that never making eye contact during flight made it easier to talk to my male colleagues. I maintained a friendly back-and-forth sparring with most of them. Some of them even forgot that I was female.

Drake shifted in his seat. He was a mover, someone who was

always active, even in the cockpit. "When are you going to get married and start spitting out some kids?"

Well, evidently Drake wasn't one to forget I was a woman. I snorted. "When you manage a smooth landing instead of those two-for-one specials."

"My touch-and-bounce landing isn't that bad. People like the little lift it gives them. Maybe I'll do better when I make captain like you."

It seemed like a harmless jab, that I had made captain before Drake, but there was a force behind it, one that contained a hint of bitterness. Getting upgraded to captain was a matter of seniority, not merit-based or favoritism. Drake understood this. But I knew what was said behind my back: that my father, who was also a captain, had helped me get hired. Most American Airlines commercial pilots were retired Navy and Air Force officers, and most military men had felt women didn't belong in the cockpit.

I glanced back at our third crew member, Marty, a friendly guy older than both Drake and me, who'd had a career flying for the Navy before switching to commercial aircraft. At first, he acted as though he hadn't heard us, and I wondered if he felt the same way as Drake, even as he was always very polite toward me and never treated me differently than our male counterparts.

But then Marty asked about my French boyfriend, which was odd, because I hardly ever mentioned Henri at work. "You still seeing that Frenchman?" he asked.

"As a matter of fact, yes." Somehow, having a boyfriend made me less threatening to them, and to their wives. Not that there was anything wrong with being an independent woman who didn't need a man. Not that they'd admit, anyway.

"I've heard the French guys are real charmers."

I nodded. "They are quite gentlemanly compared to Americans."

Drake smirked. "I thought women didn't want that anymore. Holding their own doors and stuff. You know, all that feminism BS."

"You mean, like making captain?"

"Don't get me wrong," Drake said. "You're just as good as any male pilot. And it's not that you don't deserve it," he added somewhat begrudgingly. "I just don't get what's in it for you."

I frowned. "What's in it for me? The same thing that's in it for you, Drake. Or don't you think women should have career aspirations?"

He put up his hands. "Sorry. It was just a question."

Could Drake not imagine a woman wanting the same thing as him: to fly around the world, explore other countries, and make a decent salary, all while doing something you love? That a woman could have dreams of her own? At least he'd admitted I was good, that I deserved my position.

I reminded myself that *I* was the captain. Most of my male fellow pilots, like Marty, accepted women in the cockpit and treated us well, even though there still weren't as many of us as I'd hoped by now.

My father had sat me down before I started flight school. He said we needed to have a "talk." He always looked handsome in his uniform and had aged gracefully. He reminded me a bit of James Garner with his dark hair, but with more gray flecks. He was a well-respected captain, and I wondered if I could live up to his reputation, if I would be able to make him proud of me.

"Are you sure you want to do this?" he'd asked.

"You know how much I love flying, Dad. This is my dream."

He'd nodded. "It will be harder for you than the rest of them. They'll say you got in because of me, and it won't matter how smart or capable you are. And a lot of them will hate you because you're a woman. There are instructors who will resent you being there. That's a plain fact."

"I know all that." I was up for the challenge. But I hadn't asked Dad up front before what he thought. He'd always encouraged me. Still, I had to know for sure. "Do *you* think I should do this?"

He'd put a hand on my shoulder. "Hell, yes. You're just like me, and I wouldn't think of trying to stop you."

Of course, he'd been right about it all. But I'd proven myself a thousand times over, and damn it, I deserved these four stripes. I'd worked my way up from flight engineer, flown three years of all-nighters and back-to-back trips, and later was promoted to co-pilot. I'd put in the flight hours and paid my dues, finally making captain two years ago. I had loved flying from the moment I set foot in a cockpit. The first plane I'd piloted had been a small Cessna, one I nicknamed Bug and still thought of as my favorite. Once I flew that, there was never a question of whether I'd become a professional pilot. It was only a question of when. I'd never quit believing in myself.

Still, it was an uphill battle sometimes.

Beverley Bass, who had made captain before me, had told me, "It's okay to want more," when I'd confessed my own ambition to make captain someday. I thought of her being the first female captain at American Airlines, and all that she had to go through to pave the way for women like me.

We were cruising at thirty-one thousand feet. I did another round of eyeing the instruments before engaging autopilot and relaxed back into my seat. The bottle and the handwritten message had picked at my brain throughout this entire trip whenever I had a few moments to think about it. A hidden message underneath a label had to be important, even if the bottle of wine itself wasn't. I'd done some reading and knew that the French Resistance operated during World War II, and a bottle from that time period might be used to relay messages.

Before I'd left, I'd peeled the labels off the two empty bottles of wine, but both were blank underneath. I was grateful we hadn't drunk the remaining bottle, the only one we'd left unopened.

I'd decided to hide the bottle of wine in the back of my closet before I left. I didn't want my roommates to drink it while I was gone, and if I left it out on the counter, they would assume it was fair game. Since I owned the apartment and paid the lion's share for it, I had a room to myself, while the other two shared a room.

My copilot yawned. I wanted to ask him something before he left the cockpit for a short nap. "Hey, Drake, I have a philosophical question for you. If someone gave you something and it turned out to be valuable, would you feel an obligation to share the proceeds with the person who gave it to you?"

"If you're talking about that box of Valrhona chocolates that guy in first class gave us, you'd better be sharing that with me."

"No. It's not chocolate. Suppose someone gave you a gift and it turned out to be valuable. But the person who gifted it didn't know it was valuable."

"You know me well enough to know what I'd say, Montgomery. Their loss."

I nodded. Of course that's what Drake would say. Would Henri feel the same if he was the one who had received the gift instead of being the giver? I suspected he would.

"How about you, Marty?" I asked the other crew member.

"That's a tough one," he confessed. "Part of me would feel guilty if I didn't at least let the person know."

"You've got to be kidding," Drake teased him. "This is a no-brainer."

"For you, it is," I told Drake with a smirk. "But for those who have a conscience, it's more complicated."

"You two must be drinking the crew juice," Drake replied. "Just because I'm not a pushover doesn't make me unethical. You said it was a gift."

The more I thought about it, the more I agreed with Drake. But it didn't make me feel good about myself. On the other hand, the bottle might not even be worth anything, so I wouldn't have to tell Henri. He hadn't called me before I left for my trip like he'd promised.

When I made it back to Paris a week and a half later, I realized that Henri hadn't called at all. I usually called him when I got back from trips, as my schedule was too hard for him to keep straight, so that wasn't too unusual. When we met up again, would he apologize for not calling, or simply not address it at all, as if it wasn't important enough to bother him?

I checked the bottle of wine to make sure it was still hidden. I didn't know much about wine, but I did have a friend who taught history at Sorbonne University. He would be able to translate the message and help me understand what it meant.

I arranged to meet Paul at a small café near the university, where we sipped wine in the shade of an umbrella and talked about mutual friends. Paul was seventy years old, known as a beloved and masterful teacher by all the students lucky enough to enroll in his classes. I'd gotten to know him on numerous flights, where he always made a point of chatting with and thanking the crew before he departed the plane. He made frequent trips to the US through the university, and he'd often invited me for dinner at his apartment when his wife was still alive. Their hospitality and kindness were part of the reason I fell in love with Paris.

Paul ordered a Nutella crepe as we watched the traffic and tourists of the Latin Quarter fill the boulevard, the gray dome of the Chapel of the Sorbonne in the distance.

"To be French is to embrace life," he said, taking a bite of the succulent crepe. "And to embrace food." He patted his protruding middle for emphasis and let out a deep laugh.

That was what I liked about him. He had lost his wife just last year to cancer, but he still found occasion to laugh and be happy. He said his wife made him promise not to become despondent after she was gone, that a happy soul like him needed laughter in his life. And he said that teaching gave him both laughter and life and kept him from being too sad.

I hoped the university didn't have a mandatory retirement age.

Finally, I brought the bottle out of my oversize bag.

"I attended an auction at Hôtel Drouot two weeks ago, and this was one of the items in a box of wine," I said. "It was supposedly taken from the wine cellar of a German aristocrat."

I showed him the original label. "I peeled off the label and found this writing underneath. Can you translate it for me?"

He looked at it, peering closely at the faded writing. "It claims this bottle as his child's inheritance. It is supposedly a rare vintage, and the proceeds of its sale are to provide for her until he can return. He says she is a true artisan, a vigneronne in heart and soul."

So, it wasn't part of the Resistance. It was a note for his daughter. "I wonder what happened to her. Perhaps the German aristocrat in whose cellar they found it purchased the bottle?"

He shook his head. "Doubtful. Most of the good wines were confiscated during the war as the Germans took over properties. Many vintners would bury their best wines in their yards. Others hid their wine in local caves or built fake walls in their cellars to conceal it, gathering spiderwebs to put in the corners and sprinkling dust over bottles of inexpensive wine to make them look vintage. A false label was another method to trick the Germans into thinking it was a useless bottle. But since this turned up in a German cellar, chances are that it was seized rather than sold."

"So, is this a rare vintage?"

"A 1920 Roberge? It well may be. Roberge was a noble family from the Burgundy area of France. Their wines often fetched good prices. The best way to determine the worth of this wine would be to take it for an appraisal. I know someone who may help."

He wrote down the name and address of his acquaintance.

"Can you read the signature on the note?" I asked.

"It's hard to read. Too faded. Perhaps Zachariah? The last name is Viner, which would match the label that was on top. Not a name or label I recognize. He may have been Jewish. Most of them lost their vineyards during the war."

"That's awful! How sad." A father's last wish for his daughter's safety. The thought of a child losing her inheritance, perhaps her life, was disheartening.

More disheartening perhaps because I was still upset at Dad for putting Grandpa's vineyard on the market, although I couldn't blame him for it. He said it was a money trap that he couldn't afford. If I were rich, I'd buy it and hire someone to keep it going, if only as a way to honor my grandfather.

"Thanks for your help, Paul. I guess you see these kinds of things all the time?"

"This is the first time I've seen a note hidden underneath a label. It's a testament to what a man will do for his family. I fought in that war too, you know. I was young like you, eager to protect my country. I had no idea what was in store. I know how devastating it was, how many families were torn apart. So, I consider each of these finds a miracle, and a reminder of the resilience and strength of my countrymen."

"I'd like to know what happened to this Viner fellow," I said.

"I can do a bit of searching, see if I can find out anything about him in the Jewish records," Paul offered.

"Thanks. I'd appreciate it."

Later that night, I sat alone on my pink suede couch that the previous owners had left behind. It was a cabriole-style sofa, with curved legs and sides, and only fit two people comfortably. The whole apartment was a mishmash of décor. My parents had visited once, and my mother had dubbed it "Heinz 57 style": a round glass sofa table, a floral chair, and various baskets from different locales that substituted as magazine organizers. A collage of artwork lined the wall, from bold swirls and prints to pictures of scenic rivers. I'd bought many of the items on a whim at thrift stores, what the French called *au coup de coeur*, which translated into *a blow to the heart*. Tall red plastic chairs butted up to a white countertop that separated the kitchen from the living area in our tiny 400-square-foot apartment.

What others regarded as outlandish I preferred to think of as bohemian. My roommates were never there long enough to care. They were just grateful not to have to stay in a hotel room during their layovers.

I held the bottle of wine in my hands and traced my finger across the crown on the label, wondering if I should contact Henri and tell him about what I learned. I knew he wouldn't have given it to me if he believed it was valuable. That's why he'd kept those other two bottles.

I had thought Henri was someone special, perhaps someone I could make a life with. But he hadn't even called since our night together, as though it held no importance. I think that was how he viewed our relationship. Maybe trying to find lasting romance with an irregular schedule was impossible. But the men pilots didn't seem to have this problem.

There were so many men who were intimidated by a female pilot, especially a captain. That narrowed the field to begin with. And finding someone I felt passionate about was even harder.

I needed another opinion. I dialed Jane, one of my roommates and my best friend. We'd met when I was a junior flight engineer. She was ten years older, an experienced flight attendant who'd taken me under her wing and made sure I was always taken care of on layovers. She'd attended Stewardess College in Fort Worth back when the emphasis was more on poise and beauty, before they changed the name to flight attendants. The few female friends I'd had in flight school had all been hired by other airlines and we'd lost touch.

"How's Paris?" Jane asked. She sounded out of breath. "Gorgeous as always?"

I let out a sigh. "Is this a bad time to call?" It was seven hours earlier in Chicago, which would make it around one p.m.

"Oh, no. What is it? I detect a romance crisis. And no, it's not a bad time. I just carried a heavy load of laundry up the stairs. I can talk and fold at the same time."

I imagined her with the phone propped against the side of her head while folding towels. "You make it all look so easy, Jane. Marriage, kids, a career."

"It's not easy. None of it. Simon took a hit during a soccer game yesterday and chipped his front tooth and got a bloody mouth. I was lucky I was here. I mean, I know he would have been in good hands. Stuart is only fifteen minutes away at the office, and my parents watch the kids for us when I'm gone. But they need their mom when they get hurt. I was lucky to be at the game when it happened."

"I'm glad you were there. I can't even manage to get the marriage part figured out."

"Trouble with Henri?"

I sighed again. "I thought he was someone I could have a relationship with. After an incredible night together, he just blew me off the next morning. He promised he'd call before I left town. Of course, he didn't."

"You've always had a plan, Charlotte. And look at how much you've accomplished? But marriage isn't a box to tick. It's not something you can plan for. And look at how many pilots and flight attendants are divorced."

I knew more divorced pilots, both men and women, than I did married ones. "But you made it work," I said.

"I have a very understanding spouse. But even Stuart gets jealous. The reason he encouraged me to sublet your apartment was so I wouldn't be spending time at the hotel with the male pilots. It has nothing to do with convenience."

"I just never thought this was the price I'd have to pay for being a pilot," I said grimly. "I feel like time is running out for me."

"Remember, Henri is French. You're smart and independent, and there is a cultural difference."

"I come across as too assertive," I admitted.

"Of course you do. It's who you are. But Charlotte, are you sure about Henri? I know there's passion. But is there more than that?"

I paused, thinking it over. "That's exactly what I've been asking myself."

"Amber and I only met him that once, when he came to pick you up at the apartment. Amber thought he was a hunk. But family life is hard for women in our industry. It takes a big commitment on the part of both to make it work. Honestly, Henri seems like a player. And I'm not sure he's good enough for you.

"Not that he couldn't change," she quickly added.

Jane understood men more than I did, even though I worked with them nonstop every day.

"You're right. He checked all the boxes except the one that really matters."

"There isn't a perfect guy out there. Just try to find someone who treats you good and loves you for who you are. You deserve it."

"Thanks, Jane. You always know what to say. When are we going to fly together again?"

"Soon, I hope. In any case, we'll be in Paris in another week or so."

The conversation turned to work, and Jane filled me in on

Amber's latest boyfriend, one she'd met on a recent flight. I hung up the phone feeling foolish. She'd seen through Henri in a few minutes, and it had taken me a whole year. And yes, I kept thinking that I could be with Henri now, having dinner at a nice restaurant instead of sitting by myself in a low-lit room, the traffic below reminding me that the rest of the world was still enjoying this beautiful night.

Jane was right: I had a sense that Henri was a player. I noticed when he checked out other women, how his gaze lingered on them. And then there was his lack of emotional intimacy. We never talked about a future together, as if we were on opposite frequencies.

I'd had my share of romantic hookups when I felt too young to settle down. I was thirty-three, and I was past that phase of my life, and thought Henri was too. I'd even mentioned him to my mom, the first guy I'd ever talked about.

She promptly sent me a copy of *Bride* magazine. The woman on the cover was smiling in her Dior wedding dress, while her new husband, who resembled Henri just a bit, hugged her from behind.

Mom thought that once I'd married, I'd have kids and forget about flying. As if marriage and family was a trade-off I'd gladly accept. Of course, she never considered I could have both. Mom spent all her time caring for me and Dad and the house. When I was young and Dad was gone on a trip, she'd spend her time practicing new recipes on me so that by the time Dad returned, the chicken marsala would be perfected. I'd be sick of it by then, and Dad would scold me for refusing to eat Mom's delicious dish.

Only Dad understood my need to fly. He'd often say I was the son he never had, as though that made it more acceptable for him to encourage me. He never mentioned grandkids. He understood that being a pilot was more than a job; it was a vocation. And his understanding was that, as a woman, I had a choice: my vocation or a family.

I wanted both. I didn't need marriage and family, but I wanted it. Not as a substitute for flying, as a complement. Going home to an empty apartment was less than satisfying. My male colleagues went home to hot meals and loving families. Why couldn't I at least get the loving family?

I decided to wait before I called Henri. First, I would see if the wine was indeed valuable. In the meantime, I would search for Zachariah Viner and his vineyard, if either of them still existed.

CHAPTER SEVEN

THE APPRAISAL

"UNNECESSARY."

That's what Gérard Benefiel, the sommelier who knew about French wines and vineyards, told me when I mentioned that I was interested in locating a winemaker named Viner, who had operated a vineyard in Burgundy, and who originally owned the bottle of wine.

"So many of those small vineyards are gone, especially in the Burgundy region. Besides, if you purchased this at an auction at Hôtel Drouot, it now belongs to you."

"It was most likely requisitioned by the Germans."

"Stolen, actually. But that makes no difference now. This bottle is a very lucky find," he said, his voice rising. "I see no signs of age or wear, and the label is intact." He stroked his long mustache that reminded me of every cartoon villain I'd ever seen and appeared to subdue his enthusiasm by adding, "Although you must understand that the value of wine is only what someone will pay for it."

He was examining it closely, holding the bottle up to the light. I felt a sudden protectiveness toward it and clasped my hands together to keep from grabbing it back. I remembered that Paul had said he was a knowledgeable wine professional who would give me a free estimate of its worth.

"Not all old bottles of wine are valuable," he said. "Much has to do with the grapes from those vintages, the weather conditions that year, how many bottles were produced, and how it was stored."

"Would it still be drinkable?" I asked.

"If it was stored on its side under prime conditions and temperature, then perhaps so. But that is irrelevant. Collectors don't purchase these bottles of wine to drink."

He continued to examine it. I raised my eyebrows, waiting. Finally, after a long minute, I grew impatient and asked, "So, do you think this one is valuable?"

He looked at me. "Of course. Roberges are from Côte de Nuits region and are known for their exceptional longevity. This wine was part of a small, coveted collection. About three thousand bottles of this were made, most of them exported to Germany. They loved the rich Pinot Noir."

He set the bottle down on the counter. He tapped the top and nodded. "Only nine bottles remain in existence. Ten, counting this one."

So, the bottle did have some worth. Perhaps as much as the thirteen-hundred-dollar bottles Henri took home?

"Can you give me an estimate of what it might fetch?"

"Of course, this is just an estimate, but I would guess, oh, about . . . seven hundred thousand francs. Perhaps more."

I put a hand to my chest. I calculated the exchange rate in my head. My voice pitched higher. "That would be what? One hundred and twenty-five thousand dollars?"

"Roughly," he said.

My God! I had heard that rare bottles of wine fetched enormous prices, but this changed everything!

"I see," I said, trying to act casual, as if I weren't blindsided by the information.

"If you would like me to get a more precise estimate . . ." he said, reaching for the bottle.

This time I quickly put my hands on the bottle, wrapping it in the towel I'd brought and depositing it in my bag. "Oh, I'm not interested in selling right now. I just wanted to see if it was worth anything. And it obviously is, so . . ." I couldn't think of anything else to say. My brain had completely shut down.

He handed me his card. "This is a very rare find," he finally admitted. "If you should decide to sell it," he said, "I can make you a very good offer. And make sure it is stored correctly in the meantime."

I nodded and mumbled some thanks, then left. I stood outside the door and brought a hand to my heart, trying to calm the rapid thumping. Only the shoppers passing by kept me from screaming out. One hundred twenty-five thousand dollars!

And to think how close we came to drinking this wine, never knowing its full worth!

I had to tell someone. Henri? No. Not yet. But did I owe it to him to tell him? After all, he was the one who'd bid on the bottle.

And what of the man who had hidden the note? Zachariah Viner? There must be some record of him. He would be an old man like Paul, if he had survived the war.

The sommelier seemed to think it wasn't necessary to locate him. After all, even though he'd originally owned it, it now belonged to me. But the sommelier didn't know about the note.

Did I owe an allegiance to Henri or Zachariah Viner? Perhaps not. But what about the girl who was supposed to inherit this bottle? Was she even alive? I didn't even know her name.

I quickly returned to my flat and secured the wine bottle at the back of my closet, thinking that I should buy a safe for something this valuable. I couldn't stay here. What if Henri called? What would I tell him?

I paced the floor of my bedroom. I was a ball of nervous energy. My gaze fell upon the one thing I'd kept from my grandfather's estate after he'd died: a small wooden box with an image painted on the top of *The Red Vineyard* by Vincent van Gogh.

Grandpa had kept an old corkscrew in it, a simple one with a walnut wood handle and stainless steel screw that twisted around. He'd bought it in France, both the box and corkscrew, and said it reminded him of why he'd become a vigneron.

The first time I'd noticed the box, I was just six years old. I'd picked it up off his cluttered desk, fascinated with the picture on top that showed men and women toiling in a vineyard while a man drives a horse and wagon in the background.

"Can I play with this?" I'd asked.

Grandpa took it from my small hands. "Someday you may have it. When I'm gone. I need it now to remind me of something."

"What?"

"That in between the bombings and guns and death, there were these beautiful vineyards scattered across the land with little grape nubs of hope and light and the possibility of new life. War sometimes makes you do things you regret. When the darkness came and the bad thoughts made their way into my head, this box and the thought of the vineyards made me feel better. It made me decide to grow my own vineyard when I returned home, to bring the light and hope with me. The box is my constant reminder that there is still hope for the world. And hope for me."

"Does it keep the bad thoughts away?" I'd asked.

He placed the box gently on his desk. "Most of the time it does."

Even as a young girl I sensed a great sadness in him that only subsided when he was tending the vines, as if losing himself in the task was the only way to forget what he'd left behind. No matter what I did, I couldn't take away the sadness that lurked behind his eyes, and I felt bad that I couldn't make him happy.

It was only later that I learned that Grandpa suffered from PTSD, and that the vineyard was more than a respite for him.

But I felt it was more than that, even. Grandpa had also left a piece of paper in the box on which he'd scribbled lines from a poem written by Emily Dickinson:

Remorse is memory awake,
Her companies astir,—
A presence of departed acts
At window and at door.
Remorse is cureless,—the disease
Not even God can heal;
For 'tis His institution,—
The complement of hell.

I was convinced that Grandpa had carried around a lot of guilt for something that happened during the war. I wasn't sure what it was, but I was certain it had contributed to his PTSD and had affected the rest of his life.

Maybe I could buy Grandpa's vineyard now! His lot was small, only twenty-five acres, and I could beg Dad to give me a good deal on it. I knew what Dad would say, that it would be a foolish investment and a waste of money, that it wasn't profitable. And how would I oversee a vineyard when I was constantly flying?

But, still. Maybe this was the reason the bottle came to me. The money it would bring was a gift from Grandpa, meant to keep his legacy alive.

I packed a bag. I didn't have to fly for another two days. Although I had explored Paris, and had been to the coast, I'd never visited the Burgundy area. To be honest, I rarely traveled outside of this magnificent city, feeling it had more than enough to offer.

Today was a beautiful day, the perfect kind of day to rent a car and take a three-hour drive to the Burgundy region of France. Burgundy, where a certain winemaker named Zachariah Viner once lived.

The sommelier had dismissed the idea. But I had received an unexpected gift, a very valuable one, and despite what others might tell me, I felt a responsibility to explore the origins of this gift, wherever that might lead me. And when I felt I'd honored that obligation, then I could spend the money on whatever I wanted.

I told myself I was doing it for my grandfather.

CHAPTER EIGHT

TANTE ANNA

MARTINE

1942

PARIS, FRANCE

MARTINE HAD BEEN TO DIJON WITH PAPA ONCE. SHE REmembered seeing cars, bicycles, and horse-drawn carriages on the wide streets. They had visited the Palais des Ducs de Bourgogne and walked across the large open square to a sidewalk café, where they'd eaten mousse au chocolat. She was only five at the time, but the large buildings, the paintings and gold carvings, and the wide streets had impressed her so much that she talked about it for months afterward, and she'd never forgotten it.

She had thought that Dijon was huge, but *this* . . . Paris stretched forever. She'd seen pictures of the ocean that extended out beyond France's border. This was an ocean of buildings and streets that had no beginning or end.

Martine had fallen asleep for much of the train ride, her head propped against the kind woman's arm. Once they'd arrived, her eyes had widened at the tracks that crisscrossed each other, and the large platform overflowing with people.

The woman, who said she was Mademoiselle Tridon, had arranged for her transportation to Tante Anna's apartment building.

She had even paid for the taxi, refusing to accept the two francs that Martine offered her.

"I wish you a good life with your aunt," she said, before putting Martine in the taxi.

"Thank you," Martine had said, feeling small in the back seat, wishing the nice woman was her aunt, then feeling guilty for thinking that. She didn't remember much of Tante Anna. She had come to visit last year during Hanukkah and had brought soft cheese with her, and while staying with them she had done all the cooking, making delicious potato pancakes she called latkes and round jelly doughnuts. She had the same thin face as Papa and the same brown eyes, but unlike Papa she frowned much of the time, and had yelled at Papa, which frightened Martine. She said that things were getting bad in France.

"Perhaps we should leave while there is still time."

Papa patted his sister's hand. "You are all gloom and doom, Anna. France has survived war before and will survive again."

"But will *we*?" she'd asked.

"If you fear Paris, stay here with us in Albertine. What would the Germans want with an unimportant Jewish winemaker in a small village that is but a dot on the map?"

"They are like hunters, searching under every rock for their prey. They are coming for all Jews."

That was when Papa had told Martine to go to bed. She heard the muted sounds of them through the walls, her father's voice occasionally rising to meet his sister's urgent appeals. And when Tante Anna left on the train, she knew Papa was happy to see her leave.

Now Martine stood in front of 15 Rue Chauchat in the 9th arrondissement, the street behind her busy with bicyclists and pedestrians and the occasional vehicle. She looked in awe at the five stories of windows that rose up into the sky, some of the windows open, one with checkered curtains fluttering in the breeze.

All the buildings on this street matched. Their gray-brick façades extending down both sides of the block reminded Martine of the tall, straight vines of Papa's vineyard, only higher. But the brick looked cold and lifeless, unlike the green plants that held life and sustenance.

She sniffed and recognized the strong, distinctive aroma of Papa's cigarettes, the kind that came in the blue package with a picture of a helmet on the front. Was Papa here? But the smell was coming from a passing bicyclist who rode one-handed as he smoked.

She clutched her stuffed rabbit to her stomach, which rumbled with hunger. She had eaten the biscuits on the train, giving one to Mademoiselle Tridon. She hoped her aunt would offer her something to eat soon.

She didn't really know Tante Anna well and had never been to her flat. What if she wasn't home? And which apartment was hers? She stepped inside a hallway and saw a list of names on the wall. She knew Tante Anna had the same last name as her, and she could identify the *V*.

There was only one with a *V* in the last name. She made her way up two flights of stairs along a winding staircase and knocked on the door with the number six above it, patting down her wrinkled dress as she waited. She had no coat or luggage, only her rabbit, which she held close.

An older woman, with a thick waist covered by a plaid apron with pockets, opened the door. A feather duster stuck out from one of the pockets.

"Who are you?" the woman asked, peering down at her.

Martine peeked around her, wondering if her aunt was inside. Perhaps this woman was her housekeeper? Behind the woman were unpacked boxes.

"I'm Martine. I've come to see Tante Anna."

The woman narrowed her eyes. "I live here."

Martine was flustered. She pointed to the piece of paper still pinned to her dress.

The woman snatched it off her dress and read it. "Anna? Do you mean the Jewish woman who lived here before? She's been taken away with all the other Jews who lived in this building."

Taken away? Like Papa? Martine shrunk back, fearing that German soldiers would emerge from the room and grab her up too.

The woman sneered. "You look like her; dark hair and sneaky eyes. If she's your aunt, then you're a Jew too." The woman reached out to grab her, but Martine ducked her head and escaped down the hallway.

"Yes, you'd better run," the woman shouted as Martine fled down the stairs. "But you can't hide, little Jew. The Germans will find you."

Martine ran down the two flights of stairs and out onto the sidewalk, feeling dizzy from the winding staircase. She darted down the street, turning corners, trying to get as much distance between her and that woman as she could. She wanted to run all the way back to the train station, but she had no idea where it was.

Sounds and smells from cafés and shops swooped across her as she ran. She squeezed through crowded sidewalks and bumped into people, filled with terror that a hand would reach out and grab her. She saw German soldiers but kept going, afraid that if she stopped they would see her and know who she was and it would be the end of her. She ran and kept her head down, despite the pang of hunger in her stomach, the dryness of thirst in her throat, and the low shadows that flitted across the buildings, making it hard to see.

It wasn't until the sting of blisters on the back of her foot made it too painful to walk that she finally slowed to a limp. Her wooden heels echoed on the pavement. It was dark out; most of the cafés and shops were closing up. She realized she was alone on the street except for a distant figure walking in the opposite direction.

One café was still cleaning plates from tables. She spotted part of an apple on a plate. While the worker had his back turned, she grabbed it. Her hand was quick, and as she heard a shout behind her, she sped up again, the pain in her feet exploding. Papa wouldn't approve of stealing, but she had to ease the pain in her stomach.

She had no idea where she was. What would she do now? And where would she go? If only she were to see the kind woman who had helped her on the train. But even she knew how impossible that would be in this Goliath city.

There were no bushes to hide behind here, only dark, uneven streets with curbs that she tripped over, and rows and rows of tall buildings. She finally stopped near a doorway underneath an awning. The building was triangular, which matched the narrow street that came to a V. There were all sorts of posters in the windows, most with pictures of objects: lamps and framed paintings, vases and statues, and all sorts of furniture. It must be a business that sold these items. There was also a picture of a bottle of wine, and that made Martine feel better, even though it reminded her of the one she'd lost.

She studied the letters on the door, even though she couldn't understand the words: Hôtel Drouot. Exhausted, Martine curled up in a corner by the doorway, making herself as small as possible so the Germans wouldn't see her.

The day had been warm, but now she was filled with the dampness of her cold sweat and the cool night air. She shivered and tucked her hands between her knees, pulling her dress down to cover her legs. She took small bites of the apple, thinking of the wet sloppy licks on her hand when she fed apple slices to their horse, Cédric, wondering if anyone was taking care of him now. Did the Germans take him away too? Would she ever see her beloved home again?

The apple didn't take away the soreness in her throat nor the emptiness in her stomach. She felt hot and cold at the same time, and wished she had a blanket or a coat.

Most of all, she missed Papa. She had no one now, not even Tante Anna. She was truly alone. She thought of that mean woman at her aunt's apartment and shivered again. She no longer felt brave.

She still had the two francs in her pocket, and she had her rabbit, which she laid her head on. Perhaps tomorrow she would buy some food. That was the only plan she could come up with, as she had nowhere to go, and it was becoming too hard to even think.

"Papa," she cried. "Papa, please help me."

She finally let the exhaustion overtake her, despite her fear and sadness, and fell into a fitful sleep.

CHAPTER NINE

SISTER ADA

AN ABBEY OUTSIDE PARIS, FRANCE

A WARM HAND PRESSED AGAINST MARTINE'S CHEEK. IT WAS softer than Papa's, whose plum-stained fingers were often sticky and calloused from walking the vines and picking the plump grapes. She remembered how he taught her to check the grapes for dimples and ripeness.

"Papa," Martine mumbled, before opening her eyes.

"I am Sister Ada," a voice replied. "I found you on the doorstep of the Hôtel Drouot last night. You were very sick. I brought you from Paris to the abbey."

Martine looked up. The pretty brown eyes that regarded her belonged to a woman she recognized as a nun, with what looked like a starched white bib and black-and-white headgear. She had seen them in her village in their long, flowing black robes tied at the waist with beads and a cross. Her eyes looked kind, but Martine worried she would be like the woman in her aunt's apartment and would call the Germans to come and get her.

She struggled to sit up but was pushed back down. "You need your rest. Don't be afraid, little one. You're safe here."

Martine wasn't sure she knew what safe felt like anymore. She thought Papa would come and rescue her from the armoire. She thought Damien, who had worked as Papa's cellar master her entire life, would keep her safe, but he had abandoned her as well. She thought she would be safe at Tante Anna's apartment, and instead she had run for her life.

But she was too tired to resist the woman's strong hands. She had eyes that reminded Martine of the woman on the train, Mademoiselle Tridon. Perhaps this nun was as kind as her and would help her find her Papa. It was this thought that helped her relax as she fell asleep once again.

The next time Martine woke up, she was being nudged awake, with a glass of water held to her lips.

"You need to drink," Sister Ada said, as she helped Martine raise her head. "Now that your fever has broken, you must regain your strength."

Martine took a sip, then drank down more. Her throat was still sore, but the cold water felt good going down.

"Not too much," the nun said, removing the glass from her lips. "How long has it been since you've eaten?"

"I don't know," Martine said. But then she remembered the apple she'd stolen. She didn't want to mention that.

Sister Ada sighed. "Your stomach is likely the size of a walnut now. We'll try some broth soon, which will be more nutritious."

Broth sounded good. It felt like such a long time since she'd eaten anything. Her stomach growled in response.

"That is a good sign," Sister Ada said when Martine put a hand on her rumbling stomach. "Can you tell me your name?"

"Martine."

"Martine, what were you doing wandering alone around the streets of Paris at night?"

Martine didn't want to answer so she ignored her and looked around the room. It was simply decorated, with a small table next to the bed, an open window that was covered with heavy curtains, and a large cross on the wall near the foot of the bed, one that made Martine look away, because a man was nailed to the cross and he appeared to be in great pain. Why would anyone put such a thing on the wall?

The small slit of light that came in through the part in the curtains was the only way she knew it was daytime. She wondered how long she had been here.

Martine suddenly sat up. "Where is Annabella?"

"Who is Annabella?"

"My rabbit." Martine couldn't go anywhere without her little rabbit. Had Annabella been taken from her too?

Sister Ada reached out and plucked the faded rabbit from under the covers. "She is right here beside you."

Martine hugged her stuffed animal and allowed herself to relax a bit.

"We are not in Paris?" she asked, her mind still a bit fuzzy.

"No. Our village is about fifty kilometers away. I was in Paris to visit a priest, and that is when I found you. I was afraid to take you to the hospital, so I brought you here to the abbey."

"What is an abbey?"

"An abbey is a monastery, a sort of house where a community of religious people live. You don't have to worry that you're not Catholic, Martine. But while you're here, you must pretend to be Catholic."

Martine had no idea how to do that. Still, she asked, "How do you know I'm not Catholic?"

Sister Ada tilted her head. "Only Jewish children are running in the streets of Paris at night. Were you trying to escape the Germans?"

Martine looked away and didn't answer.

"Did your parents tell you to run?"

She shook her head, not wanting to admit they had already taken Papa.

"Do you have family looking for you?"

Martine's lips quivered as she shook her head no.

"You must have been very frightened. I'm surprised you didn't encounter other children like yourself."

There were others? Her heart broke as she remembered how scared and alone she felt. She hadn't looked for other children. The whole night seemed like a terrible nightmare, one she was still waiting to wake up from.

"I don't know how to be Catholic," Martine confessed, still worried she'd be turned back out onto the dark streets.

"Don't worry," Sister Ada said. "I will teach you. I'll go get some broth for you now."

Martine spent the next five days recovering before she was allowed out of her room. During that time, Sister Ada taught her the Lord's Prayer and Hail Mary, two prayers she said all Catholic children should know. She also showed Martine how to make the sign of the cross.

"You are the only child at the abbey," Sister Ada said. "As far as anyone knows, including the other nuns, you are my niece, and I brought you here after your parents died. All except Mother Superior, who knows the truth."

Another thing for Martine to remember, another part of her real life taken away, as if the girl from the vineyard was someone who was no longer a part of her. The prayers reminded her of how Papa put her to bed each night and said the Shema with her: "Hear O Israel, the Lord is our God, the Lord is One."

Sometimes he would hum Jewish lullabies, songs that had no words, but that always put her to sleep. Sister Ada said she must keep Papa's words and music in her heart, but never repeat them in front of the nuns.

Martine felt a tear run down her face as every day she repeated the words that Sister Ada taught her, knowing that her heart would always remember another prayer, and another life.

CHAPTER TEN

BOURGOGNE

CHARLOTTE

1990

BURGUNDY, FRANCE

IT WAS HOPELESS. I HELD A MAP BETWEEN MY LEGS AS I DROVE from one winery to the next. I'd planned this trip with the same detail as charting a flight plan, plotting out a specific route that would produce the best results. I'd started yesterday with a map of the Côte-d'Or, the nickname of the area south of Dijon. I'd already had four glasses of wine today, although I'd only drunk a third of the last one, knowing I wouldn't make much progress if I got drunk before I made it to the next town.

What I hadn't counted on was the number of wineries and vineyards. I had no idea there would be so many. In one small village alone, there were over fifty wine producers! Two days wouldn't be enough time to cover the entire region. And so far, no one had heard of Zachariah Viner.

I did now know more about wine making, including how the mild winter and cool, wet spring promised a good vintage year. But the summer was hot and dry so far. If rains came in the autumn and the warm weather continued, 1990 had potential for good wine.

And I learned the names associated with the area wines: Gevrey-

Chambertin, Vosne-Romanée, and Nuits-Saint-Georges. I saw vineyards behind stone walls and iron gates to protect the valuable grapes. I learned about wine-making monks in the Middle Ages and the limestone-rich soil that gave the area wine its trademark superior-quality grapes.

I'd concentrated on older wineries, thinking someone might remember Zachariah Viner.

I'd visited one château that included a majestic castle on its estate, complete with a courtyard with fountains and terraces, and a gated entry. After speaking with younger guides, I was able to find an older man named Ferdinand who worked at the winery. He had lived in the area before WWII. I asked in my shoddy French if he remembered Zachariah Viner or his vineyard.

He shrugged. "There were perhaps a couple of Jews who owned vineyards. They disappeared after the war."

"How did you know he was Jewish?" I hadn't mentioned it.

The man seemed a bit flustered but shrugged it off. "Zachariah is a Jewish name," he responded.

"Do you know where his vineyard was located?"

He looked down a minute before responding. "Do not fish in a pond; you may catch a shark."

What kind of answer was that? I squinted at him. "Does that mean you do know or don't know?"

"You are American, yes?"

"Yes."

"You cannot understand. Even Mitterrand faithfully served the Vichy government during the war."

"The president of France? He collaborated with the Germans? I've never heard that before."

"French politicians are careful not to expose one another. They all have something to hide."

"I still want to find the vineyard," I said.

He shook his head. "I cannot help you."

I'd seen a look of recognition in Ferdinand's eyes at the name, and he certainly had tried to discourage me. If there were only a couple of Jewish vineyards, certainly someone would remember him. Despite the man's warning, I vowed to keep looking.

But everyone told me the same thing: It was war. The German army had rounded up Jews, Roma, and Communists and killed them all. Whole villages were razed, thousands of villagers shot. In the small village of Comblanchien I'd learned that people had hid in the vineyards as their whole town was burned down. Some weren't so lucky and were burned alive in their homes. Others were arrested and deported to work camps in Germany. People just disappeared. Who would remember a man who'd been gone almost fifty years?

People had moved on with their lives, rebuilt them, some from scratch, having lost everything. But that was in the past. And no one seemed to want to talk about the past.

That night I called my friend Paul from the château where I was staying.

"It is like looking for a needle in a haystack," I said. "I've checked phone books in every place I stop, and there's no Viner."

I could almost see Paul shake a finger at me, his voice scolding me. "You are correct. There are thousands of vineyards. This Viner fellow was most likely a small country winegrower, and chances are no one remembers him. This does not sound like you, Charlotte. It's so . . . impulsive."

I frowned. Calling a pilot impulsive was a low blow. It was considered one of the worst traits a pilot could have. No, I was anything but impulsive. I always used appropriate decision-making techniques when evaluating a situation. Except, perhaps, when it came to Henri.

"I'm not impulsive," I objected. "I came up with a good plan.

I'm just trying to do what's right. No one here cares, though." I didn't add that even Paul didn't seem to care, but I knew he would pick up on it.

"The French are a complicated people," Paul said with a sigh. "Many were complicit in the war during the Occupation. There were enablers who tried to make money from the war. They have their own guilt that they are trying to forget. To face the past is to be embarrassed by it once again. Better to let the dead rest in peace."

I'd read books about the Resistance, but none that talked about the collaborators, those who enabled the Germans. And today I'd learned from Ferdinand that the president of France might also have been such a person.

"I'm not trying to make anyone uncomfortable," I said, defensively. "But you don't know for sure that he's dead. People were displaced during the war. And what about his daughter? Perhaps she is alive."

Even as I said this, I knew it was a long shot. If they were Jewish, there was a good chance they were no longer alive.

"You should have called me before you left. I found the name of a small village called Albertine where the name Viner showed up. Not that far from where you're at. I could have saved you all this time driving around. But why do you feel this obsession?" he asked. "Is it guilt over finding a valuable gift, one that through no effort of your own has fallen into your lap?"

Was it guilt? An unknown guilt passed down from my grandfather? He'd named his vineyard Dragoon Orchard. It wasn't until he died that I found out why he called it that. Dragoon was the name of a battle he'd fought in France during WWII. I'd looked it up. Operation Dragoon was a smaller version of D-Day. It took place in southern France. I imagined that's where my grandfather discovered his love of growing grapes.

I'd heard stories of how people had lost everything in the war: their homes, businesses, and their lives. My own grandfather had come back shell-shocked, according to my father. He'd spent the rest of his years retreating to the vineyard he'd purchased. The vineyard had become his sanctuary, but Dad saw it as a place where he hid away from the world, and he resented him for it.

"There's a reason van Gogh painted vineyards," Grandpa had once told me. "It's a spiritual place, where one can find peace and forgiveness."

What horrors did my grandfather see in France, and why did he find peace in a vineyard? Why did he need a spiritual retreat from the world? And what did he need forgiveness for?

"No," I now told Paul. "It's not guilt. It's . . . retribution."

"You owe no retribution," he said. "If you feel uncomfortable with this gift, then sell it and donate the proceeds to a charity."

"I should have called you before I took off on this wild-goose chase," I admitted. "I didn't know you'd found anything. I just want to know what happened to him. And his daughter."

He sighed. "Fine. Go to the village. But don't expect much in the way of results. They may not remember him. My advice is to enjoy the picturesque rolling hills of Burgundy, walk down the cobbled paths, and savor the excellent wines. And don't forget to eat some crepes. And perhaps some crème brûlée."

Of course, Paul would mention food. But it was true. I hadn't had time to explore the beautiful cities and historic villages. There were gorgeous cathedrals and ancient castles that I'd passed by. Perhaps Paul was right. There was no reason to search for someone who most likely was deceased, another victim of the war. And even if his daughter was alive, I didn't even know her name. She would have married and changed her name by now, making it even more difficult to find her. Did his daughter even know about the note?

What difference did one bottle of wine make when there was

so much devastation and tragedy, and when no one seemed to want to revisit it?

Hadn't I done enough to assuage Grandpa's guilt? So why continue? Was I doing this as a way to avoid telling Henri about the bottle of wine? Or admit to myself that Henri was a mistake in my life? Was I more in love with the idea of marriage and family than I was with Henri?

Henri was the first man I'd considered marrying. I'd had a steady boyfriend in high school, but at the time neither of us was ready for a commitment or a long-distance relationship. I avoided men in flight school, but after I became a pilot I met Raul, the Spaniard, who eventually broke it off because he was too macho to date a woman pilot. And then there was Carl, a flight attendant, who also ended our relationship mostly because of the constant barrage of jokes he faced due to our reversed roles. Both relationships had started out well, at least I thought they had. I knew my career made things more difficult.

When I'd been in flight school, I was one of three women in a sea of men, and it hadn't changed much since then. Tom Cruise and *Top Gun* had only helped perpetuate the "boys club" mentality. My manager had asked me several times if I had plans to marry, and if so, how would I manage family life with being a pilot? None of my male counterparts was ever asked that question.

It hadn't bothered me before, when I was in my twenties. But now that I was over the thirty mark, it did. Why did I have to make sacrifices when the men pilots didn't? It wasn't fair! How could I even go about forming a relationship when I was gone so much of the time?

I took one last sip of wine and set the glass on the small nightstand next to my bed. I'd barely even registered the décor of my room, which included muted brick walls and a rugged fireplace. The hotel was a renovated eighteenth-century farmhouse that managed to maintain its authentic style. All this beauty around me, and I was missing it to restore my grandfather's reputation, to amend his shame when I didn't even know what he'd done to warrant such remorse. And to make myself feel better about spending that money when I sold the bottle of wine.

Tomorrow was my last day. Why not enjoy it? I decided I would visit the village Paul mentioned before heading back to Paris.

After I returned from my next trip, I'd call Henri and meet with him. It was the least I could do. And then I could make a rational, *unimpulsive* decision about him.

CHAPTER ELEVEN

MADAME'S MEMORY

ALBERTINE WAS A DOT OF A VILLAGE SOMEWHERE BETWEEN Dijon and the commune of Vosne-Romanée, where the famed estate of Romanée-Conti produced some of the best wine in the world. I was lured by the sign with grapes drawn on it, and the winding tree-lined road that held some kind of promise. Paul had warned me that it might be a fruitless stop, that I might find no one who remembered either the man or his vineyard. Perhaps it was Paul's directive that steered me, one that commanded me to savor the beauty of this region. Either way, I couldn't resist at least trying.

A thin mottled road curved up a steep hill, which led into the little town, a charming place that reminded me of some picturesque postcard, with its church steeple rising above the colored tiled roofs and a river that meandered through town, complete with a stone bridge above it.

It looks like a fairy tale, I thought, feeling glad I'd stopped.

I had started the trip by visiting wineries, but there was more to learn about the history of a place by searching for a museum or history center, usually located in the center of a town. The few I had visited hadn't produced any results, and unfortunately, I didn't see such a place in this small village either.

Other than museums and history centers, there was the municipal center, which every town and village usually had. I looked for a brick building with a large clock in the middle of its façade, which was usually where the municipal center was located. I found it on the corner of a block that held an outdoor café, an inn, a flower shop, a souvenir store, and a restaurant.

Beneath the clock was the municipal center, and inside, a small office with two desks, so I assumed a small staff as well.

A middle-aged woman sat at one desk, her short grayish hair tucked behind one ear, glasses perched on top of her head.

I fumbled with my French, asking the same questions I had practiced the last two days. If she knew of a man named Zachariah Viner, who had owned a vineyard in 1940 and produced wine under the label Viner. Or of his daughter, whose name I didn't know. That they may have been Jewish.

Finally, the woman grew impatient. "You are American? You speak English?"

"Oh, yes," I said, wincing at the woman's annoyance. "I need to practice my French more."

"I have never heard of anyone by that name."

"Oh. Is there anyone else I can ask?"

The woman sighed. "Madame Reza might know. She is one of our oldest residents, a former schoolteacher, and she dines every day at the café next door. She should be there now."

"Does she speak English?" I asked.

"No. But I can translate. That would be faster. And much easier on her ears!"

She stood and led me out the door. I plastered a limp smile on my face as I followed, thankful she was helping me, even if she had insulted me in the process.

Madame Reza was a tiny white-haired woman. Her stooped shoulders barely cleared the table. She was taking miniature-size bites of a custard, her shaky hands barely able to hold the spoon. But behind the black-framed glasses, her eyes looked sharp, and perhaps a bit cross, judging by the way she was scowling at the custard.

Another woman sat with her, perhaps her daughter? She tucked a sweater around Madame Reza's shoulders. And then Madame Reza scowled at her too.

"Bonjour, madame," said the woman from the municipal office. After making quick pleasantries in French, she introduced me as an American who was looking for someone who may have lived in the village by the name of Viner.

"He would have lived here around 1940," I said in English, "and he owned a vineyard."

The woman, whose name was Patrice, translated, and added something else, which might have been another insult. Of course it was. I could tell by the smirk on her face. This woman Patrice didn't seem to like me, but she'd been kind enough to leave her desk, and I was indebted to her for that.

But something sparked in Madame Reza's eyes, which suddenly changed focus from the custard she was eating to the woman standing before her. Her forehead creased, then she finally spoke. Two words.

"Fille. Martine."

My heart leapt.

"Was Martine his daughter?"

Madame Reza nodded. "Oui." She spoke fast now, too fast for me to keep up. I looked to Patrice to translate, almost grabbing her arm to hurry her.

"She remembers them," Patrice said. "He was a single father. The mother died at birth, and he owned a vineyard west of here. She taught his daughter, Martine."

Patrice asked Madame Reza something else, and there was a flurry of conversation between them that I couldn't understand. It was infuriating not to know what they were saying.

Finally, they looked at me. "They were Jews, and as far as Madame Reza can remember, they were taken away. She heard from Zachariah's neighbor Madame Moreau that he was sent to Dijon Prison. And that Martine died. All the Jews disappeared shortly after that. Martine was, how do you say, a bit slow?" Patrice said.

"What do you mean by slow?"

Patrice asked, then turned to me. "She could not read like the other children."

"How old was she when she was taken?" I asked.

Patrice asked Madame Reza, who rolled her eyes as she answered.

"She says she was about seven or eight. She says that Martine carried a filthy stuffed rabbit with her everywhere, and she couldn't get her to leave it at home. Her father was very . . ." —she searched for the word— ". . . lax and permissive, which Madame Reza says was a detriment to her education. She blamed him for his daughter's laziness in learning. He allowed his daughter to work in the vineyard, and her head and heart were with the grapes instead of her schoolwork."

"Oh." I was taken aback by this attitude. To me, it sounded like Martine's father had loved her dearly. He'd taken care to arrange for her future with an expensive bottle of wine, as a vintner may have seen fit. I felt an urge to defend Martine and her father, who was raising a daughter as a single parent while a war raged around him. Of course he'd want her in the vineyard with him. And how could she label a child who didn't read at seven years old as lazy? Perhaps there were other issues with her learning?

The idea of a young child carrying a ragged stuffed rabbit to school made my heart ache.

Patrice turned to go. "The vineyard is now called Clos Lapointe. It's about five kilometers west of here. Madame Moreau is still alive and still lives on the property next to the vineyard. But she is older than Madame Reza. She may not remember much."

"Merci." I thanked Madame Reza and Patrice, who clearly was finished with me, as she was heading back to her office.

I drove the three miles to the vineyard. This was a sign, after all. A woman who actually remembered the Viner family, who remembered his daughter. Even as the news about their very probable deaths was disheartening, at least I had found out something about them. I had the daughter's name now. And perhaps the owners of the vineyard might share some insight? Or the neighbor, Madame Moreau?

The road was paved, although I doubted it was when they lived here. But I wondered if much else had changed in the last fifty years, as I drove past sturdy farmhouses that looked far older than that. The paved road turned to dirt, and dust coated the outside of the car. At the crest of a hill I came to a pale stone house set between a valley and forest. The road leading to it announced CLOS LAPOINTE. The sloping valley was filled with a swath of green vines. Behind the house was the winery, and a subterranean cellar with a sign above it, VIGNERONS. Winemakers.

I drove past it to the next farmhouse, one with a half-dead tree in front of the faded small stone building with square windows, which looked as though it had been there for centuries. Outside the tiny house a woman sat on a wooden chair with a cat perched on her lap. She wore a wide-brimmed hat over her white hair and looked as ancient as the stone house. It must be Madame Moreau.

I stopped the car and got out. I gave a friendly wave to the woman so as not to frighten her. The only one who seemed frightened was the cat, which dashed off Madame Moreau's lap and ran behind the house. Madame Moreau merely frowned at me, looking down through thick glasses that covered milky-blue eyes.

"Madame Moreau, I am Charlotte Montgomery," I said in French. "I spoke to Madame Reza, and she said you remember a man and daughter who lived near to you. Zachariah Viner and his daughter, Martine? C'est possible?"

Madame Moreau sat up straighter and squinted. "Américaine?"

"Oui. Do you know what happened to them?"

Madame Moreau made a sour face. "Morts."

Dead! I couldn't hide my disappointment. "Oh. Even the little girl? Martine?"

The woman shrugged. "She came to us, wanting help. I told my husband she was trouble. But he wanted to help her. He took her to the train station, but she died on the way when a German soldier stopped him and bayoneted her in the back of the cart."

I instinctively put a hand on my stomach. "That's awful! C'est terrible!"

"Oui. It is what my late husband told me. He was only spared because he gave the soldier my tomato and mustard tart. That is what happens when you try to help a Jew." She looked around. "Where is my cat?"

I cursed under my breath, then looked around for the straggly cat, a yellow tabby who had seen better days. I found it near the door to the house and picked it up, hurrying to deposit it on Madame Moreau's lap as it scratched up my arms the entire time.

Then I hurried back to the car, wondering why I'd bothered to help that old woman. She didn't seem the least bit sympathetic to the plight of poor Martine. I couldn't help but think how unfair it was that a little girl died while that wretched woman lived well into her nineties.

I drove back to the vineyard and parked in the small lot designated for customers. A few other cars were there as well. I started to get out but stopped. What would I say to them? I had no idea how long the current owners had lived here, or whether they would appreciate me bringing up a previous owner who had lost his vineyard during the war. They might feel I was accusing them of stealing the vineyard. They might be suspicious of me.

I slumped back in my seat. What had felt so right before now felt wrong. I now knew that both the owner and his daughter had died during the war.

What bothered me most, as I had learned from Paul, was that the current owners most likely *had* stolen the vineyard.

CHAPTER TWELVE

THE ABBEY

MARTINE

1942

MARTINE ATTENDED DAILY MASS, ALWAYS KNEELING NEXT to Sister Ada, her chin coming just to the top of the pew as she pretended to mouth the strange words they spoke in unison. She turned the pages of her missalette with the thick black cover when Sister Ada turned hers, trying to keep up even though she couldn't read the words, and even if she could, she didn't understand Latin, which is what Sister Ada said was the language of the Mass.

She avoided looking at the front because a giant cross, just like the one in her room, was mounted behind the altar. Sister Ada explained it was a crucifix, and the poor suffering man affixed to it was named Jesus.

Martine preferred the statue that occupied the far side of the altar, the one with the pretty woman and the chubby baby, who reminded her of a cherub without wings. She later found out this was also Jesus, as a baby. How could one look from that peaceful baby to the wretched man on the cross without feeling completely miserable? This Jesus met an awful fate and was a constant reminder that her own papa had been dragged away by the Germans. Would she ever see him again?

When it was deemed safe, when no Germans were near, Martine was allowed outside. She helped the nuns with their large garden, where they grew potatoes, corn, onions, carrots, and radishes in orderly rows just like the pews in the church. Martine would pick the weeds that threatened to crowd the plants.

She enjoyed being outdoors, but just like in Papa's vineyard, she was prone to wandering off, exploring the grounds of the abbey. Sister Ada threatened her with extra chapel time.

"You can help in the garden, but I have no time to search for you every day," Sister Ada said. "You will get lost."

Martine didn't mind being among the plants, which reminded her of the vineyard that she missed, although the flat land on which the garden was located was nothing like the rolling hills of the vineyard. Next to the abbey was a small cemetery, where she'd hide behind tall tombstones when Sister Ada came looking for her, because Martine had to explore despite her promise to stay nearby.

Behind the garden was a thick forest. She knew that if the Germans came, she was supposed to hide in a room that connected to another tiny room. The tiny room was a confessional, and the wall opened up to another long room that held candles and was dark and musty. The little confessional Sister Ada had shown her reminded her of the armoire, and she shivered just at the thought of going in there, remembering how Papa had disappeared last time.

If the Germans came when she was outdoors, she was to run and hide in the forest, behind a tall tree that was split in two and had a yellow ribbon tied around one limb.

The Germans had only come once, she learned. That time they had taken all the food before they left, something Sister Ada seemed to worry about now as their scant provisions dwindled. They prayed daily that the crops would produce an early yield, before the Germans returned.

Sister Thérèse, an elderly nun who had trouble bending down to work in the garden, had begged a local merchant for extra material and sewed a plaid dress with a white collar for Martine. It also had a deep pocket in which she kept her rabbit, Annabella.

Although Martine had no playmates, she didn't mind being around these women, most of whom were nice, except for Sister Jeanette, who complained that Martine needed more supervision and would be better off at the village orphanage.

When Martine assisted in the kitchen, helping to dry dishes, she often broke a cup or chipped a plate. Each time she dropped a plate she remembered the wine bottle Papa had given her, and she started to cry.

"You are too old to act like that," Sister Jeanette admonished her with a puckered mouth. Martine thought that Sister Jeanette didn't like children, or at least she didn't like her, but Sister Ada said that was just her personality and she was always in a foul mood.

Martine finally asked Sister Ada about Papa, admitting that he had been taken away by the Germans. Could she help Martine find him?

"I will try to find out what I can," Sister Ada promised, but she looked quickly away.

One day, Sister Ada handed Martine a thick black book to read.

"It's called a Bible," she said. "The first books in it are the same as the Torah. We will start with Genesis. You must practice your reading."

Martine accepted the book with a heavy heart. Papa had read to her every night from the Hebrew Bible, and she knew the stories from Genesis. But her throat went tight, and tears sprang to her eyes.

"I cannot read," she blurted out, crying. "I am an imbecile." Would Sister Ada turn her out now that she knew? Would she send her to the orphanage? She wanted to stay here, near Sister Ada. Because, despite the danger of the Germans and the fact that she had to pretend to be Catholic, Martine was beginning to feel safe once again.

She felt the long black robe surround her body as Sister Ada gathered her in her arms. "You are not an imbecile, Martine. Whoever told you that was a terrible person."

Sister Ada bent down and put her face in front of Martine's. A wisp of red hair stuck out of her white headdress. Her soft, smooth skin and thin arms made her look younger than the other nuns.

"Shalom, my child. I will teach you to read," she said, with a force in her voice that left no question. "We will start tomorrow."

Martine nodded, still worried she would disappoint Sister Ada the same way she disappointed Papa. Madame Reza had declared her a hopeless case. But Sister Ada's determination was contagious. Perhaps this time she would be able to make sense of the symbols. She would try again, she decided. If only to please Sister Ada.

And even more important, if she could learn to read, when she returned home she would show Madame Reza that she was *not* an imbecile.

CHAPTER THIRTEEN

LEARNING TO READ

THE FIRST THING SISTER ADA DID WAS CUT PAPER INTO small pieces. On one side she wrote a letter, and on the other was a picture of something that started with the letter.

"These are called flash cards, but since we have no money to buy them, I made some for you. Sister Thérèse drew the pictures. She's much more talented in art than I am," Sister Ada explained.

Martine had to agree that Sister Thérèse was talented. She'd used a pencil to sketch out pictures for each letter. From the detailed nest she'd drawn for *N* (*nid*), to the flamingo for *F* (*flamant*), they were each intricately detailed. Martine's favorite was for what she would learn was the letter *R*, which was *raisin*. Grape. It reminded her of where she came from, and she kept looking at the picture over and over. The cluster of round, plump grapes looked like they could be hanging in Papa's vineyard. The grapes in his vineyard would be ripe by now and there would be much activity. She missed the sounds of the vineyard: the rumble and squealing of trucks during harvest, and the pickers chatting or singing tra-la-la after a long lunch.

The letters on the flash cards stuck in her brain this time, as if the pictures held some kind of magic glue. Papa had said she was smart, and she was eager to prove him right. She would make up for her biggest disgrace: dropping her inheritance, the bottle of wine Papa had warned her not to lose.

But the biggest difference in learning was Sister Ada's patience. She didn't become exasperated like Madame Reza had, she never hit her hand with a ruler or made Martine feel idiotic, and she never said a harsh word. But most of all, she made Martine feel hopeful, as if this was a simple puzzle, and she had been missing some of the pieces until now. Even as she progressed slowly, Sister Ada always praised her. And by fall, when the leaves were turning and the grapevines at home would be whispery brown instead of green, she had learned all the letters and sounds of the alphabet.

Martine thrived under Sister Ada's tutelage, and soon she was reading about Babar, le petit éléphant, and was learning to write. Printing her own name made Martine feel powerful, even as paper was difficult to come by. She was allowed to write on old hymnals that had been discarded.

Martine still had to hide when there were rumors of German troops nearby. Sometimes, she had to run into the thick forest near the abbey. It was different than the forest that bordered the vineyard at home. It was dense, and dark, and she was glad that she didn't have to spend much time there.

Martine still had nightmares, ones in which she heard Papa screaming, and others in which she was lost on the streets of Paris where she dropped a bottle of wine and the Germans were chasing her. She woke up, sometimes crying. Often, Sister Ada was near and would come to comfort her. But occasionally Martine had gone to Sister Ada's room in the middle of the night to ask her to keep her company until she fell asleep again, and sometimes she was not there. She never asked her where she'd gone, but it worried Martine to find her empty bed.

On this particular night, when Martine woke, barely catching her breath from running in her dream, Sister Ada was again not in her room. Rather than return to the nightmare, Martine walked down the darkened hallway, clutching her stuffed rabbit, Annabella.

The barely perceptible thud of her bare feet on the stone floor was the only sound as she made her way toward the kitchen, looking to find a piece of bread to comfort her grumbling stomach.

But as she passed a doorway, she felt a cool breeze, and noticed that the door was propped slightly open with a rock. She stopped and looked outside. Why would someone leave the door ajar?

She was about to remove the rock when she heard voices, soft, but distinct, as though they were standing outside around the corner of the building. One of the voices belonged to Sister Ada. Martine couldn't see anyone, but the faint voices drew her outside. She stopped and peeked around the brick edge, holding very still even as a cold wind rippled through her nightgown and the bottoms of her feet felt like ice.

Sister Ada was talking to a man. He wore a thick coat and beret, and had a dark mustache and matching dark hair. They were standing very close to each other. A bright moon shone down upon them, and they huddled close to the building as if afraid of being seen.

"It's becoming more dangerous," he said. "You should stay here, where you're safe."

Sister Ada shook her head, her black habit whipping around in the wind like a flag on a pole. "Not while my people are being taken like cattle to slaughter. I've heard what those camps are like."

Martine shrunk away from the corner of the building when she heard this. A newfound fear braced her. She had known the Germans had taken Papa and Tante Anna. But now she knew how bad it really was. They sent them to camps, which she didn't quite understand, but it was bad enough that they might not survive. The nightmare that had woken her just a few minutes ago now had added power.

"They have executed entire villages when they suspected the Resistance was operating there."

"The abbey has been left alone so far," Sister Ada said.

"But if you're caught . . ."

"I know. I'm putting the nuns at risk. And Martine. I will be careful."

Martine peeked around the corner again.

The man reached out and touched Sister Ada's cheek. "The Russians have stalled the Germans in Stalingrad."

"We need more help," Sister Ada said, covering his hand with hers.

They stayed like that for a long moment, his hand on her cheek, as they looked into each other's eyes. The man finally spoke again. "We have to stop them. We can't wait for the Americans or British to save us."

"But who will save you, André? I couldn't bear it if anything were to happen to . . ."

She didn't finish her sentence. Sister Ada had stopped talking because the man named André was kissing her. And Sister Ada was kissing him back!

This was nothing like a peck on the cheek, the way Papa kissed Martine goodnight. She was confused. Martine didn't think that nuns were supposed to be kissing men, especially the way Sister Ada was kissing André.

Martine turned and fled then. She ran to the door and kicked the rock aside, letting the door slam behind her as she ran back down the hallway to her bed.

CHAPTER FOURTEEN

SECRETS

THE NEXT DAY MARTINE WAS ALONE IN HER ROOM, READING to herself, or trying to. The story she read contained many words she was unfamiliar with. Words like *parable*, and *transgression*.

A slant of afternoon light filled part of her small bed and brightened the drab wall that held only a small crucifix.

She turned to Annabella. "Don't you hate this scratchy blanket and hard mattress?" she asked her stuffed rabbit.

"Sister Jeanette says I should feel grateful for a roof over my head. But it's always cold. Not like our snug bed at home with the warm quilt. Even the sunshine feels cold here."

She felt someone standing behind her. She hoped it wasn't Sister Jeanette, who would scold her for being ungrateful again. When she looked up, Sister Ada was there, twisting her hands together over her rosary beads, smiling nervously.

"You have been so quiet today, Martine. You barely said anything at breakfast this morning, and you looked sullen at Mass."

Martine didn't know what *sullen* meant. What could she say? Everything about Sister Ada didn't make sense, but she didn't know how to ask her. She only knew that the trust she'd felt had been shaken. And she didn't feel as safe as she had yesterday.

So, Martine said nothing, and continued to focus her eyes on the book folded open between the pleats of her skirt. Her rabbit,

Annabella, was propped next to her as if she was reading along with Martine.

But then Sister Ada was kneeling down in front of her, and she felt a hand turn her chin so that she was face-to-face with the woman. Sister Ada gently swiped a piece of dark hair from Martine's face that had fallen from her braid.

"If there is something you want to say to me, please do," Sister Ada said. "You can ask me anything."

Martine wanted to understand. She loved Sister Ada, who brushed and braided her hair every morning, taught her school lessons, and who seemed more like a mother than a nun. In fact, if Martine could choose a mother, she would have picked someone just like Sister Ada.

She blinked and took a breath. "Do nuns kiss men?"

"I'm not sure I understand," Sister Ada said.

Martine thought about what she really wanted to ask. "Do nuns have boyfriends?"

Sister Ada's cheeks flushed. "No. They don't."

"But don't you have one?" Martine said, stating what she was sure was a fact. "I saw you kissing a man."

Sister Ada pursed her lips, as though trying to decide what to say. Finally, she stood and closed the door before she spoke. "You're right. I do have un petit ami."

She sighed. "You must not tell anyone, Martine. Not Mother Superior or any of the other sisters. I want to tell you this so you know that you can trust me, so you know who I really am."

She sat on the bed next to Martine.

"I am not a nun. Mother Superior saved me like I saved you."

"What do you mean?"

"I am a Jew."

"But you're a nun!" Martine's eyes were wide.

"No. I'm not a nun. I was a teacher in Paris before the war. I had a Catholic friend who knew Mother Superior, and she sent me here. I am pretending to be a nun like you are pretending to be my niece."

Martine considered all that Sister Ada had said. This would explain why she knew so much about the Jewish faith. And why she sometimes crept out at night. They were both pretending.

"What is his name?" she finally asked. "Your boyfriend?"

"His name is André."

"Where does he live? In the village?"

"He used to live in the village. Now he lives in the woods. He is a member of the Resistance. Do you know what that is?"

"No." But she remembered that Damien, who worked for her father, was taken away for being part of the Resistance, and it frightened her.

"They are mostly men from the village. André is Catholic. But he is fighting for France, and for our freedom. If he is caught, he will be shot. I don't want André to be caught, or shot. So we cannot tell anyone. And we must pray for their success."

"If they win, will I see Papa again?"

"I don't know. But I hope you will. Will you keep my secret?"

"I'm not very good at keeping secrets," Martine confessed. She'd already had to keep so many. First, Monsieur Moreau had asked her to use a different name. Then she'd had to act as though Mademoiselle Tridon was her mother during the train ride. Now she was pretending to be Catholic, and that Sister Ada was her aunt. It was all so confusing. She was afraid she'd make a mistake. She remembered how she'd dropped the bottle of wine, how she'd made mistakes from the very beginning.

"This is a very important secret, though," Sister Ada said, her voice becoming stern. "If the nuns find out, they will send me away. And I have to say this, even though it will frighten you, Martine. They may send you away too."

Would they send her to the orphanage? Sister Jeanette would certainly do that. Martine wanted to stay here.

"I will try," Martine said.

Sister Ada shook her head. "No. You must do more than try. You must never tell anyone. Not a soul, no matter who it is. Do you remember when I taught you about covenants? You must think of this as a covenant, one that cannot be broken. Like the one God made with Abraham."

"I won't tell anyone," Martine promised. "And I will pray for André. But I am not very good with my Catholic prayers."

"Then perhaps we should spend more time learning those prayers, as well as the prayers of your ancestors."

"I know the Hamotzi," Martine said. At least she knew most of it by heart. It was the blessing over bread before meals that Papa always recited.

"Very good," Sister Ada said. "But again, this must remain our secret. Mother Superior would not approve of Hebrew prayers, and the other sisters would suspect us of being Jews if they heard us. And that would be dangerous for all of us. So, you will have to learn both Catholic and Jewish prayers. And you may only say the Catholic prayers out loud. The Hebrew prayers must be kept here," she said, pointing to Martine's heart. "Can you do that?"

"Yes," Martine said. She still remembered the address of her aunt in Paris. She had turned eight years old. She hadn't told anyone that Sister Ada wasn't really her aunt. And if she could learn to read, something that had seemed impossible before, then she could remember all her prayers.

"Sister Ada," she said. "Can I ask you one more thing?"

"Yes, of course."

"Are you part of the Resistance too?"

Sister Ada paused for a long moment, then shook her head. "No, my child, of course not."

Was she being honest? Martine wanted to believe her. She wanted to feel relieved so she wouldn't have to worry that Sister Ada would be shot. To lose Sister Ada would be almost as bad as losing Papa.

Martine hadn't known that Damien was part of the Resistance. Did Papa know?

After Sister Ada left, Martine cuddled her rabbit in her arms and spoke to her. "I don't understand, Annabella. Was Papa taken away because he knew that Damien was part of the Resistance, or because he was Jewish? Why do Germans hate Jews?

"We must pray for André," she told her rabbit. "And for Sister Ada, and Damien, and also for Papa."

She paused, thinking, then whispered, "And perhaps we should say our prayers in both Latin and Hebrew, Annabella. That way, everyone will be protected."

CHAPTER FIFTEEN

THE WINERY

CHARLOTTE

1990

MADAME MOREAU HAD LEFT ME FEELING UNSETTLED. BEtween her and the teacher, it seemed clear that Zachariah Viner and his daughter had been treated poorly even before the Nazis arrived.

I needed to find out more. Next to the rolling vineyard, and behind the pale house, was a low building that looked like a cellar, with a small barn to the side. The low building had a sign on it with grapes. CAVE AUX VINS. Wine cellar. It was the only building with a sign, so it must be the winery. Very different from the châteaus and stately residences that had been transformed into the wineries I'd visited during the last two days.

I entered an arched stone room and was pleasantly surprised by a brightly lit row of fluorescent lights above polished wooden tables, half-filled with wine drinkers. Festive music muted the sounds of their voices. Behind the tasting room was the tank room, and tall barrels lined the entry. According to a brochure I picked up at the entry, the winery had been updated with stainless steel tanks for fermentation.

Under the biography section in the brochure, there was a paragraph on wine history in Burgundy dating to 50 BC, with additional information about Burgundy I'd already seen before. Nothing of note about the personal history of this particular winery or how long they'd owned it.

A young man stood behind a counter. He spoke French, asking if I wanted to taste the Pinot Noir, their specialty.

"Can I speak with the owners?" I asked in my stilted French.

He gave me a quizzical look, then nodded toward the back. "Une minute."

He left, and I wasn't sure if I was supposed to wait or follow him. I took out a notebook I'd brought along to jot down notes, thinking I could possibly pass myself off as a journalist. It was the best I could come up with on the fly.

The young man returned, followed by a tall, heavyset man dressed in a sweatshirt and jeans, his dark hair flecked with gray.

I extended my hand, hoping to make him feel more comfortable, and stumbled through my introduction in French. "Bonjour. I'm Charlotte Montgomery. I'm doing some research on local wineries, and I wonder if I could have a moment of your time."

"Do you prefer we speak in anglais?" he asked, and I nodded gratefully.

"That would be nice, thank you, Mr. Lapointe."

He guided me to an open table. "Call me Georges. My English is not as good as should be, but I have many English patrons who come to the winery. I keep practice."

"Your English is much better than my French," I reassured him. "And thank you for taking time to talk to me."

I opened the notebook, as if to take notes. "What can you tell me about your winery? How long have you been here?"

"Since 1962. We move from Lille in Nord-Pas-de-Calais. Wine

was my passion, and now my son, who you met, he will take over someday. A family business," he announced, with evident pride.

"How nice." I wrote it down in the notebook.

"Do you want to see tanks and cellar? We modernize some things, but cellar is still old, antiquated."

"Yes, I'd love to. Do you remember who you bought the winery from?"

"It was a local man, who almost destroyed the vines. He had no idea how to care for the grapes or run a business. We had to start at the beginning. It took many years to rebuild."

"He was local? From the village?"

"I think, yes. He died not long after I buy this winery. Left the house in ruin and disarray too."

"Do you remember his name? And do you know when and how he acquired the property?" I asked, preparing to write it down, but when I looked up, he was frowning.

"I'm sorry," I said, "did I say something to offend you?"

He folded his arms. "What is the real reason you ask?"

I was never a good liar. My mother said my face always flushed when I lied. I resisted the temptation to touch my cheeks because they felt warm. I closed the notebook and set down the pen. "I want to be honest with you, Georges. I'm inquiring about a girl who lived here during World War Two with her father, who owned the vineyard. They were Jewish."

I shook my head. "I'm not here to cause trouble. But I found a note from her father underneath a label on an old bottle of wine, and it made me curious. I was able to talk to her schoolteacher today, and from what she and your neighbor Madame Moreau told me, both Martine and her father perished in the war. There is no family left. When I found out where their vineyard was, I just wanted to see it and know who this girl was, where she lived, and know what her life was like. And I was curious about who took over the vineyard when they were sent away."

Georges's thick arms were still crossed. "You think I steal from a Jewish family?"

"No, of course not!"

My cheeks were burning now. I wrinkled my nose. "Well, actually, the thought crossed my mind, if I'm still being honest. Or perhaps it was the man you bought it from?"

He stared at me a long moment, then let out a loud belly laugh. "I like you. You are *too* honest. I rarely meet an honest American, but here you are."

"Well, you'd be the first in this village to say you like me. I haven't made any friends today."

"Villagers put up with Americans. They don't really like them."

"I had that distinct feeling," I said. "But I thought it was just me."

He shrugged. "Do not feel bad. They don't like me because I speak ch'ti dialect from north. They say I speak too fast."

"That makes me feel a little better."

"I can get you the name of the man who I bought it from. Maybe he was a thief. Who knows? I own it legal now and have for many years. But there is also something I can show you."

He stood. "Come with me."

He spoke as I followed him. "When we did renovations, we found a fake wall. Was very common for them to do this, to keep wine hidden from Nazis. My father fought during the war."

He walked fast for a big man, and I had to almost run to keep up.

"Did your father return?"

"Yes, but it was hard time for us. No food, and we were very poor. To have this vineyard now, to come from nothing and prosper . . ."

He stopped, and I almost ran into him. "It is dream come true for me," he said, and it looked as though he might cry.

"Here," he said, leading me down cement stairs. We were in the cellar, a cavernous room filled with barrels stacked upon one another like cheerleaders forming a pyramid. And opposite the barrels were shelves stacked to the ceiling and filled with bottles of wine. A wooden ladder, the kind that rolled and looked like you'd see in a library, leaned against the shelves.

He walked down the rows of shelves, rubbing his fingers across the ends of the bottles as dust settled behind him. Finally, he stopped and pulled out a sooty bottle. He wiped his fingers across the front, and I recognized the distinctive *V* of the label, the same label I had seen on the bottle at my apartment.

Georges shook his head. "He hid dozens of bottles of his wine. Perhaps he thought they were his best vintages and saved them, but I have tasted many of them and it was not very good wine. Most wine does not taste good after fifty years, though."

"Why did you keep it?"

He shrugged. "Is part of the history of my winery. I must honor that history. But I make much better wine. This climate is best in France."

"Do you mean the weather is best?"

"No. Climate not related to the weather. It refers to vineyard. This one has high concentration of clay and limestone, and vines must make more effort. Roots go deeper and affect the structure of wine. You can have different climate in same vineyard too."

I remembered this from Grandpa's vineyard, which did not have a very good climate.

He handed me the bottle. "I would not advise to drink this, but you can have the bottle."

"Thank you. I'll pay for it . . ."

"No, it is gift. For Martine. There is also a picture I have in my office at house. You can have as well."

"A picture? That's so nice. But why are you giving it to *me*?"

"You are the first person to ever inquire about her. It must mean something."

I hugged the dusty bottle. I thought I was doing this out of some feeling of obligation. But I now knew it extended beyond that. The note had bound me with a connection to a young girl that was deeper than mere duty.

Paul, and everyone else, said I should forget about it. Maybe it was as simple as that: I needed to remember the little girl that everyone else had forgotten about.

Or maybe it was figuring out what drew my grandfather to the vineyards during the war. How had it kept the darkness and bad thoughts away? What had he found here that helped him after the war?

Georges was right. It did mean something. I felt a stab of gratitude, and a feeling that I was meant to be here.

"Thank you, Zachariah. Thank you, Martine," I whispered as I left the cellar.

CHAPTER SIXTEEN

THE PICTURE

"SHE'S ADORABLE," I SAID, WHEN GEORGES SHOWED ME THE little girl with curly dark hair that stuck out of her pigtails, as if her hair couldn't be contained. She had a serious expression on her face, as though she was already facing tough challenges in life. The black-and-white photo showed a small girl wearing a light dress with dots and a white collar. On her feet were black Mary Janes, and she stood in the doorway we had just passed through. Martine was also clutching a stuffed animal, the shabby rabbit Madame Reza had mentioned, only in this picture it looked dazzling white and brand-new.

On the back of the photograph, a date was written, along with her name and age—*Martine Viner, quatre ans*, four years old.

"When I see this picture, I am filled with sadness now that I know they were Jewish," Georges said. "That this could happen in my lifetime. That I was allowed to grow up and she was not. No one told me this land was confiscated from Jews during the war. I had no idea. I thought it was just old picture."

I couldn't help but think of how Paul preferred to ignore the note I found, to think of it as inconsequential. And the people bidding on the wine at the Hôtel Drouot preferred to ignore the fact that the wine was most likely stolen by the Nazis from their fellow Frenchmen.

But none of it was Georges's fault. He'd paid for this property. "I didn't mean to make you feel guilty. Maybe the man you bought the vineyard from didn't know either," I said. "And I certainly don't intend to draw attention to the history of your winery. You have no need for worry, Georges. I'm not looking for retribution. I just wanted to find out what happened to them."

I didn't know how much guilt people should be responsible for, but burying history was also a mistake. Maybe if Grandpa had shared his story, we could have helped him more. We could have understood his pain.

Georges pressed the photo into my hands. "You are a good person, Charlotte. You take this picture."

He seemed reassured that my intentions were honorable, that I wasn't trying to take his winery from him. And I wasn't. As far as I was concerned, the story ended here. Both Martine and her father were deceased, and I wasn't about to go searching for any other relatives.

We talked for a long time after that, sharing a glass of his best wine. Georges was impressed that I was a pilot. "I think you make a better pilot than a journalist," he told me, which made me laugh.

When I left, I thanked him for the tour and the picture. "I'm glad I met you, Georges."

Georges nodded. "Ah, we cannot pick our relatives or our past. Only our friends. And today I'm glad to count you as one."

"So true. It's been a pleasure meeting you," I said. I would make certain to purchase several bottles of wine before I left. It was getting late, and I was due back in Paris this evening. He made me promise to return.

On the drive back, I thought about the little girl in the picture. Oddly, I didn't feel sad. Perhaps because I had found the winery, had seen the rolling hills and the quaint home Martine had lived in, and I had an actual picture of her. It was like visiting a historic site and discovering the people were real and not just caricatures. Despite the sad tale of what happened to them, I knew that Zachariah and Martine had a loving relationship. And I knew that Zachariah had stood up for his daughter.

I also knew that Georges was someone who had kept the winery going, someone who put care and love into the vineyard, and who hoped to pass it down to his own son.

How would Zachariah feel about Georges owning the vineyard now? I hoped it wouldn't matter. At least it still existed.

And now I was free to sell the wine, to buy Grandpa's vineyard. I'd done everything I could think of. It was time to let it go.

THE SUN WAS LOW WHEN I ARRIVED BACK AT MY APARTMENT. There were several messages. One was work-related, the others were all from Henri. He sounded frantic to meet me.

I hadn't meant to make him that worried. Or had I? I'd been avoiding his calls the last week because he hadn't called me that one particular day. It seemed so foolish now, to place so much importance on one phone call in light of all I'd recently learned.

I called his number, and he picked up after one ring.

"Where have you been, Charlotte? I have been ringing you for the entire week."

"Um, I've been busy."

"Busy with what?"

"Flying? It's what I do, you know. And then I've been seeing some friends." Henri didn't know if I had friends in Paris. Come to think of it, he didn't know all that much about me.

"Did you get my messages?"

"I did, and that's why I called you now."

"Can you make time to see me tonight? I need to talk to you."

Damn. How did he make my heart flutter like that?

"I don't know. I have to be up at five to leave tomorrow, and I still have to pack. I'm not sure I can make it tonight." It felt good to talk to him this way.

"It is extremely important, Charlotte. Very, very important. Please? I promise I will not keep you out late."

I kept my voice even, not wanting him to know how fast my heart was beating. "I guess I could make some time."

"Merci, Charlotte. Meet me in one hour at La Grenouille."

"Sure. I'll be there."

Maybe Henri was feeling my absence as strongly as I felt his. Even now, my body generated a sudden warmth. But I couldn't let desire overtake my mind.

"Absence makes the heart grow fonder, but presence puts the heart in danger," I said, as I went to pick out something appropriate to wear.

CHAPTER SEVENTEEN

CAT AND MOUSE

PARIS, FRANCE

LA GRENOUILLE—THE FROG—WAS A RESTAURANT THAT specialized in greens of all kinds. My favorite was salade Parisienne, which contained boiled ham, Emmenthal cheese, hard-boiled eggs, mushrooms, boiled potatoes, and lettuce.

Tonight, I was thinking of having a simple French bistro salad, though. Something light and clean to go with a white wine.

As always, the place was packed, and there was a line of people waiting for tables that spilled out from a sleek, modern interior onto a traditional patio, the tables covered in white linen. I hated the idea of a two-hour wait, which wasn't unusual here. Luckily, Henri had come early and was already seated at a table inside, and he smiled and kissed both of my cheeks when I arrived.

I sat down across from him. "Thank you for arriving early. I know they don't take reservations."

"I promised not to keep you out late," he said, looking rather earnest.

"That's so nice, Henri." He could be thoughtful when he wanted to be. That's another thing I found attractive about him.

He was dressed casually, in a blue soccer jersey, the one with the name Bruno on the back, who he said was the goalkeeper.

He had ordered a bottle of wine, and his glass was just a quarter full, which meant that he had been here awhile. He now filled my glass. It was red wine. I pushed the glass back.

"If you don't mind, I prefer white wine with my salad."

"This is a Bichot Pinot Noir, which goes very well with the salad I ordered for you."

"You ordered for me?"

"I knew you were in a hurry," he said, as though that was reason enough. "A French woman would appreciate it," he added.

"Right. Well, American women would consider it rude."

I usually drank red wine with him because he expected me to, because I let him have more control in our romance. But I'd told him several times that Chardonnay was my favorite. Or a good Sauvignon Blanc. After all this time, he still didn't know what I liked to drink? Or he didn't care?

A waiter approached and I asked for a glass of Chardonnay, which made Henri frown and shake his head. And when the waiter placed the white wine in front of me, Henri complained that the glass had a smudge on it and ordered him to get me another glass. I gave the waiter an apologetic look. Henri frequently sent back silverware and plates that he said weren't clean enough.

After the waiter placed the white wine in front of me for the second time, Henri raised his glass.

"I propose a toast."

I gave him a confused look but lifted my glass. "To what?"

"To good fortune."

I smiled and clinked my glass against his. "I can toast that. How was your week?"

"I attended another auction at Hôtel Drouot," Henri said, taking a sip of his wine. "I made two more good wine purchases, thanks in part to Max."

"That's nice," I said, shifting in my chair as I thought of the wine bottle hidden in my closet. The bottle I hadn't told him about yet.

"Yes, I am contemplating investing in a portable cellar, perhaps a built-in that will fit my apartment. I want to make sure I obtain a secure one, though. Something that will protect my collection."

"Well, you have a good start on your collection."

"Yes, well, about that. I heard some very interesting news. At the auction there was talk of a bottle of wine that a local sommelier had recently valued. A 1920 Roberge. Very rare, and very valuable."

I almost choked on my wine. I tried to keep my voice light. Even so, I felt my mouth tremble slightly. "Really? That's interesting."

Henri had his hands folded on the table He was staring at me, his eyes boring into mine. As if he knew.

I put on my game face and smiled at him.

He spoke slowly. "The owner of that bottle was an American woman."

I didn't react. I just kept up the fake smile, as though this was not a punch in my gut that was threatening to bowl me over. As though it wasn't an accusation.

It all made sense now. This was why he called, why he'd been so insistent to see me. It had nothing to do with our relationship, nothing to do with me at all, in fact. He hadn't missed me, like I'd thought.

It was the wine. Only the wine.

"So . . . ?" I finally said, feeling my voice shake.

"I just thought it odd, is all," he said. "Supposedly the bottle was bought at an auction at Hôtel Drouot, mixed in a box of other wines. The only wine auction recently was the one we attended."

He was watching me closely. I closed my hand tightly around the glass of wine, trying to keep my composure. Had I mentioned that to the sommelier? That the bottle of wine had been purchased recently at Hôtel Drouot? Or did Paul tell him that?

"Is it odd? There were so many people at that auction. I'm sure I saw several American women there," I said, although truth be told, I'd only seen a handful of women at the auction, and I didn't know if any of them were American. "I'm sure in this big city there must be many wine collectors. And I know there are many Americans too. Lots of expats and people on business, and tourists and such . . ." My voice trailed off. I was talking too much, and my cheeks were on fire.

He tapped his fingers on the table. "I have the name of the sommelier. Gérard Benefiel. I intend to speak to him."

I held my breath. Did the sommelier still remember my name? I'd introduced myself to him.

"Why are you going to speak to him? Are you interested in buying it?" I finally asked. "Wouldn't that wine be expensive? Can you afford such an expensive bottle of wine?"

"Normally, no, I could not afford it," he admitted. "But there's a possibility . . ."

The waiter was there then. He served the salads, although I had lost my appetite. I focused on individual pieces of lettuce, trying to keep the wetness from filling my eyes. I felt like such a fool.

Henri hadn't touched his food yet. I knew he was still watching me. I felt like we were playing some sort of cat and mouse game and I was the mouse. Was he toying with me? Did he know it was me? Or was he just suspicious?

He filled his wineglass, then cleared his throat before he spoke. "By the way, did you ever drink that bottle of wine I left with you?"

He asked it in a casual way, but it was a loaded question, one he'd been waiting to ask the entire evening. Because of course, this was the reason he'd asked me to meet him. He wanted to know if that bottle was the one he was looking for. If I was the American woman who had taken it to the sommelier.

I had to blink several times. And even then, my eyes still felt wet. I tried to think of something funny to say, a flippant remark, but my mind was blank. I'd meant to tell him about the wine, but this wasn't how I'd imagined it, under such scrutiny.

I forced another smile when I looked up at him and met his eyes.

"Yes, I did," I lied.

"Oh," he said, sounding disappointed.

It gave me a little pleasure to see him this way. I had no intention of telling him the truth now. Not after it had become clear that he wasn't the least bit interested in me, but only in that damn bottle of wine. "Are you all right?" he asked. "You seem upset."

I took a napkin and blotted my eyes. "My allergies are acting up." Because of course Henri didn't know I didn't have allergies. He knew nothing about me, and I realized he'd never been all that interested to begin with.

"You didn't think that bottle of wine was valuable, did you?" I asked innocently. "Both you and Max examined it."

He cleared his throat again. "No, of course not. Max said it was not worth anything. But I just was not sure, you know, such a coincidence, with the woman being American, and the timing and all. But of course, that is ludicrous. You would have told me if it were you."

"That bottle had a different label too. It wasn't a Roberge," I added.

"Yes," he admitted. "That is true. But there was some uncertainty about the label."

I wasn't about to let him off the hook that easily.

"So, what did you want to talk to me about? You said it was very important."

He checked his watch and stumbled for an answer. Now he wouldn't even look at me. "I, um, just wanted to make certain you were not angry at me, you know, for not calling you last week. I was completely bogged down at work. We have been working extra hard this time of year. . . ."

He kept talking, but I had stopped listening. I was no longer interested in his excuses.

I was no longer interested in Henri at all.

CHAPTER EIGHTEEN

ANDRÉ

MARTINE

1943

THE WEATHER TURNED COLD, AND MARTINE WORE SWEATers knitted by Sister Thérèse, plus an oversize coat they'd procured for her, as she walked the gardens one last time looking for anything that could still be harvested. The potatoes and beans were long gone, but a few leeks still stood tall despite the frost that had covered the ground.

She had been at the abbey for five months, had celebrated Christmas with the nuns, and still the war raged on. Other than the kindly priest who performed Mass for them, and a few neighbors who traded objects for food, they were isolated most of the time. The nuns were used to this, to their small, cloistered family, but Martine missed the energy of a busy village, the sounds of dogs barking and children playing games. The church bells that rang were all that reminded her of the village she'd left behind.

Due to their remote location, the nuns were spared from seeing many Germans, or from having their abbey requisitioned like so many others had. Sister Ada said Martine was safe here.

But she still missed Papa.

She looked up to see Sister Ada outside, cupping her hands around her mouth.

"Hide in the forest, Martine," she shouted. "Run!"

Martine dropped the vegetables in her hands and ran. She didn't turn around until she reached the tree that was split in two and held a yellow ribbon around one of its limbs. The Germans were at the abbey! There were now several of them shouting, trampling through the garden, kicking at the barren dirt, holding their rifles pointed at the nuns, who kept their heads down, barely looking at the soldiers. Other men in uniform were walking around, smoking cigarettes, and surveying the abbey's stone walls.

A man wearing a French uniform, the visor of his kepi low over his eyes, yelled at the nuns as he translated what the Germans were saying.

"You fat sows! You cannot have eaten all this food! There must be more than what we found in the cellar."

Mother Superior looked up and met the eyes of the German officer. "We gave you all we have. All of it was stored in our cellar."

"Liar!"

How could a Frenchman talk like that to Mother Superior? She didn't act frightened at all by him or the Germans. The other nuns were visibly shaken, though. They stood together. A few held hands.

Martine moved from the tree and hid behind a tall oak nearby, which is what Sister Ada had told her to do, in case the Germans saw the ribbon. She stayed there as she was told to do. She must wait for Sister Ada to come give the all-clear signal, which was holding her hands up in the air above her head in a prayerlike stance. But the Germans were still there.

What if they decided to stay at the abbey? Would she have to remain in the dark forest all night?

As she waited, several leaves drifted down from the tree and landed on her head. Martine looked up, expecting to see a mischievous squirrel, but instead she saw a man in the tree. He was looking through a pair of binoculars at the abbey.

Martine covered her mouth to keep from screaming. But when she looked up again, she recognized him as the man Sister Ada had met outside last month. He had the same dark hair and mustache and was wearing the same beret on his head. She knew his name was André. She had been praying for him every night.

Did he know Martine was right underneath him? He didn't acknowledge her presence. She watched him for several long minutes, wondering if she should say anything.

She picked up a dry leaf and played with it for a while, picking away at the edges of it until there was nothing left but the stem. When she looked up, André had moved to a different branch. He was still watching the abbey, seemingly unaware of the girl beneath him.

Finally, she felt brave enough to speak. "Monsieur?"

André jumped and fell back on the branch he was standing on, dropping the binoculars, which crashed to the ground beside Martine.

He grabbed a gun out of his pocket and aimed it below, and Martine cried out. Was he going to shoot her?

But when he finally realized it was a small girl at the base of the tree, he put the gun away and climbed down.

Martine took a step back, afraid.

"Who are you?" he demanded in a low voice when he reached the bottom.

Martine felt her throat close. She couldn't speak.

"Are you Martine?" he whispered. "Are you alone?"

She nodded.

"What are you doing out here?"

"Hiding," she said in a small voice.

He looked toward the abbey. "From the Germans?"

She nodded. "How do you know my name?"

Just then a shot rang out. Martine jumped and started to cry. André put his hand over her mouth.

"Shh . . . We mustn't make noise."

What if they shot Sister Ada? Or Mother Superior? Martine trembled. She felt a stream of liquid run down her leg. She was too frightened to be embarrassed.

"It's okay," André whispered. "It was a warning shot into the air meant to frighten them. The Germans do it all the time. There isn't anyone lying on the ground."

But his eyes were wide, fixed on the abbey.

Martine held her breath, waiting for another shot, and felt André's body stiffen beside her as if he was waiting too.

A few minutes later the Germans herded the nuns inside.

André relaxed and took his hand off Martine's mouth. "I'm sorry to have scared you. You must have sneaked into the forest while I was resting. I have been known to fall asleep in trees, sometimes even falling out of them," he said, rubbing his backside. He wore a thick gray scarf around his neck that looked like one that Sister Thérèse had been knitting. He was dressed in a faded dark brown coat that had twigs and leaves stuck to it. He picked up the binoculars, which had landed in a pile of leaves, and rubbed off a lens with his sleeve.

"Thank God, they're not broken."

Martine felt a cold wind nip at her ankles and was now ashamed of the wetness between her legs. She worried André would smell the foul odor. He acted as if he didn't notice.

"Are the Germans gone?" she asked.

"I think they are. But I would not go back just yet, to be safe."

Safe. A word that Martine couldn't rely on anymore. "I must wait for Sister Ada to give me a sign."

"Sister Ada?"

André took a cigarette out of his pocket and put the end in his mouth. He struck a match against the bark of the tree, shielding one hand over the cigarette as he lit it. He sucked on it, then blew out a long white breath that swirled up in the cold air. Martine watched the smoke and took comfort in the smell, as it reminded her of Papa.

"What do you think of Sister Ada?" André finally asked.

Martine thought about what she should say. Sister Ada said she shouldn't tell anyone the truth about her. But André knew Sister Ada, and he knew she wasn't a real nun. Martine had seen them kissing.

"I love her," she answered, telling him the truth. "Sister Ada is my friend. She found me on the streets of Paris. She brought me here. I was very sick, and she took care of me. I am supposed to tell people she is my aunt. But she is not my aunt."

André frowned and looked concerned. "And why do you tell me the truth? Don't you know that it is dangerous to reveal Sister Ada's secrets? Especially to a stranger you meet in the forest?"

"You are not a stranger. I can tell you because you are her petit ami, André."

His eyes widened. "Ouh là . . . did she say that? Did she tell you my name?"

Martine's face felt warm, even in the cold forest. "Yes. Aren't you her boyfriend?"

He sighed. "I love her with all my heart."

"But you are not Jewish. You don't care that she is a Jew?"

"You seem to know a great deal about me, Martine. My heart does not care about whether Ada is Jewish or not. It is no consequence to me. But we are at war."

Martine knotted her brows together. "You are fighting the Germans. It is very dangerous."

"Yes," he said, looking around. "I would be a fool not to admit that."

"I pray for you every day," Martine said. She didn't tell André that her prayers were often Jewish ones. But she didn't think he would mind.

"That is the best thing anyone has ever done for me," André said, bending down so his unshaven face was in front of hers. Even with all the hair on his face, he still had pretty blue eyes that reminded Martine of a cloudless sky.

"Thank you for your prayers."

"Will you marry Sister Ada when the war is done?"

He stood back up. "I would marry her now if it were possible. I had hoped to get both of you to the Free Zone. But the Germans have just invaded that region. So, she is in the safest place right now, as are you, my little friend. Even though you must hide in the forest."

The forest didn't seem nearly as bad with André here with her. She was hungry and cold and wet, but she felt safe next to him. She pulled Annabella from her pocket.

"Would you like to meet my friend Annabella?"

He smiled, and his face looked younger, and more handsome than before. "Oui. I am happy to make your acquaintance, Annabella," he said, shaking the rabbit's paw.

"What is that?" he asked, leaning closer to the rabbit, lifting its ear up. "Annabella wants to tell me a secret."

Martine laughed. "That is silly. Annabella cannot talk."

"She is talking to me," André said. He leaned close to the rabbit's ear, and Martine could smell his woodsy scent, as if he were part of the forest he hid in.

"Oh, I see," André said, nodding at Annabella, as if he were having a conversation with her.

"What did she tell you?"

"It is a secret," he said, folding his arms. "And I can keep a secret, unlike you."

Martine frowned and stomped her foot. "I can keep secrets. I have not told anyone that I saw you kissing Sister Ada. Or that you are part of the French Resistance."

André's eyes widened. "I have underestimated you, Martine. But you must be very careful who you talk to. It is a matter of life and death. Not only for me, but for Sister Ada. And even you."

His blue eyes looked into her dark ones. "Can I trust you?"

"Oui," Martine said, and made the sign of the cross, even though she wasn't Catholic. She knew that André was, and that it would make him believe her.

"Très bien."

Martine looked past André and saw Sister Ada in the garden with her hands held up in prayer.

"I must go," she said. She looked at André. "Are you coming to say hello to Sister Ada?"

André shook his head. "No, I must leave. But don't tell anyone else about Sister Ada's real identity," he repeated. "You don't know who you can trust."

"I won't," she promised, hoping he wouldn't tell Sister Ada what she'd done.

"Annabella told me she would deliver a message for me. It is important. Perhaps you would like to help Annabella deliver it?"

Martine stood taller and held on to her rabbit. "We will."

"I want you to give the message to Sister Ada but tell no one else. Tell her André said yes."

Martine nodded. "Yes."

"And don't look back when you leave. I don't want the nuns to know I was watching."

Martine nodded again and turned to leave. She didn't look back but ran out of the forest and waved at Sister Ada.

She was intent on delivering her important message. Did this mean she and Annabella were now part of the Resistance too? She hoped so.

She wanted to help fight the Germans. Especially the ones who had taken Papa.

CHAPTER NINETEEN

THE RESISTANCE

THE GERMANS HAD RAIDED THEIR SUPPLIES, TAKING ALL the bounties of the garden they had painstakingly nurtured and harvested and that were stored in the root cellar. The nuns, who weren't known to complain, muttered among themselves about how thieves and wickedness profit nothing, and they hoped the onions the Germans took would give away their location with their foul breath.

"It would serve them right to feel God's vengeance against them," Sister Thérèse said.

But Martine knew they would be praying for the Germans the next day, asking God to forgive them and to guide them on a more righteous path, even after the Germans had removed the gold-plated crucifix that hung in the chapel and taken it with them, saying it was banned. Luckily, Mother Superior found another one to replace it.

The nuns were left to scrounge for food remnants that the Germans had missed, and there was little to be found until it was discovered that Sister Ada had hidden a portion of their garden vegetables in the secret room.

Even as they rejoiced in this find, some of the nuns were upset.

"That was very clever," Sister Jeanette remarked, as they brought the bounty to the kitchen. "But also dangerous if they were to find out. You should have consulted us first. You put all of our lives at risk."

"That's why I only hid part," Sister Ada explained, her cheeks flushing. "If I had concealed all of it, they would have known. And yes, they yelled and threatened us, but we still have the food, do we not? If I had told all of you, there was a chance someone might have slipped up and divulged that information. Sometimes, the less you know, the better off you are. If the Germans had discovered the food, I would have taken full responsibility."

Sister Jeanette frowned. "I know you meant well. But wasn't that an impulsive act? Who knows what they would have done."

Sister Ada bowed her head. "I didn't mean to put you all in danger. I only meant to help."

"What is your opinion on this matter, Mother Superior?" asked Sister Thérèse, before Sister Jeanette could complain further. The other nuns gathered in the kitchen and clutched their rosaries as they looked to Mother Superior. She was their leader and spiritual guide. They would abide by her wisdom in this matter.

Mother Superior clapped her hands together. "Thanks to Sister Ada, we won't starve this winter. Although we will have some meager meals."

She made the sign of the cross. "Our fasting will lead to spiritual reflection, and we shall offer our prayers for those who are struggling during this time of war."

The other nuns made the sign of the cross as well and nodded in affirmation.

Martine was impressed that Sister Ada, who wasn't a nun at all, and was actually Jewish, had saved them all with her quick thinking.

When Martine had given her the message from André, Sister Ada had run to the window as if she might see André waiting for her there. Martine wanted to ask what the *yes* meant, and why it was such an important message, but Sister Ada had shuffled her off to help with dinner, and she hadn't offered an explanation.

It was during another nightmare that sent Martine in search of Sister Ada that she noticed the nun had left again, and the rock was propped in the door.

But there were no voices outside this time. Martine sat down away from the cold doorway and waited. She'd almost fallen asleep when Sister Ada returned. She wasn't dressed in her nun habit but wore a plaid shirt and pants underneath a heavy coat. Her red hair was long and wavy, and if Martine hadn't known it was really Sister Ada, she wouldn't have recognized her. She looked so young!

Sister Ada didn't notice Martine right away. She stumbled in and kicked the rock outside, letting the door close. Then she grabbed her side and winced.

Martine saw a stain of red on Sister Ada's hand when she removed it from her side.

"You're hurt!" she yelled, jumping up.

Sister Ada gasped. "Martine! What are you doing here?"

"I was waiting for you. You're bleeding, Sister Ada."

"Shh. Yes. I am. But I will be fine. Would you be kind enough to get some towels and bandages and bring them to your room?"

Martine nodded and ran to get them. She wondered if she should wake Mother Superior. But Sister Ada hadn't mentioned that. She hurried with her task, anxious to get back to Sister Ada.

She ran back to her room, nearly dropping the towels draped across her arms. Sister Ada was perched on the side of the bed, her hand cupped over her side. Her face looked pale and tired.

"Thank you," she said. "Could you also fetch the water bowl?"

The bowl was heavy for Martine, but she balanced it with two hands and set it on the bed. Sister Ada had put one of the towels on her wound; the other she dipped into the water, then wiped at the blood on her side.

"It's not as bad as it looks," she said, as she gently dabbed her side. "It's just a flesh wound."

"It was the Germans," Martine said, frowning.

"Yes," Sister Ada admitted. "But I wasn't followed. I made certain of it."

"You said you weren't part of the Resistance." If Sister Ada lied to her about that, did she also lie about Papa?

"I didn't want you to worry, Martine. That night I found you at the Hôtel Drouot I was there to visit a priest at the Cathedral of Notre-Dame. He is one of the organizers of the Resistance."

"So, you have been part of the Resistance since I came here?"

"Yes," she acknowledged. "There are many children like you who need saving. But I cannot bring them here without endangering the nuns. They are already at risk with the two of us here. So, some I bring to the orphanage in the village. Even then it is risky. Each one of them must have fake identification papers and a persuasive story. It's becoming harder. We must work to defeat the Germans. It is the only way to save them."

"Why did you bring me here instead of the orphanage?" Martine asked.

"You were sick. You needed extra help. And after I had said you were my niece, it made sense to keep you here instead of at the orphanage. Also, we became quite fond of you." She gave a weak smile.

Sister Ada wrapped a large bandage around her side and covered the bloody wound. "This will have to be our secret as well," she said, giving Martine a serious look. "No one can know, not even Mother Superior."

Martine thought about what would have happened to her if Sister Ada hadn't found her in Paris and brought her to this place. Those thoughts were often the source of her nightmares. That and Papa's screams.

"It is our secret," Martine said. She solemnly picked up the bloody towels and stuck them under her bed. They would have to get rid of them later where no one could find them. She knew just where to take them.

The forest.

CHAPTER TWENTY

MORE WINERIES

CHARLOTTE

1990

"IT'S THE FIRST TIME WE'VE ALL THREE BEEN TOGETHER IN, well, forever." Amber was looking out the window at the traffic below. "What with our erratic schedules and all. We have to do something fun."

She was younger than I was, in her early twenties. Amber had long blond hair with poofy bangs and was embracing her party years, something I had left behind long ago. Maybe it was my focus on becoming a pilot, or perhaps it was just my personality. I'd never been into that lifestyle much.

Jane, who was actually Amber's aunt, was slim, dark haired, and more likely to spend the evening reading a book or retiring to bed early than going to a club. But she nodded her head, which surprised me.

"I'll go, but no loud places. You know I can't handle the bar-hopping scene. Why don't we take in a few vineyards and wineries? We don't have to drive far. There are plenty just outside the city. And some of them have music too."

I swallowed back a groan. I couldn't tell them that I'd spent my last furlough visiting every winery I could in just two days.

"Sure," Amber agreed. "It's easier to talk there than a loud nightclub. And I'm getting tired of the guys I meet. I need a classier group."

She sidled up to me. "Now that you're single again, it's time to get out there and meet someone new."

I'd only met Amber a couple of years ago, but Jane had vouched for her. We'd bonded on a Paris trip that included a severe sewage problem at our hotel. It was then I'd decided to use money I'd inherited from my grandfather to buy an apartment in Paris since I was already bidding so many Paris trips. Jane had pleaded to rent out my spare bedroom when they had layovers here, and I'd agreed. It had taken a while for Amber to treat me like one of the girls instead of an authority figure, even though I wasn't that much older than her. I liked her youthful enthusiasm, even if it was a bit misplaced.

"Meeting guys is the last thing on my mind. Especially French ones," I said. Henri had left a bad taste in my mouth. I hadn't spoken to him in weeks and considered things over between us. I'd replayed that last meeting over and over in my mind, wishing I had done things differently. Perhaps thrown my glass of wine in his face? Made a scene and stormed out? At least told him what I thought of him?

But showing my hurt feelings wouldn't have made me feel better. Henri had used me and then left me with what he thought was a cheap bottle of wine. I was worried, though, about what would happen if he found out I'd lied to him. If he talked to the sommelier and the man remembered my name. Would Henri try to reclaim the bottle? Would he try to steal it back? I kept a spare key to my apartment above the door ledge. Henri knew about it, so I'd taken it down. I'd purchased a small airtight case and kept the expensive bottle of wine in it at the back of my closet where it was always dark and cool, along with the cheaper bottle of Viner wine that Georges had given me. Both of them meant something, but only one had much value. And that was the one Henri was determined to get.

I needed a distraction from this worry. For the first time in my entire career, I'd overslept through my alarm and had been late for work. I made it to my flight on time, but pilots are supposed to report two hours beforehand. I arrived just before they called in a reserve pilot. I'd never had a ding on my record before. I blamed Henri and the worry he was causing me, but in all honesty, I'd been up late reading books about WWII as well as books about wine that I'd bought at Shakespeare and Company, a local bookstore in Paris that stocked books written in English.

The mystery of Martine and her father's vineyard had been solved, sort of. Even though Madame Moreau had said Martine was killed by a German soldier, Paul couldn't find her name on any lists of Jews who had died during the war. He'd found Zachariah though.

"If you have a firsthand account from a neighbor, then you must accept that she died," he told me, but that didn't stop my obsession with finding out everything I could about wine and war, trying to understand what French vintners had to deal with, how the wineries had been ransacked, with thousands of bottles being shipped back to Germany. And how those bottles ended up at the Hôtel Drouot. It was fascinating history, while also tragic.

I was far from a wine connoisseur, but I was learning a lot about that as well.

My two roommates were looking at me expectantly. Amber was right; we hadn't spent any time together in months. And both of them were in agreement for a change, something that didn't happen often.

"Wine it is," I said. I put out my hand, which the other two covered with their palms.

"Girl time," we said in unison.

Jane, who thrived on schedules and was a planner like me, printed off a list of vineyards just outside the city and arranged to rent a car for the day. Jane would drive since she wasn't a drinker; she was more of a sipper, and always limited herself to partial glasses.

The first place we visited was Clos Montmartre, set right in the 18th arrondissement of Paris, tucked in the streets behind Sacré-Coeur.

"Nice place," Amber said after we'd walked the steep, winding pebbled streets back to the car. "But I thought we were going to get *out* of the city." She had on a cropped metallic chainmail top and leather skirt, with a black choker around her neck, what she called her Madonna outfit.

I had on a white mini shift dress but carried a jean jacket in case the weather turned chilly.

"We are getting out of town," Jane assured us, dressed in a more conservative skirt and cardigan, her short, pixie-cut hair tucked behind her ears. She headed east, away from the city. "I just thought that was a good place to start. It's amazing how many vineyards are tucked in the city in neighborhoods right under our noses."

"So where to next?" Amber asked, just as the song "Love Shack" played on the radio. All three of us sang along, our windows open, waving at passing cars. The next stop was located just outside Paris at a castle.

"Now, this is amazing," Jane said, gesturing toward the vineyard, which stretched out to the horizon beneath us as we sipped wine on a terrace. "This makes me almost forget about work."

Even though I'd had my fill of vineyards, I had to admit the view was remarkable, and I enjoyed the company of my roommates. At work I was usually the only woman in the cockpit. I never heard the gossip that was common among the flight attendants. I missed girl chitchat: talk of fashion and nail polish, and where to get a good massage. Most of us didn't talk politics much;

it was a taboo subject at work, although the recent Iraqi invasion of Kuwait was an exception. We all knew someone who was being deployed to the Gulf. But Jane and Amber's talk inevitably turned to their jobs, and the unusual passengers they dealt with. Hearing about my roommate's lives as flight attendants always affirmed that I'd chosen the right career path.

"Half the passengers were smoking on our last flight," Jane complained. "The cabin was a thick cloud of smoke. You could have cut a knife through it."

There were nonsmoking sections of the plane, but with the stale air that circulated, everyone ended up smelling like nicotine. "They banned smoking on almost all domestic flights," I said. "I think it's just a matter of time before it's banned on international ones too."

"I can't wait," Jane said, frowning. "Do you know how many holes I've had burnt into my uniform from passengers who have their elbows resting on the armrest and their lit cigarettes dangling from their hands in the aisle?"

Drake often smoked in the cabin, and I complained about it every time I flew with him. Fewer pilots smoked in the cabin, but there were still a few holdouts. Some smoked rank cigars.

"I had a man clip his toenails in first class yesterday," Amber said, wrinkling her nose. "It was so disgusting. And then he had the nerve to hit on me after that."

"You get hit on every day," I reminded her. She always had a circle of admirers, and every male pilot I flew with wanted her on his crew. She had a new dinner date almost every night.

Amber gave me a chilly smile. "Usually by a better class of man than that."

"He was flying first class," I reminded her.

"Well, he acted like a pig," Amber said. "I'm used to guys being more cultured than that. If I wanted that kind, I'd date guys from my hometown."

Most women I knew hated the unwanted attention of men during work. I'd once had to deal with a groping flight simulator instructor, who only stopped when I started bringing my partner Drake with me. Amazingly, Amber reveled in the attention she received from male pilots and passengers. Or maybe she was just so used to it that it didn't bother her.

"Eww," Jane said. "I'm so glad I'm married to a decent guy. He doesn't even take his shoes off on a plane."

"How long did you know each other before you married?" I asked Jane.

"I know it sounds cheesy, but we were high school sweethearts. We decided to break up after graduation, but then I started working for the airlines and Jake didn't see me because I was traveling all the time, and he realized how much he missed me and asked me to marry him."

Amber shook her head. "I can't imagine settling down, and I'm older than you were when you got married. You were way too young."

"Maybe," Jane said, taking a sip of Pinot Grigio. "But we've been married for twenty years now. I got a good guy, and I didn't need to date a bunch of men to find the right one."

Jane put a hand to her forehead. "Oh, God. I'm sorry, Charlotte. I didn't even think. That was tasteless of me. I didn't mean . . ."

"It's okay," I reassured her. "Henri isn't like Jake. He's not one of the 'good ones.'" I made air quotes with my fingers.

"It's tough for women in our industry," Jane said. "I mean, I love it most of the time. The pay isn't much, but there are great perks, including free flights for my family. But then there are the last-minute trip changes, the odd hours, all the safety training, not to mention jet lag. And your schedule changes from week to week. It's taken me years to get any kind of seniority. Men don't want to have to deal with that. A lot of men still think women should stay at home."

"I'd hoped that didn't matter to Henri," I said, staring miserably into my glass.

"That's too bad," Amber offered. "He checked off so many boxes: well-off, handsome, nice apartment."

"How do you know he has a nice apartment?" I asked, my voice suddenly changing.

Amber blinked several times. "You mentioned it more than a few times."

"Oh, did I?" I said, still frowning.

"You don't think I visited him, do you?"

"No, no. Of course not." I regretted questioning her. I knew Amber had standards for dating, and one of them was to never date someone who was already involved with a fellow crew member.

"Come on," Jane said, standing up. "We have time for one more stop on the way back. And there is music at this one."

I didn't know if I could summon the energy to visit another vineyard. But I followed my roommates to the car. Jane drove back toward Paris and stopped at a little vineyard, one that sort of reminded me of Clos Lapointe near Dijon. It had the same quaint atmosphere, and instead of an expansive terrace, we found ourselves seated at a table on a small circular patio while in the center a violinist played soothing music. Rows of lavender surrounded the patio, wafting a soothing scent.

Amber was on her third glass of Chenin Blanc, and she munched on soft goat cheese and grapes as she watched people mingling around us.

"I'm a bit disappointed, Jane. You promised me French hunks, and the only one I've seen is that guy pouring wine at the table opposite ours."

I followed her line of sight. A man with curly dark hair, a bit shaggy, was setting a bottle of wine into an ice bucket. He looked up, and his eyes focused on our table. I looked away, afraid he'd think I was checking him out, because, of course, that's what I'd been doing.

He was handsome in a rough kind of way, judging from his jeans and flannel shirt with the sleeves rolled partway up, as though he enjoyed hard labor. His dark eyes were intense and serious. And when I looked back, he was staring at us. Or, most likely, he was staring at Amber, whose long blond hair and blue eyes always drew men. Even now, I caught several men discreetly eyeing Amber from nearby tables.

I doubted Amber would date a waiter, even if he was a hunk. He didn't meet the well-off item on her checklist. But Amber wasn't necessarily against one-night stands, at least from what I'd heard Jane say, and Amber was sounding three sheets to the wind as she ordered another glass of wine.

"Give me another glass and that guy over there," she asked the waitress, pointing toward the man opposite us.

Jane put a hand on her forehead, as if she couldn't believe what she'd heard.

The man disappeared, and Jane seemed relieved, but a moment later he stopped in front of our table, holding a bottle of wine. "Bonjour, American friends. Would you like to try the house specialty?"

"How did you know we're Americans?" Jane asked him.

He smiled at her. "You left a tip when you paid for your wine earlier."

"I forgot to tell you that a fifteen percent service fee is automatically included," I told Jane.

Amber looked at the man and tilted her head. "But what if the service is *exceptionally good*? Should we tip then?"

She was turning on the Amber charm. The poor man didn't stand a chance.

His lips turned up slightly. "Tipping is not expected, but I certainly can't prevent you from doing so if you're so inclined."

"You speak excellent English, by the way," Jane commented.

"Thank you. I studied at Oxford."

Amber's eyes went wide. "You're an Oxford man? What are you doing working at a winery?"

"Amber, really." Jane rolled her eyes.

He waved away Jane's objections as he poured three generous glasses of white wine. "No, it is all right. This is a family business. I came back to help when my father passed away, and I never left."

"Well, please tell your family that this is one of the best wineries we've visited," I said. "It's quaint and beautiful, and you have excellent wine."

He set the wine bottle on the table and turned to me.

"My mother is the owner. Perhaps you'd like to tell her yourself. I'm sure she would appreciate hearing this."

I didn't expect that. "Uh, sure. Is she nearby?"

"Yes. I'll take you to her."

Amber flashed a hurt look at me, but I just shrugged. What else could I do?

I stood and followed the man into the main building, where customers were milling about, selecting bottles of wine, while others sat at tables drinking.

"My name is Julien. And you are?" he asked as we walked.

"Charlotte. It's nice to meet you," I said, noticing his deep tan that most likely reflected time spent among the vines.

He led me to an office at the back of the building. A thin older woman was seated at a desk, talking on the phone in rapid-fire French. She was yelling about something, none of which I could catch. She wore a fashionable blouse and pants, and her reading glasses were perched on her curly gray hair.

I stopped and pulled back. "Maybe we should come back later?"

"Oh, no. This is how she always does business. She's fine."

"And she speaks English?"

"Very little. But if you are sincere, she will understand."

"I don't know . . ."

He gave me an imploring look. This was evidently very important to him for some reason.

"How long has it been since your father died?"

"Three years. I have two sisters, but they are married and have families of their own, and my mother insisted I come back and help."

"I'm sorry. It must have been hard on you."

He shrugged. "I do not regret it. But it is a struggling business, as it has always been, even when my father was alive. Some days, I think she would give it all up, were it not for a promise she made to him. She works harder than me, frankly."

I understood responsibility, although my father had rejected the obligation placed on him by my grandfather. It had been the ruin of their relationship.

"I know this is unusual. But she has been very depressed about the whole business lately. Perhaps a good word from a beautiful tourist would cheer her up."

He thought I was beautiful? He was standing so close I could smell a hint of wine on his breath, and coconut. Was that coming from his hair?

He cleared his throat, as though he realized what he'd just said. "And you seemed very sincere in your compliments about our winery."

I felt unsettled, but I forced a half smile. "Well, I meant every word. And I'm happy to speak to her."

"Good. And your last name?"

"Montgomery." I tugged on my short dress, as if I could will it longer. If I'd been in uniform, I'd be more prepared for this.

The next thing I knew, Julien was making introductions to his mother, who was now off the phone. I didn't catch all of it, but heard my name, *Charlotte Montgomery*, and *américaine*, which seemed to pique the woman's interest. She sat up straighter and fussed at the short gray curls that framed her face. She had dark, intense eyes like her son, but her expression was not as carefree as his. It was as if she'd had a great deal of sadness in her life. But, of course, she had lost her husband and inherited a struggling business. That was all terribly sad.

Finally, Julien motioned to me. I stepped forward. "I'm very happy to meet you. I told your son what a beautiful, quaint winery this is. I've been all over France, and this is my favorite of all that I've visited."

"Favorite?" She smiled brightly at this, and I wondered if this was the only word she'd understood.

"Oui." I looked at Julien, who beamed at his mother. His devotion was admirable.

"Merci, beaucoup," his mother said. "Your words are a . . . gift. It is difficult without . . ." She stopped, and covered her mouth, as though she couldn't let the words escape.

"I'm very sorry about your husband. My grandfather owned a vineyard in California," I offered. "But now it is being sold. I miss it, and him."

Julien translated my words to his mother.

The woman was fast; she had crossed the space between us and enveloped me in a tight hug before I even knew what was happening. I've never been the hugging type, and I'd thought most French people weren't either, but I tried not look as awkward as I felt.

She spoke French words of comfort, and when she pulled back her eyes glistened.

I unexpectedly felt my own eyes filling up. Maybe it was contagious. I sniffed and smiled. "I will bring all my friends here," I promised.

The woman clapped her hands and smiled back. "Please. Drink more wine. My son pour for you."

"I will," I said. "It was very nice meeting you, Madame . . ." I realized I didn't know her name.

"Élisabeth," the woman said, taking my hand. "Je m'appelle Élisabeth."

"That's a beautiful name. How long have you owned this winery?"

"Since I married. But it felt like my home long before that, as I was orphaned. My father died during the war."

My heart quickened. Her story sounded very familiar. But the orphan I had been searching for had not been so lucky. "I'm so sorry."

"As am I. I know he would have loved his grandchildren."

She turned to her son. "Thank you for bringing me this beautiful American woman. I suspect you had other reasons for wanting me to meet her?"

Julien's face reddened. "I only wanted you to know that our winery is popular with tourists," he said.

"It makes me very happy," she said. "Go now and drink more wine."

CHAPTER TWENTY-ONE

INVITATION

THERE WAS SOMETHING ABOUT JULIEN'S MOTHER. I FELT A sudden connection to the woman, who seemed so full of warmth and passion, from the way she had argued on the phone to the way she had embraced me. Even with the sad demeanor that her body seemed to carry, she was so personable.

The way Julien fawned over our table after that made it all worthwhile. He wouldn't allow us to pay for the bottle of wine he served us, as well as a puffy pastry coated with a sweet apple concoction that he placed between us on the red-and-white checkered tablecloth.

Amber fluffed her bangs and leaned in toward him almost to the point of falling out of her chair when he approached our table. He was courteous, but somehow escaped her flirtatious signals. Normally, she'd already have plans to hook up later.

As we left, he asked if I'd consider coming back in a few weeks. "It is our fall festival. My mother would like you to be there. As would I," he added.

I cursed the way my stomach quivered at those last words, at how I noticed the dimple in his left cheek. I didn't need another French boyfriend. Especially one who was as busy as I was.

I would have politely declined, but something about the way he was asking, as though it was the most important thing in the world, made me reconsider. And it also made me think of his mother, of how insistent she'd been.

"I travel a great deal for work," I said. "But if I'm in town, I'd be delighted."

He handed me his card. "Would you let me know? You would be our special guest."

"That's sweet. I didn't really do anything, though."

"But you did. You made her smile, and my mother does not smile often. We would be honored to have you attend."

"I'll try to come," I said, almost adding that if I came, it would be for his mother. Only his mother. But those words stayed inside.

"Thank you. All of you are invited," he said to Jane and Amber, who had her arms folded and was scowling.

"He didn't even invite me," Amber complained as she slumped into the back seat of the car.

"Yes, he did," Jane said.

"He threw out a last-minute invite as we were leaving. That doesn't count. He could care less if we showed up. He's only interested in Charlotte. Did you see the way he was looking at Charlotte?"

I turned to look at my roommate. "Honestly, he only asked me because of his mother. There was nothing between us, I assure you."

"And if there was something there, it's not like you had dibs on him," Jane said, addressing Amber in the rearview mirror. "So don't sulk."

Jane winked at me. She was Amber's aunt but seemed more like a second mother to her sometimes.

Jane's scolding seemed to work. Amber reached over and patted me on the shoulder and said in her sloppy drunk way, "I guess I should be happy at least one of us scored a hunk."

I rolled my eyes. "As if! I didn't score anything. And I'm not interested in *scoring* anyone."

"Sho, you're not going to festival?" Amber slurred.

"I doubt it very much. But *if* my schedule permits it, and *if* I do attend, it won't be because of Julien." I didn't need to get involved with anyone right now. My relationship with Henri had gone nowhere and everywhere, and I needed time to regroup. I wasn't like Amber, who enjoyed a brief fling and moved on without regret.

No, I had no intention of getting involved with another Frenchman.

"We won't be back in Paris for another month," Jane said. "Except for a few brief layovers. The whole thing is a moot point. So, none of us is going. You were disappointed over nothing. Right, Amber? Amber?"

Amber was already asleep in the back seat, her face plastered against the upholstery. I couldn't help but smile at the jagged lines she'd wake up to, later, on her perfect porcelain skin.

I ALMOST FORGOT ABOUT THE FESTIVAL. IT WAS WEEKS LATER, when I was looking through the pocket of my jacket, that I found the card. I was in Paris for one day; I had to fly out the following afternoon.

I remembered the woman's sad eyes, and how Julien had said they were struggling. The winery had been bustling with customers the day I'd visited, but I didn't really know all that much about the business aspect of owning a vineyard and making wine. I did know that there were thousands of wineries in France, and smaller ones had to balance tradition and innovation, which was costly.

Georges Lapointe had made the transition, and his winery was now doing well. But many wineries couldn't keep up with new techniques and increasing competition.

I had things to do; I needed to tidy up the apartment and submit my bid for next month's trips. I had seniority, so I did have some say in my schedule, which meant that I always put in as many trips to Paris as I could get.

I was also tired, having completed four days of flying. Extensive travel and time changes affected my body even though I was used to it.

But as I looked through my closet, I instinctively pulled out a skirt with a flowered pattern and a yellow peasant top. Exactly what I'd wear to a wine festival.

I put them on, still wondering if I should go. Then I arranged to rent a car, my doubts fading as I drove out of town.

I'd told Amber and Jane that I doubted I'd attend. But I felt drawn to go, much like I'd felt drawn to drive to Burgundy. There was something about that woman, the way she'd hugged me, as if I were her long-lost daughter and not some total stranger.

I'd go. For Élisabeth, Julien's mother. And only for Élisabeth.

CHAPTER TWENTY-TWO

FALL FESTIVAL

TABLES WERE SET UP BEYOND THE PATIO, WHICH HAD BEEN converted into a dance floor. Sparkling lights twinkled above them, and a jazz band was playing. People were dancing; some on the patio, others next to their tables, and one person danced on top of a table.

I barely recognized it from our last visit; it had been transformed into a dazzling French oasis.

"This is amazing," I murmured.

I spotted Julien sitting at a table with Élisabeth and several others. I felt suddenly self-conscious. I should have called first.

Élisabeth was wearing a green dress, which complemented her curly gray hair. She wasn't smiling, but she still looked happy in that way that mothers often do when they're surrounded by family.

My eyes were drawn to Julien, who wore the same outfit as the waiters: black pants and a white shirt, although his sleeves were rolled partway up. I wondered if he'd been working the event. He was talking with his hands, the way many Frenchmen did. And his wavy black hair had been combed back.

Julien looked my way, and an immediate smile engulfed his face. "Charlotte! You have come!"

He was so effervescent, so animated. So unlike Henri.

"I should have called," I said, approaching the table. "It was a last-minute decision."

"No matter," he replied, and he stood and motioned me to take his chair. "We are very happy to see you."

"Oh, no, I couldn't," I objected, but he insisted. I sat next to Élisabeth, who patted my hand and offered me an empty glass.

Julien introduced the others at the table. His two younger sisters, Adrienne and Suzette, who were both thin and had long dark hair, and his brother-in-law, Charles, a studious-looking man with glasses who reminded me of a younger version of my friend Paul.

And lastly, he introduced his three nieces, all young girls with wispy hair who looked to be around five and six. Two were siblings.

I nodded at the group. "Enchantée."

"Le toast," Élisabeth shouted above the sound of the lively music.

"My mother wants you to make a toast," Julien said, standing above me and filling my glass with pink wine, which I remembered was one of the house wines I'd tasted last time. "It is customary that each person who joins our table offers a toast."

I raised my glass. "Will you translate?" I asked Julien.

"Of course."

"To an excellent harvest," I said, which he translated to the group.

"Santé!" I added, and everyone clinked their glasses with mine and replied with "Santé!" *To health!*

"We must all take a drink before setting down our glasses," Julien instructed me.

I took a sip, noticing that the young girls had cans of soda in front of them.

Élisabeth reached over and touched my hair and said something in French. I looked to Julien to translate.

"My grandmother had hair the same color as yours," he said. "Red is my mother's favorite color."

"Merci," I said, turning to Élisabeth, wishing I had spent more time practicing my French. There was something about Élisabeth, about her sad smile and struggling business. I was reminded that the girl I had searched for would be roughly her age now, a girl who had been robbed of her heritage, and her life. What might Martine be like if she'd lived?

Suzette, Julien's sister, spoke some English too. "How is it you come to France?"

"I'm a pilot for an airline," I said.

"Pilote," Suzette told the others, and there was some gasping and *ahh*ing and comments that I didn't understand.

Élisabeth seemed especially impressed. "Intelligente et belle."

I understood that compliment. Smart and beautiful.

"Merci," I said again, feeling awkward at all the attention.

The music had changed to a slow, soulful song. More people crowded the dance floor.

Julien extended his hand. "Please, a dance?"

I was glad to escape the focus of the table for a few minutes. I took his hand gratefully and we squeezed into the middle of the floor, away from his family.

"I hope you're not too overwhelmed," Julien said. "They are impressed because there aren't many women pilots. But I'm sure you know that."

"Yes, it isn't always easy being the only woman in the cockpit," I admitted.

"It's admirable," he said. "You are a pioneer."

"Just call me Amelia Earhart."

That made him laugh. A tip-back-your-head kind of laugh. Julien was taller than Henri, and more rugged looking, even with his hair slicked back. His eyes were full of expression, unlike Henri, who was always so guarded and hard to read. Was this what was meant by the expression "an open book"?

I didn't want to talk about myself any longer. "What did you study at Oxford?"

"Law."

"You graduated from Oxford Law?"

"Yes," he said.

I couldn't hide my astonishment. "You could practice anywhere in the world! How could you give that up?"

"I admit I feel bad for my professors, who taught me in good faith that I was committed to studying and practicing law. But how can I not do what my mother asks of me? This vineyard has been in my family for four generations. How can I be the one to end the dream?"

"But what about what you want?"

Julien tilted his head. "I thought I wanted to work as a solicitor, perhaps in London, or in Paris. I didn't see myself here. But now, coming back has been a chance to reflect, to appreciate my roots and heritage. There is something about growing up in a vineyard and playing there as a boy. Making wine is personal and close to my heart. I'm not unhappy. I have my family and a purpose, although it's not the purpose I expected."

"I'm sorry, but I couldn't imagine giving up my career for anything."

"You are not the son of a winemaker."

"My grandfather owned a vineyard. My father is selling it now. I never blamed my father for wanting something else, for having different ambitions than my grandfather."

I *did* resent that Dad stopped visiting him, though. And I regretted that the only time I had with Grandpa was summer vacations.

"Perhaps it is different for Americans. Family matters a great deal to the French."

I scowled. "Family is important to Americans too. But so is happiness. And following your dreams."

"I would never forgive myself if I turned my back on my family."

I stopped dancing and crossed my arms. "My father didn't turn his back on his family. He just followed his own interests."

Julien immediately put his hands up. "I'm sorry. I have insulted you, and that was not my intention. I appreciate that it must not have been an easy decision for him."

I could feel my blood pressure rising. He'd gotten under my skin. I knew how hard it was to follow my own dream. I couldn't begin to understand how he could have given up on his so easily. But what bothered me most was Julien saying it was not an easy decision for my father. Because it was very easy. Perhaps too easy? Was that why I wanted to buy Grandpa's vineyard?

"You haven't insulted me," I said with too much conviction. "It's just that I've had to work twice as hard as most men in my profession, one that women are often expected to give up when they marry or have a family. How can I fault my father for wanting to follow his own path instead of doing something he hated just to please *his* father?"

"No one can fault him. Perhaps I can admit that I don't have your father's resolution. Or yours, for that matter."

"And perhaps I can admit that I admire your dedication to your mother," I said, feeling foolish for getting upset.

"We agree then." Julien sighed. "It may all be in vain, however, as we may not last much longer. This year our harvest is good, but we need at least five years like this to stay afloat. We must somehow adapt, perhaps change our wine making, but I haven't ascertained how to do that yet. When I try to bring it up to my mother, she says 'I'm a grape grower, not a winemaker. Your father made the wine. I know how to grow exceptional grapes, and that is the most important part of good wine.' That is true, but is only one part of our business."

I thought about Georges Lapointe. Julien and I hadn't made

much of an impression on each other, but I felt a sudden urge to help his business, even if we didn't see eye to eye. "I happen to know someone who is a winemaker, who has a small vineyard like this. He's incorporated new methods, and his business is thriving now. Perhaps your mother would like to meet him?"

Julien's face lit up. "Yes, I am sure she would very much like that."

"He lives a few hours away, in the Burgundy region. I'm free in another two weeks, if you want me to go with you and introduce you both."

He smiled. "That is very generous. I know you are very busy with your travels."

"I'm happy to help." I didn't mention that it would help me as well, since I wanted to buy Grandpa's vineyard. The more I knew about vineyards, the more it would help me make a good business plan, which would also convince my father.

"I insist that I drive, and pick you up," Julien said.

"I accept, since I don't have a car," I said. If I could help a struggling winemaker, well, it gave me some satisfaction in knowing my quest for Martine ended up helping someone else.

I only hoped that Julien didn't get the wrong impression, because I wasn't the least bit attracted to him. And I doubted he was attracted to me.

It wasn't that he was unattractive. Amber had fallen head over heels for him. There was just no spark between us, and that was as important as looks; at least it was to me.

But a minute later he took a step closer. "I look forward to it," he said, and leaned forward as if to kiss me. I abruptly pulled back. "I have to leave now. Please tell your mother goodbye for me."

I rushed off, leaving him alone on the dance floor.

CHAPTER TWENTY-THREE

THE VILLAGE

MARTINE

1943

MARTINE FOLLOWED SISTER ADA ALONG THE DIRT ROAD toward the village. This was her first visit since coming to the abbey almost a year ago. She wore a dress that was too big on her, but she might soon grow into it; the nuns made sure she ate even as they went hungry. Their long habits didn't reveal the undernourished bodies beneath, but Martine noticed how their cheeks were gaunt and they moved more slowly.

She didn't understand why Sister Ada was taking food to the village while the nuns were starving. But she was excited to go. It had been so long since she'd seen other children.

"What if the Germans stop us?" she asked Sister Ada, feeling a sudden chill on her arms even though the sun was hot on their backs.

"We have papers," Sister Ada said, pulling the cart full of vegetables from their garden, hidden beneath liturgical missals. They had planted an early harvest, and some of the vegetables were not ripe, but Sister Ada said the children in the village orphanage were starving, and if they waited, the Germans would raid their shelves and nothing would be left.

Sister Ada also provided potatoes and radishes to the Resistance hiding in the forest, including André.

Martine flashed a worried look. "Don't worry," Sister Ada said. "Your name is still Martine. But your last name is now Blanchet. And you are still my niece. Can you remember that?"

"Of course I can," Martine replied. Hadn't she learned to read? Hadn't she memorized prayers of both the Catholic and Jewish faiths? She gave Annabella a quick squeeze in her pocket.

"What are the children like?" Martine asked Sister Ada. "Are they all Jews like me?"

"Some of them are Jewish. They are like all children. Like you, Martine. But their bellies are empty. It is hard to play and learn when you're hungry."

Martine hadn't played with another child in so long. She barely remembered what it was like. She didn't admit it to anyone, not even Sister Ada, but she hardly remembered Papa. She knew he had a kind, thin face, or at least that was what she remembered of him. She thought she knew the sound of his voice, but even that was beginning to escape her memory. Father Pierre, who said Mass at the abbey, was the voice she often thought of when she tried to conjure up Papa's voice.

Along the way they passed a vineyard, one that had straggly plants that barely passed for grapevines. But a sudden breeze blew across the road and the aroma made Martine stop. Lavender, combined with the sweet scent of flowering grapes. She knew these sensations, these smells. In an instant she was back among the vines and the plump grapes, and when she looked up from the vines, she saw Papa's face. She felt his coarse beard on her cheek; she heard the melodic tenderness of his voice as he recited the Shema. She saw his calloused, purple-stained hands that he said were the mark of hard work. She remembered!

"Martine. Are you all right?"

Sister Ada was far ahead of her and had set down the cart.

"What is it, Martine?"

She looked at Sister Ada. She felt tears stream down her face. She wanted to stay here and keep the memory alive, just for a little while. She wanted to be with Papa. What if she forgot? She couldn't bear to lose him again.

But then a boy appeared. He was older than Martine, taller by at least a head, with thick dark hair, wearing pants that had holes in them. He carried a basket that held grapes.

"Bonjour," the boy said. "Who are you?"

Martine didn't answer. She wiped her eyes with the back of her hand and ran to catch up with Sister Ada. She felt him watching her, but she didn't look back until they were far down the road, and he was gone by then.

The spire of the Catholic church was what Martine saw first when they reached the village. The streets were narrow, cobbled mazes lined by blue and green shuttered half-timbered houses and stone buildings with purple wisteria climbing the walls. It was smaller than the village Martine had lived near before, or maybe it just seemed that way. It was eerily empty. Sister Ada had said that more than half the population had left before German forces arrived, but Martine didn't see any cars or people on the streets at all.

"Where are all the people?" Martine asked.

"I don't know," Sister Ada said, slowing down, her steps more cautious. "Stay near, Martine." But she pushed on with the cart.

They passed a café and a store, but there were no lines outside waiting to use ration cards. Instead, there were German soldiers.

Two sat outside the café, and several others were standing outside the store. Martine cowered at the sight of them, wanting to turn and run. She held on to the sleeve of Sister Ada's habit.

"It isn't the Germans we need to worry about," Sister Ada said in a low voice, pulling her cart defiantly down the middle of the road. "It's the French police."

Martine didn't understand. "Why should we be afraid of the French police?"

"Because they are carrying out Hitler's orders," Sister Ada said, and she spat on the ground as though she had swallowed a bug, which Martine didn't think was something a nun should do. What if the Germans saw her?

As they turned a corner, Sister Ada abruptly stopped and put a hand over Martine's eyes, but not before she caught a glimpse of the two bodies dangling from a scaffold in the town square. It was a man and a woman, but that was all she saw before her eyes were covered.

"Don't look," Sister Ada warned, although she didn't seem to realize it was too late. "I'm going to take my hand away because I need to pull the cart, but you must only look down until I tell you it's okay. Hold on to my skirt."

Martine nodded and did as she was told. The stench of death was all around them, and she couldn't erase the image, however fleeting, of the figures hanging there. Who were they, and why had they been hanged like that?

"You may look up now." Sister Ada had waited until they'd passed beyond the square.

"What was . . ."

"We'll take a different route back," Sister Ada said in a firm voice, and Martine knew she shouldn't ask any questions. Now she understood why the village had been so quiet and empty. The people were hiding in their homes, afraid to come out.

The orphanage was on the other side of the village, and surprisingly, the two French policemen they passed didn't stop Sister Ada to inspect her cart. Maybe it was the missals that scared them off.

"I must go inside for a moment. There are children playing. You can join them for a bit," Sister Ada said, motioning toward a group of children outside the orphanage. It was a welcome sight after the deserted streets they'd passed.

How could she play after what they'd just seen? Plus, Martine barely knew how to play. It had been a year since she'd attended school. But she nodded, and Sister Ada went inside. Martine stood at the edge of the field where some children were chasing a ball, although their running looked halfhearted, as though they didn't have the energy for it, while others played with marbles. All of them were thin, like the nuns at the abbey. Their clothes hung on them like limp rags, and many were barefoot with dirty faces and arms.

Martine thought about Sophie, her best friend at school. Sophie was also Jewish, and Martine wondered where she was now. She searched the faces of the girls, but none of them looked familiar. Of course, it would be silly to think that Sophie would be here. She would still be in their village. Martine wondered if she would ever see Sophie again. If she would ever see her village again.

When Sister Ada came back out with two older boys to unpack the vegetables from their cart, Martine was still standing at the side, her hands behind her back, watching the children play. Several children came to help unload, their faces brightening at the sight of the vegetables. After they had unloaded everything, Sister Ada turned to go.

"Martine, do you want to return to the abbey? Or would you rather stay here?"

Martine felt her pulse quicken. "Stay here? What do you mean?"

Sister Ada put a hand up to block the sun from her eyes as she watched the children in the distance. "You must miss being with other children. Now that André has made up proper papers for you, you could remain here, if you want. I know you saw something terrible at the town square, but you would be safe here."

Martine ran and put her arms around Sister Ada's waist. "No! You can't leave me behind. I won't let you."

Sister Ada hugged Martine. "I didn't mean that you're not wanted at the abbey. All the nuns adore you. And I do too. But you could go to a proper school with children your own age instead of having nuns teach you, and play games and have fun. It is so stuffy and quiet at the abbey. I only want what is best for you."

"You're what's best for me," Martine declared. Who would help Sister Thérèse keep the wood floors polished? Who would help keep the garden free of weeds? Who would look after Sister Ada when she was injured, or poke her awake during Mass when she was out all night with the Resistance?

"But don't you miss other children?" Sister Ada asked.

"No. I don't care about other children," Martine said. "Please don't leave me here."

Sister Ada patted her back. "Don't worry, child. I won't leave you."

Martine looked up at her. "Do you promise?"

"I promise," Sister Ada said.

"You will always stay with me?"

Sister Ada sighed and bent down so she could face Martine. "Someday, when the war is over, we will both have to leave the abbey, Martine. When that time comes, you will want to be with your family. But I promise that until then I will always watch out for you."

"Is the war almost over?" Martine asked.

"I'm afraid not. But the Allies are bombing Rome. That is a good sign that the war is turning for us."

Martine thought about the bodies hanging in the square. That was not a good sign.

What she really wanted was to see Papa again. But until that time, Sister Ada was all she had. She took hold of Sister Ada's hand, determined not to let go until they were back at the abbey.

She didn't sneak even a single look at the children, who were still playing.

CHAPTER TWENTY-FOUR

GABRIEL

Martine looked up toward the edge of the garden. A small, scraggy dog was watching her. He had pointed ears and a tail that stuck up in the back. His coat was brown and white, and his face was brown on the sides with a white streak down the middle. He was skinny, as though he didn't get much to eat, like everyone else in France.

The nuns were planting the second garden of the summer, which they called the "Nazi Garden" because they knew the Germans would confiscate whatever they grew.

The nuns chattered among themselves, wondering where the dog had come from.

"He lives at the vineyard down the road," Sister Ada said. "Martine, why don't you take him home?"

The dog barked, and Martine ran behind Sister Ada. "Don't worry. He won't bite," Sister Ada assured her. "He's just hungry."

"Maybe he will try to eat me."

Sister Ada laughed. "No. He won't eat you. I promise."

Martine peeked at the dog. "How will I get him to follow me?"

"Remember the story of Hansel and Gretel?"

Martine's eyes lit up. "I'll drop breadcrumbs behind me?"

"Exactly. He will be your best friend then."

Sister Marie, who did most of the cooking, reprimanded her. "Just make sure you take a stale heel. Not a fresh loaf."

Even the fresh loaves were thin and hard, as eggs and yeast were hard to come by. Every cake and dessert now contained carrots, which grew in abundance and were a staple of all their meals. Martine worried that her skin would turn orange from eating so many carrots.

She went to the kitchen and came back with the bread. Martine approached the dog and dropped a few crumbs, which the dog eagerly licked up. It looked to her for more, then leapt up, putting its paws on her dress. Martine screamed and backed away.

"He just wants more," Sister Ada said. "Start walking and he'll follow you."

Martine started walking down the lane, throwing breadcrumbs behind her, which the dog eagerly lapped up. But soon she had to run, as the dog jumped at her side, trying to get more of the bread. She dropped a big piece, which the dog stopped to eat, and which gave Martine more time to run ahead. But soon the dog was next to her again, nipping at her heels.

She finally dropped all of the bread left in her hands and ran the rest of the way to the vineyard, panting as she ran up the stretch of lane from the road to a brick house. The boy she'd seen before was there, sitting on the front steps.

He stood as she approached, then saw the dog chasing her.

"Oscar," the boy called, and the dog ran past Martine toward the boy, who bent down and rubbed his head. The boy was thin and wiry, just like the dog.

Martine was still panting, trying to catch her breath. "He chased me all the way here."

The boy stood up. "He must like you."

"I was feeding him bread," Martine said between gasps.

"Well, that explains it. Oscar will do anything for food."

"I wanted him to follow me. Not chase me."

"But isn't that sort of the same? He *was* following you."

Martine didn't like this boy. There was definitely a difference between being followed and being chased. She was about to leave when she got a whiff of the vineyard and the memories flooded her again. Memories of home, of tending the vines with Papa. She went to look at the vineyard. The boy followed her.

Instead of the neat lines of vines that she was used to, the plants grew haphazardly. She picked up a clump of dirt. It was rocky soil, different than the limestone clay of Papa's. But she remembered what Papa used to say: "The more a vine struggles, the stronger it becomes."

"Those branches need pruning," she said, pointing at the unattended plants. Weeds were everywhere.

"I know. I have to do it all by myself," he said. "My father died, and Mother, well, she isn't much help."

"My father is dead too." Martine repeated the lie that she had memorized, but it left a bitter taste in her mouth. She didn't want to say that Papa was dead, not even if it was pretend.

"Do you live with the nuns?" the boy asked.

"Yes. Sister Ada is my aunt." Another lie. Martine was becoming used to lying. But then she said something true.

"I used to help with Papa's vineyard," Martine said. "I could help with yours."

"You're too petite," he said. "Very small."

Martine stood straight. "I help the nuns in the garden, and I worked in the vineyard at home since I was une enfant. I know what to do."

"Why would you want to help me?" he asked. "You don't even know me."

This place reminded her of home, of Papa. It helped her remember the life she left behind. And Sister Ada was right. Martine did miss other children. She was tired of being with old nuns all day long. "Because you need me," she answered.

"My name is Gabriel," he offered.

Like the angel. "I am Martine." She pointed at three broken vines. "They need replacing," she said. "We should get to work."

CHAPTER TWENTY-FIVE

IMMERSION

CHARLOTTE

1990

THE ATTEMPT AT A KISS HAD BEEN IMPETUOUS. A RESULT OF the music and excitement, and the atmosphere. Or maybe he meant to kiss me on the cheek? He was a Frenchman, and that would be perfectly acceptable. In that case, I'd been rude to run off.

I felt a flush of embarrassment. I hoped he wouldn't try it again. I'd sent a strong enough signal. Now I was feeling awkward about our upcoming trip. I didn't want Julien to think he was anything more than a friend, nor did I want him to think I was a social pariah in not letting him kiss my cheek, if that had been his intention.

Was I sending mixed signals? I knew these things had a way of snowballing. And I didn't want to waste time with another Frenchman, especially one who had already suggested I was somehow less family oriented because I wouldn't give up my career like he had. The whole conversation had left a bad taste in my mouth.

It wasn't as though I disliked Julien. I felt sorry for him, for being so weak as to give up his dreams, his plans for his life, and attribute it to loyalty.

At least I would have Élisabeth to talk to. I went downstairs, but the car that pulled up had only one occupant inside.

Julien was driving a small red Peugeot hatchback. It was a manual transmission, which meant that his hand occasionally brushed against my leg, which I tried to move without being conspicuous.

"Where is Élisabeth?"

"I am afraid she has decided not to come. She wants me to report back what I learn."

"Oh." I couldn't hide my disappointment. This changed things. Julien seemed to sense this, as he thanked me several times before we'd even left the city.

"I again thank you," he said, as he drove out of Paris. "It is very generous to do this."

"No. Generous is giving up your career to take over your family's vineyard. I didn't mean to insult you. I have to admit, when you told me that, I felt a tiny bit inadequate."

"What do you mean?" he asked.

"Well, it's like when someone says they donated a kidney or something. You immediately put yourself in their shoes and think about whether you would do the same if you were in a similar circumstance. And if you choose differently, it makes you feel, well . . . selfish."

"I was rude to make you feel that way. If it is any consolation, I resented coming home for at least the first two years."

"But you stayed," I noted.

"Yes. I stayed."

"Do you still resent it?"

"No. Not at all."

My father didn't stay. And in my heart, I knew I wouldn't have stayed either.

"I couldn't . . ." I began.

"And that is as it should be," he interrupted. "But how do you know what choices you would make until you have to make them?"

"I just know. Even if I owned a vineyard, I couldn't give up my career. My father is selling my grandfather's vineyard. That doesn't speak much to his loyalty either."

"I guarantee I did not see myself working at the vineyard when I was eighteen. I wanted to be far away from there. But now that I face that prospect, I want more than anything to save the business. And I don't want my mother to think I let it fail on purpose."

"She wouldn't think that. Would she?"

"I hope not. She knows it has always been a struggle. But she also knows where my heart was in the beginning. I'm not certain she believes I have changed."

"Well, I spoke with Georges Lapointe. He's very enthusiastic about meeting with you, and I think he will be an excellent mentor."

"I look forward to it," Julien said, flashing a smile.

I relaxed back in my seat.

Julien shifted into fourth gear, and the car smoothly accelerated. "When did you know you wanted to be a pilot?"

"My father was a pilot, and every time I saw him leave for work, I put on one of his old hats and pretended I was flying. The sofa was my airplane, and I made more than one emergency landing when the dog jumped off."

"How rude of him!"

"I know. I had to keep giving him treats to keep him on board."

"Do you have brothers or sisters?"

"No. I'm an only child, the same as my father. But my mother came from a big family, and I have several close cousins who are kind of like sisters."

"Your parents must miss you when you're traveling."

"My father has the same occupation, so he understands. I owe him a lot. He paid for my flight lessons; I learned to fly before I drove a car. And he let me skip college and go right to flight school. But Mom is left alone a lot in Dallas, and I know she misses me, especially now that I've relocated to Chicago. She's used to it by now, of course, and she has two sisters nearby, so it isn't that hard on her."

I didn't call Mom enough; I barely thought of her during the week, which often made me feel guilty. I remembered how much I missed Dad when I was young, how hard it was when he had to miss more than one of my birthdays. How even when he brought back something special, like an expensive doll, it never made up for his absence.

"And do you miss them? Is it a difficult life to be a pilot?"

I blinked, bringing myself back to the present. "In some ways it is. I'm never guaranteed to have holidays or birthdays off, so I miss a lot of those important events. And you can't commit to regular activities."

"Are people surprised when they meet you? I admit you are the first woman pilot I have ever met."

"They're shocked. They assume I'm the copilot, and when they find out I'm the captain, they assume the copilot, who is male, is always the one *really* flying the plane."

"That must be hard. How do you cope with people like that?"

"I make jokes. Or I play dumb. When one man met me and said, 'You know what they say about female drivers,' I said, 'No. What do they say?'"

Julien laughed. "I assume he didn't have an answer."

"No. He didn't. I make it sound terrible, but I love my job. Flying to Paris is certainly a perk. I bid on it as soon as it became available for me. It's one of my favorite cities. I wish I were more fluent in French, though. . ."

"French is not a hard language to learn. And where better to learn than in France?"

"You're right. I've been listening to Berlitz audiotapes. But immersion is the best way to learn."

"Oui. I was not a great English speaker when I went to Oxford.

I had studied in school, but I was not fluent. It was sink or swim there."

"Sink or swim, huh? I'll practice during our trip if you promise not to be snobby about my terrible accent," I said. "Usually when I speak French, whoever I'm speaking to switches to English."

Julien looked shocked. "French people are snobby? That is the first I have heard about it. My guess is they're trying to be helpful."

I shot him a doubtful glance.

"Or perhaps they want to practice their English?"

"I'd like to believe both of those statements are true," I said. "Really, I do. But experience tells me otherwise."

"Well, I will prove you wrong. But if I correct you, don't consider it rude," Julien said. "I am only trying to improve your skills."

"It's a deal," I agreed.

We spent the rest of the trip conversing in French, with me switching to English when I needed to act as navigator. I directed him to the village, and past it to Clos Lapointe.

"It's there, on the right," I said, feeling proud that I was able to say it in French as I pointed to the lane at the crest of the hill. The ride had passed quickly. Julien was easy to talk to, and the thought occurred to me that none of the men I'd dated had ever asked about my childhood and family. Julien had gotten me to talk about myself almost the entire trip.

Georges Lapointe had told us to come to the house when we arrived. He was wearing a thick sweater that made him look like one of the wine barrels in his cellar. He greeted me with a kiss on each cheek and then a big hug.

I introduced Julien, who quickly shook Georges's hand as though worried he might be next in line for the hug.

I was glad we spoke mostly in English, even as it interrupted my French-language immersion.

The first thing we did was look at the vines.

"It all begins with the grapes," Georges said, leading us to the top of the hill that looked down over a patchwork of yellow and red plants attached to trellises in neat, parallel rows. It was late October and chilly. I put on the sweater I'd brought along. Julien had on a long-sleeved pullover.

The vineyard was set against a backdrop of autumn-colored forest. "This view could be on a postcard, and everyone would come here," I said.

"Of course," Georges said, with no hint of pride, as though it was a fact. "It is most beautiful place in France."

He carried a small black notebook in his hand.

"This is my vineyard journal," he said, opening it up to show us his scribbly handwriting. "I write down all the important dates each year: cane growth, first flowers, last flowers, harvest date. I have another book that I write down where I found mildew, insects, disease, pests."

He turned to Julien. "Do you have a notebook?"

Julien shook his head. "My mother is better than any notebook. She knows everything about every single plant in our vineyard, knows when a plant is diseased, and can tell the quality of the soil just by examining it in her hands."

"That is good," Georges replied. "But, God forbid, what if something happens to her?"

"We would have much trouble," Julien confessed.

Georges nodded. "And that is why you need to be prepared like me. My son will someday inherit all this." He spread his arms wide.

Julien winced at those words. Did he even realize he was doing it? And what it revealed? Perhaps his mother was right to wonder if Julien truly wanted the business to succeed. Julien said he didn't resent giving up his law career, but his actions betrayed him. I wondered if Georges's son was as enthusiastic about the vineyard and winery as his father, or if, like Julien, he had other dreams for his life?

"My son will need these notes. They will be his Vineyard Bible." Georges held the notebook to his chest as if it was sacred.

"It's a good idea," Julien agreed. "And I will start one as soon as I return."

Georges took Julien's arm. "Come. Now I show you my equipment."

I followed behind, sneaking a small notebook from my purse, as I jotted down notes for Grandpa's vineyard.

CHAPTER TWENTY-SIX

A PREDICAMENT

IS YOUR HEAD GOING TO EXPLODE?" I ASKED ON THE DRIVE back.

"Excuse?" Julien looked alarmed. "Is something wrong with my head?"

"No," I reassured him, smiling. "It's an American expression. It means that you have too much to think about."

"Then yes. Definitely. I have many ideas swimming around in my head. Some are very practical, and I can incorporate them easily. Others are quite costly, and frankly, I don't think my mother will agree to take on more financial burden to add new equipment, even if it results in increased revenue."

"Perhaps if she came herself to see his vineyard."

"I asked her to come today, but she insisted I go. With you."

I narrowed my eyes. "She's really trying to set us up, isn't she?"

Julien gave a short shrug. "Don't be too hard on her. She likes you very much."

"I felt a connection with her too," I acknowledged. "Maybe it's because my grandfather owned a vineyard. Your mother also mentioned that her father was sent away to a camp during World War Two. It must have been awful for her. My grandfather fought in France and carried his trauma back with him. Both of them were affected by the war."

Julien nodded. "My mother won't speak much of her past, but I know she suffered much during the war. She has no one except us. She says she is grateful for her little family every day."

"I'm so sorry. She's lucky to have a loving family."

"She also thinks that if I marry, I will be more settled at the vineyard, and won't resent being there. I tell her I no longer resent it, but she refuses to believe me."

"Maybe it's because you protest too much? I saw you wince when Georges mentioned his son."

Julien sighed. "I am my own worst enemy," he said. "I do want the vineyard to succeed, but I miss practicing law. There. I have revealed myself."

"Was that so hard to admit?"

"Terribly hard. I could not admit it before. That is why I was a bit rude to you at the party. You hit a nerve."

"You know that you could make a lot of money as a solicitor. Perhaps you could pay someone to run the vineyard with the money you earn."

"No. That would not be acceptable to my mother. She expects me to do it. And, as I have said, I do enjoy it. I just do not love it as much as she does. And honestly, she gets fatigued more easily now."

"That is a predicament. I wish I could help more."

"You have already done so much. And for that, I am grateful. Tell me, how did you meet Georges?"

I took a moment to reply. "I, uh, met him when I was visiting wineries in Burgundy."

"He said you are a good friend."

I didn't feel ready to tell Julien about the note or wine bottle, or how his mother had sparked a connection to a dead girl from WWII, one who hadn't been so lucky. I wanted to keep it to myself awhile longer. I hadn't told anyone except Paul about the bottle's value, or the note. Of course, there was that sommelier named

Gérard who also knew about the wine. And he evidently had been talking about me if Henri knew an American possessed a rare bottle of wine.

"Well, he's a very friendly guy."

"Yes, he is," Julien agreed. "I don't want to impose on your kindness more, but . . ."

"I'm happy to help," I was quick to reply. Perhaps too quick? I didn't want to seem too eager, especially since I could tell Julien had a slight crush on me. I actually wanted to see his mother. It was as if I'd substituted her for Martine in my quest to set the world right. Not that I had any plans of giving Élisabeth the bottle of wine. But if I could help her in some way . . .

Julien cleared his throat. "When you show up, it's like turning on a switch. She really likes you. If you could visit, she would very much appreciate it."

"Your mother would like to see me?"

"As would I," Julien said. He paused. "When I tried to kiss you, it was impetuous of me. Perhaps bad timing on my part."

"I shouldn't have run off," I apologized. "It wasn't my best moment."

The corners of his mouth turned up. "Yes. I agree."

I felt my defenses flair up. "But in truth, I wasn't expecting it."

"I wasn't either," he said, flashing a quick glance at me as he drove. "As I said, it was impetuous. I don't want to scare you away with my forwardness."

"I'm not easily spooked," I said, but my voice didn't sound confident. I liked Julien. Even though I didn't feel the passion between us that I felt with Henri, he was attractive and kind. And so appreciative. But honestly, how would a relationship work with a vintner when I was flying across the world? He needed someone who would be his partner, like Élisabeth had been for her husband. And that person wasn't me.

"Doesn't your mother worry about you dating a foreigner? Doesn't she worry I will whisk you off to America?"

"My mother knows I won't leave, and I definitely won't fly to America."

"Why is that?"

"I have a confession to make," Julien said as the lights of the city came into view.

Here it was. I'd felt there was a reason for the lack of passion between us, and now I would find out. Was he in love with someone else? Another woman? A man?

"What is it?"

"I'm afraid of flying."

I blinked. That was it? "Why?" I asked. I never could understand such a thing.

He shrugged. "I had a bad experience once. It was a horrendous flight with much turbulence. I was very sick. And ever since then, whenever I fly, I get sick again. So, I will take a train, a boat, a bus, whatever. But I won't fly."

I almost laughed but forced a concerned look. "You know, there is medicine you can take for that."

"Perhaps. Is it a deal break for you? Especially since you are a pilot?"

I couldn't help it. I burst out laughing then.

"You are mocking me," he said, flashing a hurt look.

"No. Well, maybe just a little bit. I didn't expect this."

"I thought you should know," he said, looking sheepish. "It is embarrassing to admit."

I thought about the precision of flying, the adrenaline rush I got during a soaring takeoff and the sigh I felt inside when the wheels gripped the pavement during landing and the speed brakes and reverse thrust slowed us down. The sheer joy of flying sometimes made it hard to comprehend a passenger's anxiety, even as I knew there were people who felt that way.

I put a hand on Julien's shoulder. "There are a lot of things that are deal-breakers for me, but fear of flying isn't one of them. Unless you plan on being my copilot."

"You have no need to worry about that," he said, shaking his head.

As he pulled up to the curb, I thought of inviting him to my apartment, but resisted the urge. That might convey a different intention. As much as I liked Julien and enjoyed spending time with him, I was sure we would not make a good couple.

"I've been thinking," I said, "of how comfortable your mother is in the vineyard. And how much more knowledgeable she is about the vines."

"Well, thank you for that assessment," he said with irony.

"It's just that you said that when you returned, she put you in charge of the vineyard and she took care of the business side. I wonder if you two shouldn't change positions. You might do better with the practicalities of management. And from what you told Georges, your mother loves spending time with the vines."

He raised his eyebrows. "That is actually very astute. She thought she should handle the business. But this is something to consider."

"It makes sense."

"You're right," he said, and the irony was gone from his voice.

"Thank you for a fantastic day," I said, remembering the fine wine and food Georges had provided, and the beautiful autumnal views we'd encountered. "I fly for six days and then I'm off for three days. I'll come visit then, if that's okay with your mother."

Julien got out and opened my car door. "That would be perfect. And even though you say you are not spooked, this time I will ask first. May I kiss you goodbye?"

I hesitated. I didn't want to lead him on, but one kiss wouldn't hurt. If I didn't feel anything, and Julien didn't either, it would be easier to maintain our friendship knowing we weren't a match.

"Charlotte?"

I stopped and turned toward the familiar voice. "Henri?"

"It seems I still have bad timing," Julien said, and he backed away.

"Henri, this is my friend, Julien." I made the awkward introduction.

Julien reached out his hand, but Henri only gave a curt nod of his head. "Am I interrupting?"

"I was just leaving," Julien said, pulling his hand back, then looking at me. "Thank you again for your help."

I watched him leave, feeling embarrassed, wondering what he must be thinking. It was only after he turned the corner that I faced Henri again.

"I wasn't expecting to see you," I said.

"Obviously," he said, his voice filled with accusation.

I bristled. I didn't owe him an explanation. It had been more than a month since we last met. He hadn't called once since then. "I have an early flight tomorrow. Did you want to talk to me?"

Henri's tone softened. "Can we talk at your flat?"

I felt myself weaken. He was wearing a suit, as though he'd come straight from work. Henri always looked so sharp and handsome in his suit. But then I remembered . . .

"I'd prefer to do it here."

"Right here? On the street?"

I looked around. There were pedestrians walking past and we were very public, standing on the edge of the sidewalk. But if he wanted to talk to me, this was where I felt safest, where I wouldn't succumb to his charm. I folded my arms in a determined manner. "Yes."

He stuck his chin out. The irritation was visible on his face. "Very well. If you insist. You lied to me about that bottle of wine."

I rolled my eyes. "Are you still talking about that wine? I told you I drank it."

"Did you? I spoke with the sommelier and even though he refused to give me your name, he said the woman was a tall, redheaded American, and that a different label had been attached to the bottle."

I'd feared that the sommelier would rat me out. At least he didn't tell him my name. My heart was beating fast. My mind was reeling. I waved a hand in the air. "That's ridiculous, Henri. You can't think that I'm the only redheaded American woman in Paris."

"Perhaps not. But I think if you came with me to see him, I suspect he will recognize you."

As if I'd go anywhere with him. "I have no time for this nonsense. I'm not going anywhere with you."

I turned to go, and he grabbed my wrist. I looked down at his hand and narrowed my eyes. He was really going to do this in broad daylight?

"Remove your hand," I said forcefully.

He let go and flexed his hand. "Then perhaps you will make time when I take you to court."

He was taking me to court? Righteous indignation flared up inside. "How can you sue me? You gave me that bottle!"

"And how will you prove that? I can say I left it behind accidentally."

"That's a lie, and you know it."

"I would not have given it to you if I had known it was valuable. And if you kept that information from me, then you should at least give me half of the proceeds."

My voice grew hard. "It was a gift. I owe you nothing."

"You will owe me plenty by the time we go to court. By the way, you are not the only one seeing someone else. Say hello to Amber for me."

Amber?

That stung. He said it to get a reaction, so I gave it to him. "I knew you were seeing her." I had suspected it all along. But it wasn't until I actually said the words, until I saw the look in Henri's eyes, that I knew it was true.

I remembered Amber's innocent denial that day at the winery. But later, when I'd thought about it, I'd never once mentioned Henri's apartment to Amber, who seemed to know all about it.

Henri flinched. But he didn't deny it.

My eyes filled. I didn't want to be right, didn't want him to admit that he'd been seeing Amber. God, how I hated him now.

"It doesn't have to end this way," Henri said, reaching for my hand. "I have missed being with you."

I pulled my hand back. How dare he! First he tried to bully me out of the wine, and now he was trying to seduce me out of it? After admitting he'd been seeing Amber?

Back when I was young, it might have worked. I might have given him another chance. But I was a captain now. I would never give him that bottle of wine. I had plans for that money. He'd have to pry it out of my cold, dead hands.

"Go ahead and sue me, Henri. I already have an excellent attorney."

He smirked. "You? Have a solicitor? And who is that?"

I pointed toward the direction of Julien's car. "You just met him."

CHAPTER TWENTY-SEVEN

THE ORPHANS AND THE HARVEST

MARTINE

1943

MARTINE SPENT LONG AFTERNOONS AT THE VINEYARD, helping Gabriel tend to the vines. Oscar ran between them, wanting to play, sometimes carrying a stick in his mouth.

"Where are your workers?" Martine asked, as she tied back shoots that had come loose. Some of the plants needed pruning. She remembered that Papa had many men who worked at the vineyard. Damien oversaw the workers in the vineyard. Damien, who was supposed to help her, and who had been taken away because he was with the Resistance.

"They left when we could no longer pay them. We used to have a horse, but the Germans requisitioned it."

"Where is your mother?"

"She is standing in line for rations. It is what she does most days."

"Do you make your own wine?"

"No. We take the grapes to a producer who makes the wine. You ask a lot of questions."

"I'm interested in learning," she replied.

"You already know a lot. How old are you?" Gabriel asked.

"I am eight. How old are you?"

"Twelve. I've never met an eight-year-old who is so interested in growing grapes and making wine."

"Well, I am," she said. "Papa said it was in my blood."

"I think he was right," Gabriel said, with a smile. "I helped my father, but I can't tell when a plant has disease. You find the bad parts and cut them out, and the plant thrives."

He shook his head. "I should have paid more attention when my father showed me things. I was more interested in playing."

"Do you have brothers or sisters?"

"No. Do you?"

"No." She stopped weeding and looked up at him. "But I have a secret. One that I want to tell you."

She paused. "My papa isn't dead. He was taken away by the Germans."

"Oh," he said. "How do you know he's still alive?"

Martine bristled at his question. "I just know," she replied.

Gabriel sighed. "My father was killed by the Germans. I hate them."

"Sister Thérèse says we can't hate people. We can only hate their evil actions."

Gabriel shook his head. "To me that's the same thing. And I still hate them."

Martine remembered the bodies hanging in the town square. Nothing could block out the horror of what she'd seen, even if it was for just an instant before Sister Ada had covered her eyes. She knew that she was supposed to be forgiving, that the nuns preached loving every fellow human being. But it could have been Sister Ada hanging there, or André. And the Germans had taken Papa away, even if she was certain he was still alive. She missed him so much.

"I hate them too," she admitted after a few minutes.

Gabriel looked up at the hot sun. "Ripening happens faster in hot weather. With just the two of us to pick the grapes, we'll lose a lot of the crop."

"I'd ask the nuns to help, but they have their own garden to tend to," Martine said. "And all the praying." They spent so much of their day in prayer. Martine couldn't sit still that long, and she wondered how Sister Ada, who she now knew was part of the Resistance, could sit still too. Then her face brightened. "I know other children who can help."

"Who?"

"The orphans. They're underfed, though, so they might not be able to do much work." Even Martine felt lightheaded sometimes from all the fasting that was required at the abbey. Even though Mother Superior said Martine was exempt from fasting, she didn't feel right eating in front of the starving nuns.

The orphans didn't have a choice, though. There wasn't enough food to go around.

"I'd offer them all the grapes they want to eat if they help pick," Gabriel said.

"I'll ask Sister Ada about it," Martine promised.

That same night she approached Sister Ada to ask about the orphans helping in the vineyard when the grapes were ripe.

"I think that's an excellent idea," Sister Ada said. "But you must realize that they're inexperienced. You will need to teach them. The young ones might not be up to it, but there are many who could help. I'll arrange it with the directress of the orphanage."

Three weeks later, a line of boys and girls walked up the road to the vineyard. They were a poor-looking group, many of them barefoot and wearing threadbare sweaters, but they were all eager to work. Gabriel and Martine had baskets ready for them, and Gabriel instructed them on how to tell if the grapes were ripe, how to pick the grapes, and how to make cuts at the top of the cluster stems. He handed the older children the knives to cut the bunches, while the younger ones placed them in the baskets.

They hauled the baskets to a waiting truck, which would take them to a local wine producer. Gabriel dumped the baskets into the back of the truck. The nuns supplied loaves of bread and fresh jam they'd made. And they all drank watered-down wine and ate grapes during breaks.

The orphans sang while they worked, filling the cool morning air with their high voices. Martine thought it was fun despite the work, and no one mentioned the war the entire time, as if their little vineyard was in a different realm. The orphans played with Oscar, who loved all the attention, and taught Martine how to play marbles when there was a break. At the end of two weeks, Gabriel gathered the orphans in front of him.

"You saved our vineyard. And you worked as hard as any grown man. If you ever need a job after the war, I will have one for you here." Then he gave them each a bottle of wine and small cakes that his mother had made after saving her rations.

Martine rode in the truck with Gabriel and the man who would turn the grapes into wine.

The man, Monsieur Bernard, warned Gabriel about what he could expect to earn from the grapes. "You have to follow the rules. There are no alternatives," he said. "The Germans are taking much of the profit. Everyone is being forced to accept low prices."

Martine felt Gabriel's body stiffen next to her. "Or you're taking advantage of us because we're children," he said.

Monsieur Bernard shook his head. "I would never do that. Your father was a good friend of mine. What you have done is admirable. So many vineyards are falling into disrepair. You have done the work of a man."

He added, "I will help you get the best price possible. Your father would be proud of you."

Gabriel relaxed. He turned to Martine and squeezed her hand. "I couldn't have done it without her. My best friend, Martine."

Gabriel's hand felt warm in hers, and she tried not to blush. Martine remembered how Papa had said she had a connection to the vines, how she knew how to make them grow and produce the best grapes. Assisting Gabriel with his vineyard had helped her remember her life before the Germans came, even though she was so young when she left her home. Even as Papa's face was becoming a blur, the vineyard was the one place where she felt his presence, as if he was there with her tending to the grapevines.

She had told Gabriel her secret, that Papa was not dead, but was taken away by the Germans. She hadn't told him why, though. She wondered how he would feel if he knew she was Jewish. Would he still hold her hand?

That was one secret she could tell no one. Not even Gabriel.

CHAPTER TWENTY-EIGHT

SENT AWAY

1944

THE WEATHER TURNED COLD, AND THE DANK ABBEY DIDN'T hold much warmth. Martine spent as much time as she could in the kitchen near the ovens, and her hands cramped from cold during her school lessons. Martine had heard the rumors from the orphans, especially the ones who were Jewish and whose families had disappeared. How people were sent to horrible camps. How many of them were taken on trains and never heard from again.

The orphanage hid as many children as they could. But what of the parents? Would they ever see them again?

She pestered Sister Ada every day, asking if she could find out something about her papa. How if she did find him, Martine could write him a letter so he would know where she was and come find her after the war.

Finally, one day several weeks later, Sister Ada told her she had some news. She had come to Martine's room where Martine was reading. As always, her little stuffed rabbit was beside her, keeping her company.

Sister Ada paced back and forth. "I'm afraid it isn't good news. I found out that your father was taken to the Fort d'Hauteville prison near Dijon."

Prison! Poor Papa. “Papa is not a criminal,” Martine protested.

“No, he is not. He is Jewish, and that is his only crime. But it appears he was on another list. One that took him from the prison to the Drancy Camp. I will do more searching to see if he is still at the camp, although I have not heard from anyone there that knows him.”

Martine felt tears sting her eyes. She knew Sister Ada had only done what she had asked of her. But she had hoped for better results.

Sister Ada tried to sound optimistic. “If he is at the camp, you can write to him. I can send the letters through my friend André.”

That gave Martine some hope. “What if he isn’t at the camp? Where will he be?”

“I don’t know. He could have been sent to another camp,” she said softly. “Some of the prisoners were transported to Auschwitz Camp in Poland.”

Martine thought of the trains, of Papa going away never to be heard from again, like the orphans had talked about. But she also thought of the Catholic nuns. They were constantly offering up their prayers for the needs of others. And Martine offered up hers for Papa every day. She would not give up hope. To do any less would be a betrayal to him. She remembered the bottle of wine she had lost. She had her rabbit, which was more beloved than any bottle of wine.

Still, she felt guilty for losing it. Papa had made her promise not to let go of it. She would apologize in the letter and hope that he would forgive her.

Sister Ada sat down next to Martine on her bed. “I know this is hard to hear. Why don’t you write a letter now, and when we find him, it will be ready to send?”

Martine nodded. She had so much she wanted to say. And Papa would be proud of her now that she could read and write. She could share what her life was like here so Papa would know she was safe.

"There is one other thing I must tell you," Sister Ada said, fidgeting with her hands. "The bombing is getting worse. We are close to Paris, and it is dangerous for us. There have been random roundups in the village. They take people off the streets and put them in trucks if they even look a bit Jewish. André feels that . . ."

"No! I won't leave." Martine had grown to love the nuns and Sister Ada. They were her family. And there was Gabriel, who needed her to help with the vineyard. Despite the freezing January weather, Martine often walked to visit Gabriel. The bare vines looked like they were getting a peaceful sleep under a light dusting of snow. She had helped Gabriel lay down grass cuttings to keep the roots warm.

"With your false identification papers, we could try to get you out of France and safe," Sister Ada continued, even as Martine shook her head. "It would only be until after the war ends. We will forward any letters we receive from your father. And when the war is over, you could return to the abbey and meet your father here. When it is safe to come back."

Martine barely remembered any time other than war. She could not imagine a time when there would not be war, and she felt safe here. She would only leave if Papa came to get her. Until then, she would resist. She'd run away into the forest if she had to.

"We don't know what will happen," Sister Ada said. "Just our being here makes it dangerous for the abbey and all the nuns."

We? "Would you come with me?" Martine asked.

Sister Ada continued to fidget with her hands. "I can't, Martine. I must stay and help with the Resistance."

Martine's voice was accusatory. "You promised you would always stay with me."

"I promised I would always look out for you. And I am doing that by taking you somewhere safe."

"You just want to get rid of me so you and André can get married." Martine still remembered how André said he would marry Sister Ada. Maybe having Martine around was the reason he hadn't asked her yet. At least, that was what she had conjured in her mind.

"Married? Why would you say such a thing?"

"Because when I saw André in the forest, he said he would marry you right now if he could," she answered, wondering if she had betrayed some secret she wasn't supposed to reveal.

"I don't want to get rid of you, and neither do the nuns," Sister Ada said. "That is the real problem. We would all miss you terribly."

"Then why do you want to send me away?"

"I have come to love you dearly, and sometimes I even think of you as my own child," Sister Ada confessed. "And if you were my child, I would do anything to keep you safe. And that is why I must do this. I know you don't want to go, but you must. You may go say goodbye to your friend Gabriel today."

She got up to leave, her beads clacking as she rose. "We leave first thing tomorrow morning. Write the letter to your father. Then pack your things up."

She paused at the door. "And do not tell Gabriel you're leaving because you're Jewish. Tell him it's because of the bombings. He'll understand."

And then she was gone, and Martine collapsed in tears on her bed, with only her tattered Annabella for comfort.

CHAPTER TWENTY-NINE

TOXIC NOSTALGIA

CHARLOTTE

1990

I DID SOMETHING I DIDN'T OFTEN DO. I CALLED MY DAD. I rarely saw him, except when we were both home at the same time or happened to see each other at an airport, which hardly ever occurred. Even less now that I'd relocated to Chicago and spent so much time in Paris. I hadn't been back home to Dallas in over a year. But we kept in touch by phone.

I was lucky. I called Dad's car phone, and he answered. "Hi, Dad. Are you on your way to the airport?"

"Where else? Where are you calling from?"

"Paris. What exotic location are you flying to?"

"Newark. I know, right? I'm only flying domestic flights now."

"What? Why? Is Mom sick?" I couldn't imagine him giving up those trips that only came with seniority unless something drastic had happened.

"No, nothing like that. I was ready for a change, and to be honest, I wanted to sleep in my own bed. It's a lot of short flights, but I'm home most nights now."

"You're not thinking of quitting, are you?"

"Of course not. Flying is in my blood. But I only have another five years left before mandatory retirement hits. This is a way to edge into being home more so it's not a complete shock to the system."

Flying was Dad's whole life and identity. I couldn't imagine anything preparing him to give it up or edge him into retirement. He'd talked about buying his own plane, which I fully expected him to do.

"Enough about me," he said, "what about you? You still seeing that Frenchman?"

I hated to disappoint Dad. He and Mom had gotten their hopes up after I'd told them about Henri. But it was better to rip the Band-Aid off than slowly peel it.

"No. We broke up, actually."

"I'm sorry to hear that, Charlotte. Are you okay?"

"I'm fine, Dad. I'm calling because, well, I just wondered if you'd sold Grandpa's vineyard yet."

"No. But we waited until after the harvest. It's only been on the market a few weeks."

"I know you weren't a fan of the vineyard, but what if I was able to get the money to buy it myself?"

"Charlotte . . ."

I imagined him frowning, trying to come up with the words to discourage me.

"Dad, I have an investment that could pay off big-time, and I can't think of a better way to use the money."

Dad sighed. "Even if you could come up with the money, do you realize how much work is involved? You're not going to give up flying to manage a run-down vineyard that doesn't make much profit, are you?"

"No," I admitted. "It's just that all my memories of Grandpa are tied to that place."

"You're looking through rose-colored glasses, kiddo. Your memories are ones of a child who didn't see how broken he was. That vineyard was his way of retreating from the world."

I remembered a soft-spoken man who was absorbed with his grapes. One who didn't like crowds or the Fourth of July (the fireworks, especially), and hated traveling, which is why he never visited us. "I know Grandpa suffered from PTSD. But do you even know what happened to him during the war?"

"He never talked about it. But I remember when I was about ten years old and I found him hiding behind the couch in the living room. He had this look of fear on his face I'll never forget. And he said some strange things."

"What kind of strange things?"

"Well . . ." Dad paused, and I wondered if he'd tell me. "Things like 'I didn't mean to kill him.' Stuff like that. Made me wonder who he'd killed. I've heard that during the chaos of battle that sometimes soldiers killed their own troops by mistake. Or innocent bystanders."

"That's awful, Dad. And so hard for you as a young boy."

"It's not so much that he wasn't present while I was growing up, it's that he was only present when he was in that damn vineyard. That's the only thing he cared about. It certainly made it easy to leave when I was old enough."

"I don't blame you for leaving."

"Maybe you don't. But he did. I felt bad for my mom. She was left to care for him. At least she came for visits. Always alone."

I could hear the car being turned off, and the rattling of the keys in his hand.

"I have to go, Charlotte. You understand why I'm not thrilled with the idea of holding on to the place? You feel nostalgic about it, but for me it was toxic."

"Yes, of course. I just hate to see some big corporation buy it."

"Tell you what. If I have a choice, I'll try to sell it to a family operation."

"Thanks, Dad."

"By the way, what's this big investment?"

"Oh, it's nothing, really. A bottle of wine that might be worth something."

"Wine? Well, don't drink it then. And make sure you safeguard it."

"I will. Thanks, Dad. I hope I didn't upset you."

"Nah. I'm grateful I have this great career. And I hope you're happy with yours too."

"I am. Bye."

Sometimes I forgot how lucky I was. Dad was right; I wanted Grandpa's vineyard for sentimental reasons, but I didn't want to put in the time and effort to make the vineyard work.

And Dad's advice to safeguard the wine struck a nerve. Henri knew where I kept my extra key. What if he'd made a copy?

I wouldn't have thought Henri was capable of stealing the wine, but I hadn't expected him to grab my wrist either. Or threaten to take me to court.

What if he did come in to steal the wine while I was gone? Where would be the first place he'd look? In my closet, of course.

I needed a better hiding spot.

CHAPTER THIRTY

LEARNING A LESSON

I HAD TO WAIT ANOTHER SIX DAYS TO CONFRONT AMBER. HER betrayal percolated inside me, threatening to spill over if she happened to be on my crew during a flight. I knew I wouldn't be able to face her without losing it. Luckily, I didn't see her until she showed up at my apartment.

I waited all of three minutes until I spewed out all the accusations and resentment I'd been hoarding. It was uncomfortable because Jane was there too.

"How could you, Amber? You're my roommate and a fellow employee!"

"You know I have a policy where I don't sleep with crewmates' boyfriends," Amber had said, not looking directly at me.

"But you made an exception for Henri."

Amber's eyes went wide. "That's so unfair! Why would you accuse me of such a thing?"

I folded my arms. "He told me, Amber."

That finally brought a flush to Amber's porcelain face.

Jane stood there, frozen in place, waiting for Amber to say something.

Amber finally looked at me, but there was no apology in her eyes. "I only went to his apartment because he asked me to come, to talk about you. I was trying to help. He said he needed someone to talk to."

Jane shook her head, her lips pinched together. "Amber, how could you?"

Amber looked like a trapped animal. She appealed to Jane. "He told me he was going to break up with Charlotte anyway."

"He wouldn't have told you that," I objected.

"He said you wanted a commitment. He said it was over. Did you even know he was married?" Amber asked me.

"Married? No. I've been to his apartment. He's not married."

"I saw pictures of her," Amber said. "And he told me."

I clutched my stomach. It couldn't be true. Was that why he insisted on coming to my apartment most of the time?

"Oh, Amber," Jane said, her voice filled with disappointment.

"He's French. He has mistresses," Amber said, as though it were common knowledge. As though that explained her betrayal. "Both of us were interviewing for the same position. Wannabe mistress."

I was livid. "I wasn't *interviewing* for anything. You can move out today," I said, and went into my bedroom and slammed the door like a teenager. I almost wished Amber hadn't told me he was married. It made my dreams of a life with him seem even more ridiculous and foolish.

An hour later Jane knocked on my door. I could see her packed suitcase in the other room, along with a box filled with her various toiletries and knickknacks. She was still in her uniform.

"You don't have to leave, Jane."

"I don't want to, believe me. I'm so angry with Amber."

"Then stay."

"She's my niece. My sister would kill me if I didn't watch out for her."

"I'd say it's time she started watching out for herself."

"Remember, she's twenty-three years old. She's ten years younger than you."

"Ten years ago, I wouldn't have cheated on a senior pilot or my roommate," I said.

"I know you wouldn't have. But you were more mature at that age. And so focused on your career. Amber thinks flying is all some kind of continuous party. I'm not excusing her for this. I just think she needs to grow up."

She sighed. "Are you going to be okay?"

I shook my head. "All this time, Amber wasn't the other woman. I was."

"You didn't know," Jane said. "Amber should have told you sooner."

"I probably wouldn't have believed her."

"I hate having to go back to those lousy hotels. That girl needs someone to set her straight. We're going to have a long heart-to-heart talk."

"I can't believe he was married," I said, feeling the tears come.

Jane gave me a long hug. "I'm so sorry, Charlotte. You're my best friend, and you don't deserve any of this. The bastard didn't deserve you either. But I'm glad you broke up with him, especially since we now know he was married.

"Call me," she said before she left. "Let me know if you want to talk."

I didn't watch them leave. I didn't want to face Amber again, and I hoped she'd steer clear of any of my flights.

THE NEXT DAY, I TOOK A LONG HOT SHOWER AND JUST MISSED his call. Julien had left a message on my answering machine. He was in town and wondered if I could join him for a stroll through the Père-Lachaise cemetery.

I needed to get out. It was a sunny day, and not terribly cold for

November. And I'd always wanted to see Jim Morrison's grave. I took the Métro and met Julien at the cemetery entrance.

"I'm planning to come to the winery tomorrow," I said as he greeted me with a kiss on the cheek. This time I didn't pull away.

"That will be wonderful," he said. "I had a couple of hours to wait while an order was being filled, so I thought I would enjoy the fresh air and walk. I'm glad you could join me at this last minute."

We accepted a map of the huge cemetery and strolled down the pebbled road through a thick coating of leaves, as the tall, old maple and ash trees that lined the road had shed most of their foliage. The cool fall air felt refreshing, even as I was bundled in a knee-length coat and with a scarf around my neck. Julien wore a leather jacket over his flannel shirt.

We stopped to examine the elaborate headstones and mausoleums that held entire families. Like everything in Paris, it was a testament to beauty and architecture.

Some headstones held fresh flowers and recent dates; others looked to be hundreds of years old. And some were run-down, their collapsing walls covered with moss.

"What is this?" I asked, stopping at one grave that featured a sculpture of a man on his back holding a woman's head, his eyes staring into hers. The epitaph on the grave was written in French.

"It reads, *They marveled at the beauty of the journey that brought them to the end of life.* His name was Fernand Arbelot, and his one desire in death was to gaze forever on the face of his wife."

My arms shivered. "That's beautiful. He must have loved her so much."

"I'm sure he did," Julien said, and the way he looked at me made me turn away. I wandered to the next tombstone, where a pink ribbon streamed across a large bouquet of fresh flowers with the words À NOTRE SOEUR—to our sister. In front of it sat a tray filled with spring rolls, oranges, and incense.

"Each monument tells a story of a life," Julien said. "That is perhaps why this is the most famous cemetery in Paris."

I noted groups of tourists in the distance led by a guide. "I've never been on a guided tour of a cemetery."

"This cemetery is more like a museum," Julien said. "It consists of more than forty hectares, and you can spend days here.

"Or an eternity," he added, taking my hand.

We stopped to see Chopin's grave, where Julien noted that Chopin's body was buried here but not his heart, which was buried in Poland. "He was afraid of being buried alive," Julien said. "And he wanted them to cut him open to ensure that didn't happen. As it turns out, his sister smuggled his heart back to Warsaw."

Then we passed French singer Edith Piaf's tombstone, decorated with bouquets of daisies and roses. I couldn't help but hum her famous tune "La Vie en Rose."

"They should play that song nonstop near her grave," I said, noting the quietness around us.

Finally, Julien led me to Jim Morrison's grave, a simple, unelaborate stone, but the grave that contained the most flowers and decorations left by fans, including pictures, jewelry, and even fake lizards. A small metal fence kept fans away, but even that was decorated with balloons, wine bottles, love locks, and graffiti.

"He came to Paris for anonymity," I said. "But he's one of the most famous residents of this cemetery."

"If you don't count Oscar Wilde, Molière, Chopin, and Rossini. But for Americans, yes, he is most popular."

We walked awhile longer, but I had to stop and rub my legs, which had started to ache.

"Here, let's sit for a while," Julien said, leading me to a bench to nurse my tired legs.

"When you come tomorrow, I will give you a tour of our winery," Julien said. "But I won't make you walk as far as this," he promised. "And then perhaps we can have dinner?"

I paused, wondering how to tell him. "Julien, I've been thinking..."

"Oh, no. When a woman says that it is never good."

I scowled. "It's not good that a woman thinks?"

"That is not what I mean. It's not good, because it is always followed by a rejection. At least in my experience."

I looked down. He was right. "It's just that I think we should remain friends."

"Nothing more than friends?"

"I'm afraid not," I said, meeting his eyes. I saw disappointment and hurt in them, and it made my heart wrench.

"We can still have dinner," I offered. "As friends."

"You're not even going to give me a chance?"

"I like you. A lot. You're attractive and kind and fun to be with. But we have such different lives, and we're both very busy."

"And why should that matter? We can make time to see each other. Look, we are doing it right now."

I pursed my lips together before I spoke. "I'm thinking long term."

He sighed. "You are a planner, I know. But these things have a way of working out. Do you have to chart out every relationship before you even begin?"

"I don't chart out my relationships! It's not like a flight plan."

"Isn't it? Do you have to know what will happen one year from now? Or two? Can't you live in the present?"

I hated that he was hitting on so many truths. I'd learned during the last year that all my planning was for nothing.

"I'm not as young as I used to be," I said, even though I hated to admit it. "And I don't want to just have fun. I have to look at a relationship in regard to how it will endure over time."

"And how do you know if it will endure? You are only looking at my occupation. If I were an attorney at a law firm in Paris, would you feel the same way?"

"But you're not. You're a winemaker and you live on a vineyard forty miles outside of Paris. You are tethered to the land, and that's fine. But I'm tethered to the air. And I'm gone for days on end. Why would you even want to be involved with someone like that?"

"You don't make a good case for yourself, I have to admit," Julien said. "But this is not about any of that. Sometimes it is about letting go and enjoying life, and seeing where it takes you."

"I know exactly where my life is taking me," I said. "Thirty-five thousand feet above the ground."

He shook his head. "You are so frustrating, Charlotte."

I took Julien's hand. It was rough and a bit dry. "Look, I don't want to hurt you."

He spoke softly as people passed by. "Perhaps it is not me you are afraid of getting hurt."

So, he thought I was afraid of taking another chance on love? That I was afraid I would get hurt again? There might be some truth to it, but he couldn't understand. Just yesterday I'd learned that the man I thought I loved was married.

I didn't want to hurt Julien further by telling him there wasn't any passion between us, because he obviously felt something. And I had to admit there was a little spark between us, one I hadn't wanted to acknowledge. It wasn't like Henri, but it was there nonetheless. If I was younger, if I hadn't had such a bad experience with Henri, I might have given in to this feeling to see where it led.

"For now, it's probably best we don't rush things."

He cupped my chin with his other hand. "I am not trying to rush you, believe me. I only want to spend time with you. Don't push me away."

He pointed at an elaborate tomb surrounded by a black gate across from us. "That is the final resting place of Abelard and Héloïse, two young lovers who were separated by her uncle and who never saw each other again. They only kept in touch through letters. But they professed their love forever and were reunited in death."

I felt a rush of wetness behind my eyes and pushed back the tears. Who would have thought that a cemetery would be so hauntingly romantic?

"Love follows no plan," Julien said.

Julien wanted me. And I was making it impossible for him.

"Then let me be your friend," I said.

He let his fingers linger on my cheek. "I will be your friend, Charlotte. But I cannot deny my feelings."

We walked the rest of the way back in silence. He offered me a ride home, but I insisted on taking the Métro back.

"I'll see you tomorrow," I told him before I left. "I rented a car for the day. Let Élisabeth know I'm coming."

"Oui. I will." He kissed me on the cheek.

As I sat through the roar of the train, I remembered that I had wanted to ask Julien about Henri's threat to sue me. But today hadn't been the right time for it. Perhaps tomorrow I could ask him, but in an indirect manner. I didn't want Julien to know what had really happened, how I'd gotten the bottle. Because even though I didn't think we should be more than friends, I had felt it again. When his hand had lingered on my cheek. The flutter in my chest I'd felt when I first met Henri.

This time I wouldn't act on it, though. I'd learned my lesson.

CHAPTER THIRTY-ONE

A VISIT TO AN ABBEY

THE NEXT DAY, I DROVE TO THE WINERY. I ARRIVED EARLY, before the restaurant opened. Élisabeth was waiting for me near the front door.

"Julien is at the vineyard," she said, motioning me to follow her.

I thought she was taking me to the vineyard, but instead found myself in a room off the kitchen where a large basket was packed with bread and pastries and two bottles of wine. Perhaps food for Julien?

Élisabeth struggled with the basket, which I quickly took from her. "Here, let me help," I said in French.

"Merci." Élisabeth smiled and led the way, out of the winery and down the lane I had just driven up. The basket wasn't too heavy, but it was bulky. And why were we walking, when we could drive? We passed my car, and I was tempted to stop and put the basket in the trunk. Instead, I followed Élisabeth, who meandered down the road as if we were out for a stroll. We were headed in the opposite direction of the vineyards. Was she taking me out for a picnic?

Finally, I spoke up, feeling more confident in the French that I'd been practicing. "Are we taking this to Julien?"

She shook her head. "No. To my friends."

"Oh." That gave me little to go on. But the day was sunny, and slightly crisp, as if teetering on the edge between fall and winter, not sure which way it wanted to go. We turned left at the road, opposite the direction I had driven from Paris. Élisabeth seemed to enjoy the walk, and she hummed a tune that I didn't recognize.

Julien had talked of her depression after her husband's death, of how she still rarely smiled four years later. But she seemed happy now. She stopped and pointed out a row of yellow buttercup-like flowers and said the name in French, which I didn't quite catch. Élisabeth bent down and touched one, and she seemed lost in her thoughts.

I didn't want to break the spell of contentment that gripped Élisabeth now. So, I simply smiled and nodded, wondering if I would even see Julien today. My excuse for coming had been to see Élisabeth. But I was anxious to talk to Julien, to see if I had anything to worry about in Henri's threat of a lawsuit. And I had been thinking more about Julien, of how different he was from Henri. In truth, I thought of him more than I cared to admit. He had the same warmth and kindness as his mother. I wondered if I had given him short shrift.

Élisabeth interrupted my thoughts. "My husband proposed to me here."

My French was getting better, but I wasn't sure I understood correctly. "In this spot?" I asked in French.

"Oui. I was nine years old at the time, and he was thirteen. I said no. Of course, I had no idea what I wanted then. I only knew that I missed my papa, and I didn't want to be sent away again. When he proposed ten years later, I made him go to this very spot and do it again in a proper manner."

"That's a lovely story," I said, feeling a bit envious. I was thirty-three and hadn't had a single proposal, much less one when I was nine years old. Of course, I thought boys had cooties when I was nine.

"Let us go now, before I waste your entire day," Élisabeth said, hurrying now.

In the distance I could see a turret stretching up toward the sky. It was attached to a cluster of buildings, on one of which sat a large cross.

"What is that?" I asked.

"That is where we're going. The Abbey of Saint Louise de Marillac is where I spent time as a child."

"You spent time there?"

"Yes. But I was not Catholic," she said. "The nuns helped hide me during the war. Because I was Jewish."

Élisabeth was Jewish? My arms tingled. I'd been reading a lot of books about the war. Some Jewish children were hidden in convents and private homes so the Germans wouldn't deport them. Perhaps the Martine I was searching for had survived. How much better would this ending be than the gruesome thought of her being bayoneted by a German soldier?

I tried not to get my hopes up, but found my voice was shaky as I asked, "Were any other Jewish girls hidden in the convent with you?"

"No," she replied. "Some were at the orphanage, but I was the only one at the abbey. I was very fortunate."

"Did you meet any girls at the orphanage named Martine?"

Élisabeth stopped walking and put a hand on her heart.

"No," she replied, her eyes focusing on me.

"How did you end up at the abbey?" I asked her.

"It was sérendipité."

"Serendipity?" I wasn't sure that's what she meant.

Élisabeth shrugged. "Or perhaps fate. I know they saved my life. In Jewish tradition, there's a teaching, 'If you save one life, it's as if you've saved the whole world.' I only know they saved my whole world."

"Was your father sent to the camps?"

"Yes. I hoped he'd survive, but like so many others, he perished there."

We walked up the road to the abbey, which bordered a forest. As Élisabeth led the way around the back to a door near the kitchen, she explained that it was still a working abbey, that nuns still lived there, and a few worked as nurses at the local hospital. Their mission as Sisters of Charity was to nurse the sick and aging and provide shelter for orphans. The nuns had their own garden and provided for themselves by selling handmade crosses.

"There are no orphans here now. Mostly just a few older nuns."

She knocked and the woman who answered didn't look anything like a nun. She was dressed in slacks and had a long apron decorated with daisies over her blouse. Her brownish-grayish hair was tied back into a bun.

"Élisabeth," she said, kissing her cheeks. "So nice to see you. It's been such a long time. I'll let them know you're here."

I awkwardly held out the basket.

"This is my American friend Charlotte," Élisabeth said. "And this is Olivia, who cooks for the nuns," she explained.

"Enchantée," Olivia said, taking the basket and placing it on a long wooden countertop. "They will appreciate this. Please, sit down. I will be back shortly."

We sat off to the side of the kitchen at a small table, one with an open magazine on top, a celebrity gossip type that boasted a picture of Juliette Binoche with a handsome scuba diver. Not something I expected to see in an abbey. But then again, I'd never been in an actual abbey before. I'd never had much contact with nuns either.

"I have many fond memories of this room. The kitchen seemed so huge when I was young," Élisabeth said.

It was big by modern standards. The kitchen had stone walls and wooden countertops. Dark wood beams ran across the ceiling, and a large portrait of the Last Supper was hung above one of two stone fireplaces tucked into the wall.

"I remember helping with dishes and setting the dinner table. I felt so grown-up even as I sometimes resented having to do chores. But I was useful, and that meant a great deal to me." She smiled and pointed a finger at me. "Life doesn't always work out the way we expect it will. But we must embrace that which makes us happy. Make good memories while you can. They will give your soul something to hold on to when you're old like me."

I barely remembered which airports I'd visited in the last week. They all blurred together. I did try to visit museums when I had a layover, and I always had a book to read so my mind wouldn't turn to slush.

I had met Henri at a museum, and I had developed expectations that hadn't turned out. Élisabeth was right that life didn't work out the way I had hoped. I felt disillusioned, so much so that I hadn't even given Julien a chance. Maybe I didn't feel any passion with him because I didn't want to feel it. Because I'd shut myself off.

"How do you go on when life hands you so many disappointments?" I asked.

Élisabeth sighed. "That is a question I asked myself many times after my papa died, and again after my husband died. Discover your own joy, wherever it leads you. I know you are a very accomplished woman, Charlotte. But don't confuse accomplishment with joy. You need both to survive. You must find your joie de vivre."

Élisabeth spoke with such wisdom. What was it about this woman that I connected with? Was it the sadness I saw in her determined face that reminded me of my grandfather? Or did I identify with her stubbornness, a resiliency that I had to show every day at my own job?

We both held positions that were usually associated with men. It seemed that Élisabeth was the unsung hero of her business, the force behind her husband that wasn't always acknowledged. Even now she had made Julien the head of the company when she was really the one who ran it.

Each time I was with her she revealed a bit of herself, and each bit of her was fascinating. Not only was I not aware of an abbey right down the road, I never would have guessed that Élisabeth had lived here. Or that she was Jewish. This must be the tragic past that Julien mentioned. One that Élisabeth rarely divulged to her own family, much less a stranger.

"My children think I am depressed," Élisabeth said in a low voice. "Yes, I am still sad. I mourn every day for my beloved husband. But I also have much happiness in my life. I am grateful for every person I meet. And I have wonderful memories too. Can we ask for any more in life than that?"

"That's more than enough."

"There are only two nuns left here who remember me," Élisabeth said. "The rest have all died. But when I am with them, I still feel like a little girl again. Isn't that silly?"

I started to reply that no, it wasn't silly at all, when two nuns entered. One was in a wheelchair, and the other used a walker. They were both tiny, as if their bodies were shriveling with age. Their wrinkled faces look puckered under the stiff headdresses.

"Our little chère," one said, opening her arms wide, and Élisabeth's face brightened as she went to embrace them. I could see the little girl she had once been, one who flourished because of these women. A girl who was given a future and a family until she could find her own way in the world.

This was definitely a memory I would store in my soul for the future.

CHAPTER THIRTY-TWO

JOIE DE VIVRE

IT WAS LATE AFTERNOON BEFORE I FINALLY MET UP WITH Julien. He led me to a table near the back of the winery, just off a cozy fireplace where a fire glowed warmth at our feet. The outdoor patio was now closed for the season, and the room was filling up. Julien darted quick glances at the staff to make sure customers were being waited on. Soft music played in the background.

"I'm so sorry about this," he apologized. "I was caught up with trimming a batch of diseased vines, and then my mother kidnapped you."

"It wasn't actually kidnapping. I went willingly. Sort of."

"When my mother decides something, no one has a choice. Believe me, I know this from experience."

"Really, I didn't mind. She introduced me to the nuns, who she said saved her life by hiding her during the war."

"Yes, she is very attached to them. It is so odd. She usually prefers to go alone. My mother rarely divulges information about her time there, even to her own children. I am surprised she brought you with her. The last time I went I was just a small boy."

"I don't know why she invited me along. But it was an honor to learn a bit about her past."

"We know little of her life before that. Neither my grand-mère or grand-père Katz are alive. They adopted her after her father died. She doesn't like to talk about her past, or perhaps she doesn't remember. She said she was young when it all occurred. We only know she survived the war, while no one else in her family did."

I nodded. "My grandfather never talked about the war. Maybe it's easier to repress the past than talk about it. Although she did say your father proposed to her when she was nine."

Julien's eyes widened. "I never knew that!"

I smiled at knowing something personal about Élisabeth that her own son didn't know. A lock of his curly hair drooped down over one eye, and I felt a ridiculous amount of infatuation with it.

There was an earnestness about Julien that made him appealing... but this wouldn't end well. I could tell. I should nip it in the bud right now.

I decided to focus on Élisabeth, on the connection I felt with her, rather than my preoccupation with Julien. And that lock of curly, wild hair.

"I've been reading about the children who were helped by friends, neighbors, and others during the war," I said, thinking of the pile of books by the side of my bed back at the apartment. "The trauma they experienced must have been overwhelming. And then to lose everything and everyone besides." I shook my head and shivered. "Your mother is exceptional. And her relationship with those nuns was amazing to see."

"I think she sees you as a strong woman, like her. Perhaps that's why she's so drawn to you." He reached for my hand. "As am I."

I felt a slight flutter.

A waiter brought out two glasses and a carafe of white wine. Julien poured for us and handed me a glass.

Before I could taste it, he told me to put it under my nose.

"What do you smell?"

"Flowers. Jasmine."

"Now look at it."

I held it out in front of me. "It looks sort of buttery."

He nodded. "Now taste."

I took a sip. "It's a bit fruity. With a salty finish."

"It's from some of the older vines," he said. "You are very observant. Is this acceptable?"

"It's perfect."

Julien had remembered what kind of wine I liked. And then asked for my opinion.

He gave both of our glasses a generous pour. "Did you know that wine was thought to cure many illnesses in ancient times? Hippocrates experimented with wine to treat ailments."

"What kind of ailments?"

"Bloating. Obesity. High cholesterol. They even used it for those ailing Casanovas who were having trouble with their libidos." He raised his eyebrows, and I felt myself flush.

"Actually, my libido is just fine, but I could use your legal help," I said, wanting to guide the conversation to something else. "I have a friend who was given a gift by someone. Later that gift was discovered to be quite valuable, although at the time he gave it to her neither of them knew the value. Now he says he wants it back. He may actually take her to court. What should she do?"

"She should hire a solicitor. An attorney."

"Well, you're a solicitor. I wondered if you could give me your opinion about whether she has a solid case or not."

"If it truly was a gift, then it belongs to her. He can't take it back, no matter its value."

I nodded. "But what if he lies, and claims he didn't give it to her?" Was that something Henri would even do? At one point I wouldn't have thought so. But after he'd grabbed my wrist like that. After all he'd done . . .

"Then he would have to explain how it ended up in her possession. Custody precludes ownership. Or as they say in America 'possession is nine-tenths of the law.' This has legal bearing. May I ask what it is he wants back? Is it jewelry? A ring, perhaps?"

"No. Actually . . . it's a bottle of wine."

"Now I am very curious. Who gives away a bottle of wine without knowing its worth? He must be American."

That made me smile. "No, he's French. The bottle was disguised with a fake label."

"Even more curious. Is she thinking of selling the wine? Perhaps she can split the value and make a compromise with him? One without involving the law?"

I felt my body stiffen. Compromise? Not after everything that happened.

I shook my head now at Julien, as thoughts of Amber and Henri still made me furious.

"She can't compromise," I replied, my voice too hard, perhaps giving myself away.

"I see. If that isn't an option, I would advise her to stand her ground. Be strong and unafraid. The law is on her side."

He added a small squeeze of my hand, then stood up. "I have something to show you. I will be right back."

I took a sip of wine. Stand your ground. That's what I always did, first in flight school, then as a pilot. How many times did I have to fight for what was mine?

But the bottle of wine didn't belong to me. Not really. It didn't belong to Henri, either. It belonged to a man who wanted no more than to protect his daughter, the girl in the picture that was propped against my grandfather's box on the bureau in my apartment. It belonged to little Martine, who lost her father, and then her life. She wasn't lucky enough to have nuns save her, like Julien's mother.

PERHAPS IT WAS AS SIMPLE AS REMEMBERING HER WHEN EVeryone else wanted to forget. When I first read the note, Martine didn't have a name and was nothing but a stranger to me, but now I knew who she was. Now I had a picture of her. And I knew how Martine had died, cruelly bayoneted by a German soldier, if Madame Moreau's statement was accurate. I was beginning to wonder if she'd been truthful. And I'd detected a slight reaction from Élisabeth when I'd mentioned Martine's name. I wasn't sure what that meant.

The fact that I found the note when no one else did meant something. It meant that Martine's life mattered.

And the fact that she grew up on a vineyard was connected to my own grandfather's journey through France during the war. Whatever horror he experienced, he'd found solace in the vines, much like little Martine had.

Paul was right. I should sell the wine and donate the money to the compensation and restitution of Holocaust victims in France. At least it would do some good that way and honor Martine and her father.

I had wanted to buy Grandpa's vineyard. But in running the figures, and after talking to Dad, I knew it wasn't an option.

Julien returned, placing a green notebook on the table. On the cover was a picture of a bottle of wine.

"You see? I am learning. I took Georges's suggestions to heart. I am writing down everything I can think of that I learn from Élisabeth."

"Your own Book of Wisdom," I said, smiling, thinking of the copious notes I'd taken as well.

"Yes. At least, Élisabeth's wisdom."

"Well, she is very wise."

"And she has an intuitive connection to the plants. Unfortunately, she doesn't have that same connection to the business side. I cannot blame her. She missed much school during the war and didn't continue her studies when she was older. This vineyard has been her whole life, much like her father's vineyard was before the war."

I leaned forward, choking back the wine. "Her father owned a vineyard?"

"Yes. But she was very young when she left. She doesn't even remember the name of her village."

How odd. Two little Jewish girls who both had fathers who owned a vineyard. I was reminded of the fact that there were thousands of vineyards in France. But this was another connection to the little girl who had perished. She'd brought a different Jewish girl to me, one who perhaps needed me too. Was that what this was all about?

Julien cleared his throat. "I had hoped to spend more time with you today. Can I make up for it by taking you to dinner tomorrow?" He put up his hand. "It could be just as friends, as you want."

I looked away. My impulse was to say no. Not because I didn't want to, but because I didn't want to fall for Julien. What was the point? I didn't really see a future for us. And despite Élisabeth telling me to look for joy wherever I could find it, I still felt the pressure of finding a partner and having children before I got too old. I didn't see that future with Julien.

"I'm not sure it's a good idea, Julien. I mean, how does this work? You have a winery to run, and my schedule is so crazy . . ."

"I am not asking you to choose between me and your career. I only want to spend time with you, Charlotte."

"Can I ask you something?"

"Of course."

"Why did you ask me to speak to your mother that first night?"

Julien tilted his head, prompting the wayward curl to move to the side. "Your comment about the winery seemed very kind and genuine, and my mother had been exceptionally distraught that day. To be honest, I had been watching you since you first sat down. I wanted an excuse to meet you."

I couldn't help but feel flattered. He'd noticed me. He'd been watching me. But I had to find out more. "Why didn't you ask Amber?"

"Who is Amber?"

"She was my . . ." It hit me then. He didn't even remember her. Hadn't paid attention to Amber, who turned heads with her looks. He'd only noticed me.

Who is Amber? There was power in those three words, even if he didn't realize it. What an unexpected delight!

Amber had tried so hard to get his attention too. This was the best revenge I could think of, better than any of the ones I'd dreamt up.

I felt a sudden joy. Julien had just given me back my joie de vivre that Élisabeth had referred to, my enjoyment of life.

"I'd be happy to go to dinner with you." I smiled at Julien.

I paused, then added, "And not just as friends."

CHAPTER THIRTY-THREE

A PROPOSAL

MARTINE

1944

A COLD WIND BIT AT MARTINE'S ANKLES AS SHE WALKED along the dirt road to visit Gabriel one last time. She didn't want to leave. Gabriel needed her, and so did the vines, which were still fragile after being neglected for so long.

Sister Ada needed her too. What would happen if she came back injured again like she had when she'd been shot? Who would take care of her? She wanted to cling to Sister Ada's thick robe, hide behind her, and stay until the war was over. But she had no say in the matter.

Oscar barked a greeting, running out from a shed, looking as cold as she felt. She ran a hand along his back. "I will miss you," she said.

He followed her to the door, which she knocked on, and after a minute it creaked open. Gabriel stood there, looking confused.

"It's too cold out today," he said, thinking she wanted to work on the vines, which had a light layer of snow around them now.

"I came to say goodbye." Her face felt all twisted up, and it was all she could do not to cry. "The nuns are sending me away until the war is over."

He grabbed a ragged coat and came outside. He had never once invited her in. Martine wondered if he was ashamed of his home. From what she could glimpse it looked dirty and messy all the time. But his mother made delicious bread and cakes, even if she didn't bother to clean or help in the vineyard.

"When do you leave?"

"Tomorrow morning."

"Where are you going?"

She shrugged. "Someplace safe, where there is no bombing."

"Then you will have to leave France," he said.

"Oui," she answered. Was there someplace safe? She had finally felt safe here with the nuns and Gabriel.

"I will walk you back," he said, and Oscar trailed behind. "Do you have to leave?"

"I don't have a choice. Sister Ada says I must go."

"Is it because you're Jewish?"

Martine stopped walking. She felt her mouth gape open. How did he know? She'd even taken her first Communion, which the nuns had made a huge fuss over, sewing her a long white dress and a crown of flowers. They'd taken a photo and put it up on the wall in her bedroom.

Martine knew the Mass in Latin by heart now. Sister Ada told her that it was okay to pretend to be Christian to save her life. But if Sister Ada hadn't been there to tell her who she really was, Martine might have forgotten all about her Jewish faith. And she'd never know the Jewish prayers that Sister Ada taught her.

Sometimes, Martine mixed them up. At night, after saying her Jewish prayers, she would make the sign of the cross and say, "Amen."

Now, she shrunk away from Gabriel. "Why do you say that?" she hissed, wondering what she'd done to give herself away. Was it her dark hair and eyes, or her creamy complexion? Sister Ada had red hair and light brown eyes, and they didn't look anything alike.

He put his hands up. "You don't have to pretend with me."

Martine's throat tightened. "Sister Ada said I couldn't tell anyone. Not even you."

"You didn't tell me. I guessed. And staying at the abbey? You picked the perfect place to hide from the Germans."

"Sister Ada rescued me in Paris," Martine said. She didn't reveal Sister Ada's secret, that not only was she not a nun, she also was Jewish, and a member of the Resistance. That knowledge was ingrained on her heart, and her heart would have to be plucked from her beating chest before she'd ever tell.

Gabriel stopped walking and pulled on her arm. He reached out to pick a single yellow buttercup flower on the side of the road, a hearty flower that hadn't yet withered away in the cold. He brushed a coating of snow from its petals.

"You don't have to leave. You can stay with me."

Would his mother want another child to take care of? A Jewish child?

"I don't think that is possible," she said.

"Marry me," he said, pressing the flower into her hand, his face flushed.

"I'm too young. And so are you."

"But I am the man of the house now. That makes me old enough."

He had grown since she met him. He was now another head taller than before.

Martine had grown too. Sister Thérèse had sewn her a new dress, as she could no longer fit into the other one. But she hadn't grown as much as Gabriel. Before, his face was round; now it had taken a different shape, like a pear. And even his voice had a different sound to it now.

"You're not old enough to get married." Even a young girl such as Martine understood that.

"Then at least promise that you'll marry me when we are old enough."

Martine twirled the flower in her fingers, thinking it over.

"How did you guess that I'm Jewish?" she asked him.

"When you asked me what song I was humming last month. It was 'Noël Nouvelet,' the song everyone sings at Christmas. At least, every Christian."

"I heard the nuns sing it, but I didn't know the name," Martine confessed. "You don't care that I'm Jewish?"

"No, it's good, because now I know you're not a Nazi."

She put out her hand. "I will marry you when I am old enough. If Papa gives his permission." She'd written him a letter, which was waiting back at the abbey to be given to André.

Gabriel took her hand and shook it, as though they had a deal. He looked down at her hand, not meeting her eyes. "Aren't we supposed to kiss, or something?"

"This way," she said, stepping forward to kiss him on both cheeks. Gabriel gave her cheeks a soft peck as well.

"You must come back, now," he said. "Or I will grow up and never get married. And the vineyard will miss you too."

Gabriel walked her all the way back to the abbey in the cold. She could think of nothing to say, other than goodbye when they reached the door, and so she said nothing, but ran inside without looking back as Oscar trailed behind her, nipping at her heels as he barked at her. As if he knew.

CHAPTER THIRTY-FOUR

ENCOUNTER WITH A GERMAN SOLDIER

THEY LEFT IN THE DARK, BEFORE VIGILS. MARTINE'S EYES were heavy with sleep, despite the cold air. She wanted nothing more than to go back to her warm bed. Even the cold, damp chapel sounded inviting.

Sister Ada wasn't wearing her habit. Instead, she had on a wool skirt and sweater under a thick coat and hat. Martine kept staring at her, at her long red hair and thin figure. She looked so much younger and prettier than when she wore the habit.

Martine carried a small suitcase with a change of clothes, her children's missal, and of course, her rabbit, Annabella.

André shined a small flashlight on the forest floor as he led them through the woods, which he said he knew better than anyone. It seemed a maze to Martine, one that went on forever.

Sister Ada let out a sigh of relief when it became light enough to turn off the flashlight. Her face was a mask, but Martine could see the stress beneath the veneer, a storm of fear kept bottled so as not to scare Martine. She knew they were trying to protect her.

In the winter the forest sounds carried for miles. Martine shuddered at every crunch of leaves and yelped when a deer ran in front of them.

After that, André chatted as they walked, as though they were on a merry stroll instead of stealing away. He talked incessantly. He said the only ones in the forest who would hear them were the animals.

Sister Ada peppered him with questions. "We have papers now. Why go this way? If the Germans see us, they'll be suspicious of a man, a woman, and a child walking in the forest." She was the cloud to André's sunshine, worrying over every step, which was so unlike her. She was usually so calm.

André answered each question but kept walking. "The papers aren't foolproof. They're fake, and there's a chance the Germans will notice. This way we avoid them altogether. The Germans won't see us. They rarely go into the forest."

His voice was light, and when he wasn't talking, he was humming a happy tune. But Martine couldn't help but think of "Le Petit Poucet," the story of seven children whose parents abandon them in the forest, where they're captured by ogres, who plan to eat them. The youngest child tricks the ogre into eating his own children instead. She couldn't help but wonder if there were ogres in this forest, and what she would do if she was abandoned here.

The forest didn't go on forever. André admitted they couldn't walk all the way to Italy, which had surrendered to the Allies a few months before. "You will be safer there," he said, "and it will be warmer too."

That was the only appealing part, in Martine's mind. Her fingers were icicles.

André felt that it would be better to board a train in a village farther away to protect the nuns at the abbey. But it involved more walking.

It felt strange to Martine's ears to hear André address her companion as "Ada" instead of "Sister Ada." Martine was so used to her being a nun. She had to keep reminding herself not to address her as Sister Ada while they were traveling.

"I will board the train with you, and then get off at the next stop," Sister Ada explained to Martine. "You will be by yourself for part of the trip, but someone will meet you at the station in Nice and will help you get to Italy. Can you remember that?"

"Yes," Martine said, even though she was frightened that Sister Ada wasn't coming with her. It wouldn't be so bad to leave if they were together. She also had to remember that her name was now Martine Blanchett. It was easy to pass herself off as a Catholic now that she knew her prayers. And she was carrying a missal in her suitcase to prove her faith.

They walked for hours, stopping only long enough to relieve themselves, drink a bit of water, and eat the sandwiches Sister Ada had brought. When Martine's feet hurt too much and she fell behind, André hoisted her on his back.

She clung to his neck. He smelled of oak and leaves, with a hint of sweat. She could feel the bristles under his chin, from where he'd shaved.

"It isn't far now," André said after a while, pointing ahead to a patch of light beyond the trees. "That is where we'll catch the train." But his voice had changed. It was lower, and held an edge.

He put her down, and she took Sister Ada's hand. Martine's chest tightened with each step. She remembered her last train journey, almost two years ago. How she'd had to act brave even though she'd been frightened. She was older now, but even more afraid. She knew more about the Germans and what they were capable of doing.

They walked out in the open now, and up ahead was a village, larger than the one near the abbey. It was afternoon, and the sun had warmed up enough that Martine was sweating beneath her coat.

"What is your name?" Sister Ada grilled her.

"Martine Blanchett."

"And who am I?"

"Sis . . . my aunt Ada."

"And where are you going?"

"To Nice to visit my cousins."

"Do not show fear," Sister Ada said.

"Perhaps that is asking too much," André said.

Martine remembered how she had sat with the kind woman on the train to Paris, how it had helped her to be brave.

"I will be brave," Martine told Sister Ada, hoping it would be true.

They were near the edge of the village, where houses were spaced far apart, and there was no traffic on the road.

"Halt!" a voice sounded, and they stopped. Sister Ada didn't turn around. André did, and held up his hands. They had not seen anyone. Where had he come from?

"What is the problem?" André asked, in an innocent voice.

"Where are you going?" the German asked. A cap sat low on his head. He didn't look much older than André, but his eyes held suspicion and he pointed a rifle at them.

"I'm walking my wife and her niece to the depot," André replied.

"Do you have your papers?"

"Of course." André handed over their papers, which the German studied for a long minute.

André tapped his watch. "We don't want to miss the train. It leaves soon."

The German stared at Martine. "She looks Jewish."

Martine's heart lurched.

"Show him what you have in your suitcase," Sister Ada told her.

Martine sat her suitcase down and opened it, taking out her missal. She handed it to the soldier and forced a smile. "I'm Catholic," she said.

"This isn't proof," he said. "You could have stolen it."

"She is Catholic," Sister Ada said. "She knows all her prayers."

Martine brought out the picture of her in her Communion dress. Then she made the sign of the cross and recited the Hail Mary in front of the soldier.

"Okay," he said, before she'd even finished the prayer. "You can go."

He handed the papers back to André. But as André was putting the papers back into his coat pocket, the sun caught a glint of steel and the butt of a gun protruded just enough to capture the soldier's attention.

André looked at the expression on the soldier's face, and knew he'd seen it. He took the gun from his pocket and slammed the butt of it into the soldier's head before the man had time to react.

Martine gasped as the man dropped his rifle. André hit him again, and this time the soldier fell over. A line of blood ran from his head.

"Is he dead?" Martine asked.

"No. He's just out of commission," André said.

"We must get him out of the road," Sister Ada said to André.

But before they could move him, André spotted another soldier down the road.

"Run," he told Martine and Sister Ada.

"Not without you," Sister Ada said.

André was already holding up his hands in surrender. "Go! Take her home. Back to the abbey."

Sister Ada grabbed Martine's hand and they ran toward the forest. Martine held on to her suitcase for dear life. She couldn't lose Annabella.

She struggled with the suitcase as she ran, and Sister Ada finally took it from her. Martine wanted to scream out, to tell her not to throw the suitcase away. But Sister Ada tucked it under her arm and pulled Martine along. They scurried like mice into the dark woods, not stopping until they had reached a darkness that made it hard to see even though it was still daylight.

Only then did Sister Ada stop and show a crack in her emotions, bending over and letting out a gut-wrenching howl.

"What will happen to André?" Martine asked. She thought of the soldier, bleeding on the ground, and her stomach twisted with fear.

Sister Ada finally forced herself to stand and wiped a sleeve across her face. "I don't know," she said, shaking her head. "I don't know," she repeated, tears streaming and fear in her eyes.

They didn't speak for a long moment. Sister Ada closed her eyes and said, "We can't stay here."

"Are we still going to get on the train?"

"No. They will be on the lookout now. We have to return to the abbey."

They should never have left the abbey. Now André had been captured trying to help her escape. All because she looked like a Jew.

It was all her fault.

CHAPTER THIRTY-FIVE

A BREAK-IN

CHARLOTTE

1990

I WAS CERTAIN I'D LOCKED MY APARTMENT WHEN I LEFT. BUT the door was slightly ajar. I pushed it open and froze. The kitchen drawers were flung open, and the sofa cushions were scattered across the floor. The place had been ransacked.

My arms shook and I clenched my fists.

"Damn you, Henri!" It had to be him. No one else knew about the wine or had access to my key. I'd removed the spare key from its hiding spot, but he must have made a copy.

I checked the bedroom, which was in complete disarray, as well as my closet. My heart raced. If Henri found that bottle of wine, I'd never see it again.

I hurried back to the kitchen, where I checked underneath the kitchen sink. I pulled out the messy rags and cleaning products, which I'd placed in front of the mat I used for drying dishes. I removed the large mat. The storage case that held the wine was still there, pushed back into the dark recess where I'd moved it after talking to Dad. I made sure the two bottles were still inside, the one Georges had given me, and the 1920 bottle of Roberge.

I knew my roommates would never find the case behind

cleaning supplies, which they hardly ever used when they were here. Henri must have been put off by the dirty rags too.

I hadn't thought Henri capable of breaking into my apartment. He didn't even try to hide it, either. Perhaps this was a message for me.

I picked up the phone and dialed the gendarmerie. After that, I planned to have the locks changed.

I wasn't about to be intimidated by an amateur wine collector. He thought he could scare me? Henri would find out just how badass I really was.

CHAPTER THIRTY-SIX

LOVE IS IN THE AIR

PARIS IN NOVEMBER WAS LESS CROWDED. THE MOOD OF THE city changed as the weather turned chilly and the days grew shorter. Although holiday decorations were already beginning to show up, Parisians seemed to enjoy the break between seasons, before the rush of Christmas shopping.

When Julien picked me up for dinner, he didn't tell me where we would be eating.

"How much of Paris have you seen since you've lived here?" he asked.

"Not nearly enough," I admitted. "I've been to all of the museums. And some of the restaurants. But my schedule doesn't make it easy." I was used to often dining by myself at restaurants.

I was surprised, though, to see Julien park his car near the banks of the Seine just below the Eiffel Tower, its twinkling yellow lights shining above us in the darkness. Despite the cool weather, a crowd of tourists gathered underneath to take photos. Others sat on blankets on the grass with a bottle of wine, toasting Paris's famous skyline monument.

"I hate to disappoint you, but I've been to the Eiffel Tower many times," I said.

"I'm sure you have. We're not going there. We're taking a dinner cruise on the river."

I wrapped my jacket around my short black dress. "Won't it be cold?"

"No," he assured me, taking my hand. "The boat is glass walled and glass topped. And heated."

He held my hand as we descended the steps toward the water, searching for the slip where our boat was located. Twenty minutes later we were sipping champagne and eating a pear marmalade while the bright lights of Paris floated by. Soft instrumental music played in the background.

"I didn't think anything could match the view from the cockpit," I said, as the boat slid past Notre-Dame. "You can see the whole city lit up from above. But this is truly magical."

Julien nodded. "And there is no work involved for you. All you have to do is enjoy the view."

"Yes. The only checklist before this takeoff is making sure my glass is full," I said, taking another sip.

He laughed, and we clinked our glasses.

We talked through the whole meal, even as the guide pointed out the iconic landmarks: the Louvre, the Grand Palais, the Paris Islands, the Statue of Liberty. Even as the female vocalist serenaded our table, singing love songs in French. We chatted about the winery, about Élisabeth, about flying and being one of few female pilots. We chatted about law and universities, about siblings and being an only child (we couldn't decide which was worse).

We shared tastes of our entrées between sips of wine: French duck foie gras with dried fruit chutney, French guinea fowl for Julien, sea bass fillet for me, glazed carrots and chicory, cheeses and bread, and of course, dessert, which was a Black Forest gâteau for him and an apple-almond pastry for me.

I avoided talking about my previous relationships. I never found it helpful to bring them up, as if talking about failure dampened the conversation. I figured it was the same as when people never mentioned previous jobs they'd been fired from. I also didn't mention the break-in. The locks had been changed, and the gendarmerie promised to question Henri.

But Julien was more open. He said he'd had a few girlfriends at university and law school, one he was a little bit serious about, but none he'd brought home to meet his family.

"I can't count you either," he said. "You have already met my family."

I grinned and said playfully, "Does that mean you consider me your girlfriend? This is technically our first date, you know."

His cheeks flushed. "There I go again, acting impetuous. It is a serious flaw of mine."

"I'll forgive you this time." I tried to sound cool, instead of like a flirty seventh grader, but inside I felt fireworks going off. No one had proclaimed me as a girlfriend in a very long time. Not even Henri. I was always referred to as his *American* friend.

BY THE TIME WE'D DOCKED AND GOTTEN OFF, WE HAD TALKED so much that I wondered if we would have anything left to say to each other.

But then the Eiffel Tower's light show began, and we watched as a young man from the boat proposed to his girlfriend beneath the Tower. The girl was younger, perhaps her early twenties, and I felt a tick of envy as I watched, noting how the girl held on to her boyfriend's neck and shouted yes as the crowd applauded, and how happy they looked as they kissed and smiled at the people who had witnessed this special occasion.

Not for the first time I wondered what I had given up in order to become a pilot. It had always been my dream from an early age to be in the cockpit, commanding a large jet. I couldn't imagine doing anything else.

Even though I never voiced it out loud, I couldn't imagine being like my mom, waiting while my father was off in the clouds. She lived a life that felt excruciatingly limited to me. But Mom kept busy and never seemed to be bothered by the life she'd chosen. It only bothered me, which might explain why I didn't call often enough.

And frankly, we didn't always have a lot to talk about. Mom was far more interested in my love life than my pilot life.

Julien clapped along with the others. I just stood there, thinking about the constant demands of my job, the annual checks and simulator sessions, in addition to flying time, and how it compromised any sort of relationship I might have. I'd chosen this life, yes, but somehow hadn't realized when I became a pilot that it might exclude me from being a wife and mother. Seeing young couples like this always made me realize what I was missing.

"Are you okay?" Julien asked.

I put on a fake smile. "Yes. Just a little melancholy."

"I did not want to intrude before by asking about the man on the street that day. His name was Henri?"

"Oh, him? No, he wasn't important. We weren't serious or anything." But my voice pitched higher and gave me away.

"Oh. Is it rude of me to be a little bit happy about that?"

"I'd be insulted if you weren't."

"Then let's go," he said, taking my hand.

"Where to now?"

"Now that I have officially announced you as my girlfriend, I have a standing invitation at Les Bains Douches, so tonight we're going to use it."

"Club Les Bains? Amber tried to get in there for over a year without success."

"Then you will have to rub it in."

I hadn't seen or spoken to Amber since I kicked her out of the apartment. But I would have made an exception to rub this in.

The club was located in the 3rd arrondissement on the site of a nineteenth-century bathhouse. It was glamorous and chic and attracted artists, actors, models, and rock stars. Prince was often known to perform there impromptu.

We parked several blocks away and walked to the entrance on a small street that resembled an alleyway. Julien paused in front, where red velvet ropes and stanchions kept out the riffraff.

"Are you having second thoughts?" I asked.

"Only that if I get rejected, I will look pathetic now," Julien said, and I noticed that his hand felt a bit clammy.

"Not at all," I assured him. "Well, maybe just a little bit."

He grimaced. "You're not making me feel better."

After entering the elegant foyer with David Rochline frescoes, Julien nodded at the doorman and approached the man at the counter, where he produced some secret code name, and we were let in. The club was located below the chic restaurant, down a dark stairway that I would have thought was creepy except for the sound of music floating up. It was everything I had heard about and more: under the haze of cigarette smoke the dance floor was crowded, as well as every table next to the bath-tile green walls that reflected the club's roots.

The place seemed to be a watering hole of the fashion world. Almost every style of dress could be seen, from eccentric to tuxedos. Some people arrived in costume, perhaps coming from late-night performances at local theaters. Most men sported the French turtleneck, with some in casual jackets like Julien, even a man in a top hat matching an orange suit-coat; and women in slacks, shorts, or extravagant long dresses. Some people wore dark sunglasses. It was all on display, as were the people, who all held glasses in one hand and a cigarette in the other.

I held tight on to Julien's hand as he guided me through the crowd to the bar. Most of the people were in their twenties and thirties, although a few men with gray hair sat in booths surrounded by young beauties. A man in a leather jacket who looked very much like Robert De Niro occupied a prominent booth. Heat rose from the black-and-white checkered dance floor as a thick wall of people jumped and swayed beneath a few red spotlights.

On a small stage, a DJ spun out David Bowie's hit "Never Let Me Down" through giant loudspeakers situated around the club.

We danced and drank champagne on the crowded dance floor, while trying not to spill our drinks. Besides the smell of liquor and the metallic taste of cocaine dust in the air, I caught the distinct scent of chlorine.

"Are the pools still open?" I yelled above the music.

Julien nodded. "Yes. Can you imagine bathing in the same thermal baths as Proust?"

"No. But we have to see it."

In the thick crowd, I hadn't noticed the pool adjacent to the dance floor. As we got closer, I saw women and men in the pool. Some wore swimsuits, but most had just stripped down to their underwear. Others were fully dressed, making it look like a large wet-T-shirt contest. A few women were on red inflatable rings, still wearing their dresses and high heels. Julien had ordered more champagne, and we raised our glasses toward the people in the pool.

"Venez. Come in," the guests encouraged us. "Join us."

I shook my head.

Julien tilted his head and raised his eyebrows. "I'm game if you are."

"You're joking," I said, calling his bluff.

He took off his jacket. "Try me."

So, it was a dare. I removed my shoes.

Julien, accepting the challenge, took off his shirt, shoes, and socks. Then he removed his pants, revealing his muscled physique in a French black-striped brief.

There was no way I was backing down now. I removed my dress, leaving me in my bra and my, thankfully, new underwear. Julien whistled his approval. Then he took my hand.

"Ready?"

I jumped in, holding his hand.

"I didn't think you'd do it," he said, laughing, as we landed in the waist-high water. He handed me my glass of champagne and we clinked our glasses together, and then clinked glasses with the other patrons in the water.

SEVERAL HOURS LATER WE SPILLED OUT INTO THE COOL night air, sweaty from dancing and slightly drunk, even as our undergarments were still damp.

"You impressed me tonight," I confessed. "A dinner cruise followed by a Parisian bathhouse and nightclub. I've never had such an exciting night."

He held on to my waist as we walked. "That was my intention, but I don't think I can top that, so be prepared for boring dates in the future."

"How did you get us into the club, by the way? Who do you know there?"

"An assistant to the owner did a photo shoot at the winery last year and held her engagement party there."

Why couldn't I have met Julien first? It would have saved me so much heartache. And yet, what did the future hold for us? I would still be flying out in another day and would be gone for six days in a row.

Somehow, in this moment, it didn't matter. With Julien, I just relished his company. The night had been full of warmth and laughter, and no pressure on either of us. I would have been just as impressed if we'd spent the entire time eating gelato and making conversation. There was a magic to this evening.

"I enjoy every moment with you, no matter what we do," I

replied, and I knew it was the truth, despite what the future might hold.

Julien stopped in the middle of the street and pulled me close. As he kissed me, I tasted the champagne still on his lips, and felt the longing behind the kiss.

This was a kiss worth waiting for. Sexy and sweet. A knock-your-socks-off kiss. I wasn't ready for the night to end, to leave once again and put time and distance between us. I kissed him back, deeper, with an urgent hunger, and an invitation, as if to put Henri's memory to rest, because that's just what I intended to do.

I wanted to enjoy this night, to live life to the fullest.

Half an hour later we stumbled into my apartment, stopping twice on the way up to kiss, pushing each other against the wall, as if we couldn't get there soon enough. Fumbling with my new keys, we almost stumbled down the steps as we kissed. And then we were in the bedroom, pulling off damp clothing, kissing once again, and falling together on the bed.

He ran a finger down the side of my neck, sliding it down to my breast, causing me to shiver.

"Are you certain of this?" he asked.

My heart was beating fast, and I thought of how kind he was to ask, but how silly it sounded. I was the one who led him up here. I should be asking him that question.

I pushed the curl out of his eyes. "It's not the champagne, if that's what you think. I'm not that drunk."

"Neither am I," he reassured me. "I don't want to be a one-night stand. You mean more to me."

Did I hear him right? I ran a hand through his luscious hair. "Julien, you mean a great deal to me too. I don't do one-night stands. And you're definitely not a one-night-stand guy. But I understand if you have concerns."

I cocked my head. "Wait. Are you backing out?" We were naked in my bed, and I was beyond aroused by him. I could tell by his hardening erection that he was aroused too.

He kissed me. "Not at all. But what of our different occupations? What of the too many complications you spoke of earlier?"

"What about just spending time together? Those were *your* words, Julien."

He flashed a rueful smile. "It's just that . . . my mother will kill me if I ruin our friendship."

"Then I won't let you ruin it. This will only make it better," I said, and drew him to me.

His objections fell swiftly away.

CHAPTER THIRTY-SEVEN

AN ENVELOPE AND A BUNNY

I AWOKE TO THE SMELL OF COFFEE. THERE WAS MUSIC PLAYing, coming from a radio I kept on the kitchen counter. I could hear Julien humming along to David Hallyday. And I couldn't help but catch the irony of a song that spoke of flying high and dreaming of places that your heart yearned for.

But Julien was here, not rushing off with some quick excuse even though he had a winery to run. And I had another day before I had to fly. If only I could hold on to this moment.

But I needed to pee.

I got up and used the bathroom, then threw on a pair of sweatpants and a T-shirt. Julien was wearing just his underwear and shirt, the sleeves rolled up, and had retrieved my only frying pan from the cupboard. He was attempting to make an omelet, although the pan was old and I didn't have any oil or butter to keep the eggs from sticking.

"I hardly ever cook," I apologized, as he made an effort to turn the omelet with a spatula, but half of it stuck to the pan. And then the whole thing was a mess and resembled scrambled eggs instead of an omelet.

He turned off the burner and put the pan in the sink. His hair was disheveled, and he still had his socks on, which made the whole outfit look rather silly, like a version of Tom Cruise's *Risky Business* character. He smiled and then kissed me, and even though it was a quick peck on my lips, it meant the world to me.

"Why cook when you're in Paris?" he said. "There's a good café around every corner."

"But not one where I can be serenaded by you while you're making breakfast. Or attempting to make breakfast."

"I admit I can't sing like David Hallyday, but I can dance better."

I raised my eyebrows. "How do you know that?"

"Because he was at the club last night, dancing right next to us."

I threw my arms up. "He was? You should have told me!"

Julien shrugged and wiped his hands on a dish towel. "I was too enamored with you. Let us go to the café."

"Don't you have to be at the winery?"

"They can get by without me for some time."

Time. The one thing I never seemed to have enough of. Julien was making time for me when I knew how busy he was.

"I'll just be a minute," I said, looking down at my sweatpants, realizing that Julien would have to wear the same outfit he wore last night.

"Oh, I found this on the floor by the door," he said, handing me an envelope.

"The building manager sticks all my mail under the door," I said as I took it. "It's probably a bill." But as I looked closer, I saw the name of a law firm written on the top.

I felt suddenly weak, as if all the blood was draining from my head.

Was Henri really suing me? That bastard!

"What is it?" Julien asked.

"Nothing," I lied.

He cleared his throat. "I could not help but notice the Palomer Associés law firm logo. They're well-known in Paris."

"They are? Oh, God!" I needed to sit down. I found the sofa and put my hands on my head, wondering how I'd been stupid enough to ever think I loved Henri. He'd denied breaking into my apartment, of course. And now he was suing me for something he gave me, a last-minute gift. More like payment for the night we spent together. But the payment turned out to be too high.

And then there was the airline to think of. They frowned on their pilots getting into international lawsuits. Especially female pilots. And especially female captains. How would it reflect on me when they found out?

Julien sat down next to me. "If I can help in some way . . ."

I shook my head. "I don't want to bother you. You have enough on your plate with the winery, and everything."

He put his fingers under my chin and tipped my head up to meet his eyes. "You are not a bother, Charlotte. You're anything but a bother. And you've helped me. Why not let me help you?"

My hands shook as I opened the envelope. The letter was written in French, of course. I understood none of it, only that it looked very official. I handed it to Julien.

"This is a mise en demeure," he said. "It is a letter from an attorney demanding payment or corrective measure. In this case, he is demanding a bottle of wine that it states you possess."

"That friend I told you about who wanted legal advice? It was me."

"I deduced that. You also told me it was a gift."

"It was. What if I don't give it to him?"

"Then the next step would be a summons and complaint. You would appear before a tribunal. The advocates present to the magistrate their oral arguments based upon the facts. There is no jury or testimony. It is much simpler than American law."

He patted my hand. "Don't worry. I will represent you.

"I'm very curious about this bottle of wine," he said. "Do you still have it?"

"Yes," I admitted.

"May I see it?"

"Of course." As I procured the bottle and note, I thought about how it all began at the Hôtel Drouot, a place that took no responsibility for selling other people's history. It had thrived during WWII, selling artwork from Jews across the country as they entered concentration camps. Jews weren't even allowed to bid on items during that time. And as recently as a few months ago, the auction house had sold bottles of wine confiscated from French wineries.

But what if a person had a chance to set one thing right? One tiny thing to put the universe just a little more on track?

I realized that I wasn't keeping the bottle and note for myself, or even for the little girl with the intense eyes and pristine stuffed rabbit in the picture on my dresser. I felt rage at the losses people incurred through no fault of their own, simply because others had power over them. To make money from injustice was wrong, and I wouldn't let Henri have a single cent.

I carefully handed Julien the bottle. He examined it, turning it over; his eyes gleamed with reverence, as only those of someone who appreciated fine wine would. "This is indeed a rare bottle of wine. A grand cru appellation. And 1920 was a good year for wine. Anyone who would give this away is a fool who doesn't deserve it."

"Or someone who was unaware of what he was giving me. It was hidden under another label," I told him. "And there was this note on the back of the label too."

"A note?"

He took the brittle paper and read it through, stopping to look up at me when he came to the part about the child who was a gifted vigneronne. "Very intriguing. Is this why you felt a connection to my mother? Because of the girl mentioned in the note?"

"No. Yes. The girl in the note supposedly died. But yes, I did feel a strong connection because of her devotion to the vineyard." I proceeded to tell Julien about the auction and the gift, leaving out the night Henri and I spent together. Then I told him how I'd searched for Martine and her father, and how I'd met Georges, who now owned the vineyard and winery.

Telling the story out loud made sense now. It didn't sound like the crazy pursuit I'd felt at the time, but a concentrated effort to discover someone's history. Learning Martine's story had helped me come to terms with my grandfather's history as well. Martine's father had sought a way to save his daughter the only way he knew how. My grandfather had searched for a way to save himself from the torments of war. They had both sought refuge in a vineyard.

"It is a sad story," Julien said when I'd finished. "But I am glad for one thing. It somehow brought you to me."

I kissed him, as that was the sweetest thing he could possibly say. I was past the idea of falling in love with him; it was more like a skydive off a cliff. It was too soon, I knew, after I'd let go of my expectations, to make any sort of plans.

"I will help you fight this lawsuit," he stated.

"How many times have you argued a case in court?"

"Including this time? One. But I helped prepare many arguments during my internships. I am not exactly a beginner."

"Except that you are," I said playfully.

"Then I need more practice," he said, pulling me onto his lap.

I kissed him again. "Are we still talking about law now?"

"Not at all," he said in a low voice. He groaned softly, and all thoughts of breakfast disappeared.

LATER, WE SHARED A SHOWER TOGETHER, SQUEEZING INTO the small stall that was made for only one person, letting the hot water run between the curves of our skin. Afterward, I was famished, but I knew Julien had to get back to the winery.

"You can come spend another evening at the winery, but I don't want to bore you while I work," he said, as he got dressed.

"I have some paperwork to do," I admitted, even as the idea floated through me. Another night with Julien would be worth it.

"Call me before you leave tomorrow," he said, kissing my forehead.

"I have an early flight. I don't want to wake you."

"I insist. I just want to hear your voice."

I hugged him and smiled. "Where have you been all my life?"

He reached over and straightened the picture that had started to fall from the side of my grandfather's box, where it had been perched. "Is this a relative of yours?"

"No. It's Martine. The girl from the note. Georges had a picture of her."

"Look at her expression. She looks too fierce to perish in war," he said, "although I know that doesn't make sense."

"I agree. I hope her little stuffed rabbit gave her courage. I met her former teacher, who said she had it with her all the time."

"I'm surprised it was allowed," he said, frowning. But he continued to stare at the picture, as though he was looking for clues.

"What is it?" I finally asked.

He turned the picture over and looked at the back, which had her name and a date written on it. "I don't know," he said, squinting, turning it back around and bringing it closer to get a better look. Then his mouth opened as if he'd suddenly remembered something.

"It's the stuffed animal," he said, his eyes brightening with recognition.

"What about it?"

"I know that rabbit!"

CHAPTER THIRTY-EIGHT

BOMBS FILL THE SKY

MARTINE

1944

After Sister Ada and Martine returned, things were different. Children showed up suddenly at the abbey and then disappeared just as suddenly a day or two later. The nuns were all aware of it. They helped feed the children and often gave them clothing and books to read, hiding them behind the wall with Martine when Germans were near. The tide of war had turned, and the allies were closing in. They were all part of the Resistance now.

Even though they lived in fear of the Germans, they turned their fear inward with prayer, and outward with action. Food was hidden and then distributed to the orphanage in town, although there wasn't enough food for anyone. German vehicles were tampered with by local Resistance groups. Munitions were stolen.

Sister Ada never spoke of Martine leaving again. It was as if losing André had made her more rebellious, taking more chances, but at the same time she had to keep Martine close to her.

Martine wrote another letter to Papa, and Sister Ada made sure it was delivered to the Drancy Camp. Each day Martine waited for the mail, hoping a letter would arrive from Papa. But none came.

No one could find information about André either. He could have been sent to a camp, or he could have been shot by the Germans. Martine prayed especially hard for André. Sister Ada never mentioned him. And Martine didn't say his name out loud for fear of upsetting her.

The bombings continued, although the majority occurred near the rail centers and main roads. As spring arrived, Martine and Gabriel often saw planes flying overhead as they were pruning and tying up the vines before the buds began to swell. Gabriel became adept at identifying whether the planes were American, British, or German. He stood and waved at the Allied planes, shouting encouragement.

"Yankee Doodle," he yelled, pointing to the writing on the side of one plane.

Martine wanted to pull his arms down and shush him. She'd heard Sister Ada say that Allied bombs had killed almost as many French civilians as the German bombs.

Although Sister Ada encouraged Martine to play with the orphans, she preferred to spend her time at the vineyard with Gabriel. She felt at home among the vines, and closer to Papa. She had spent almost two years at the abbey. She didn't remember a time before war. She also couldn't remember Papa's face any longer, only what she imagined he looked like, a shadow of angles and expressions that lingered in her mind. But she did remember the sound of his voice, always soft and comforting. And she remembered his hands carefully attending to the vines, the same way she was now.

Papa was here in the vines, at least the faint memory of him, and she clung to it.

Gabriel was happy to have her back. Martine hadn't mentioned what happened, only telling him that the nuns had a change of heart. To tell him any more than that might betray secrets, and Gabriel already knew too much.

On the first warm day of 1944 Martine didn't go to the vineyard, as she was helping the nuns prepare their garden for planting. The ice and snow were long gone, and although Martine could never make it up to Sister Ada for what happened to André, she tried her best to be as helpful as possible. She still felt guilt over André's sacrifice, which she felt had been caused by her Jewish appearance.

Papa had always told her she was beautiful, but now she thought he must have been lying to her. She had dark curly hair and dark eyes, and a narrow face. Is that what the German meant when he said that she looked like a Jew?

Martine looked up to see Sister Ada coming out the door, her face red from running.

"We must all take shelter," she said, hurrying the nuns into the building. "The Germans are sending reinforcements to the coast, and they're passing through the village right now. They'll be passing by on this road soon."

Anytime the Germans were near, they hid. Martine wished she could warn Gabriel, but Sister Ada was already rushing her inside.

All of the nuns except for Mother Superior and Sister Ada crowded into the long hidden room. It was stuffy and dark, but Sister Thérèse had brought a small candle, which she lit. Flashes of light flickered across their worried faces. Martine wondered what the Germans would think of an abbey with only two nuns around. Wouldn't they wonder where the other nuns were? But she didn't voice her question aloud.

Then a thought occurred to her. "I forgot my rabbit, Annabella," Martine said, moving toward the door, but she was pulled back.

"It will be there later," Sister Thérèse assured her, even as Martine started to cry for her stuffed rabbit. She knew it was wrong to act like a baby, but Annabella meant more to her than anything. It did no good, though. She had to remain until it was safe to go out.

Sister Thérèse clutched her rosary beads and began praying, her mouth silently forming the words, and the other nuns did the same. Martine tried not to cry and tried to focus on her prayers, but a distant humming put her on edge. It was the sound of airplanes. Lots of them, if they could hear it in their secured room in the abbey, sounding as if they were barely skimming the treetops.

"It's the Allies," one of the nuns said, her voice rising. "They're attacking the Germans."

Moments later they heard the whistling sound of a bomb. And more whistling as other bombs were released. Martine held her breath as the noise became louder, imagining the bombs filling the sky like raindrops.

They were all holding their breath now, waiting for the bombs to hit. And then the earth rumbled, followed by a distant explosion.

"The village," said Sister Thérèse, making the sign of the cross.

Martine thought about the orphans, hoping they were safe. She thought of the pretty village and the old buildings that would be destroyed, buildings that had been there for centuries.

More bombs dropped, some sounding closer, as if they were targeting the Germans on the road. One landed close enough that the room shook.

Martine didn't realize that she was shivering until she found herself folded into Sister Thérèse's arms. The nun was covering her with her body.

The nuns were praying out loud now, as if to cover up the sound of the bombs. Martine closed her eyes, wondering if there would be anything left when they were finished bombing. If the abbey would still be here.

Somehow, she fell asleep. She was awoken later when Sister Ada gave the all clear and opened the door to the hidden room.

"They hit the village," Sister Ada said. "And a few local farms have damage."

"What about the orphanage?" asked Sister Thérèse.

"I don't know. I'm going to check on them."

"Can I come?" Martine asked, wiping her tired eyes.

"No. You must stay here," Sister Ada said. "It's too dangerous."

"One of those bombs sounded very close," Sister Thérèse said. "It must have struck nearby."

And that's when Martine remembered Gabriel.

CHAPTER THIRTY-NINE

THE FIRE

MARTINE WAITED UNTIL SISTER ADA HAD LEFT. SHE TOLD Mother Superior that she was going to read in her room, but she sneaked out the side door. Lying was a sin, but it was a small one when she was so worried about Gabriel.

The sun was shining, and two butterflies fluttered above her head as she ran. But there was the smell of burning wood in the air, and another smell, like rotten eggs. And in the distance, dark smoke rose up from the village, and even closer, there was a plume of smoke rising up from the vineyard.

Gabriel!

Martine ran all the way to the vineyard. The smoke grew closer and thicker, and it was becoming hard to see. As she turned into the lane leading to Gabriel's house, Oscar ran out to greet her, barking at her as if to hurry.

Then she saw flames leaping up from the barn. Gabriel and his mother were throwing buckets of water at it, but it was hopeless, like tossing water at the sun. Martine added herself to the water brigade, but the pails were too heavy, and she resorted to helping fill the buckets.

Finally, both Gabriel and his mother were exhausted and realized the futility. They sat down to watch the fire, making sure it didn't spread across the grounds to their house.

"Thank you for your help," Gabriel's mother said, handing Martine a cup of water. "At least the house is intact. As are we."

"Must have been an accidental drop," Gabriel said. "There's no reason they would bomb us."

Martine remembered what Sister Ada had said; that civilians were killed just as easily by Allied bombs. But Gabriel didn't need to hear that right now.

"The smoke will taint the grapes," Gabriel said to Martine.

"They're not even buds yet," she said. "Don't be worrying about it now. I'm just happy you weren't hurt."

They looked off in the distance at the thick black smoke, and knew that others weren't as lucky.

It was hours later that Sister Ada returned, her black habit covered with gray dust, her face coated with tears and dirt.

"There is not much left of the village," she said, putting a hand over her mouth as if to hold back a scream. "Everything was destroyed."

"The orphans?" asked Mother Superior.

The nuns closed their eyes.

Martine held her breath.

"They are safe. They were having a picnic near the forest because it was such a nice day."

"Thank God they were spared," Mother Superior said, making the sign of the cross.

Sister Ada nodded. "But the orphanage is severely damaged. They have no place to live."

"Then they will stay here," Mother Superior said, clapping her hands. "Until the building can be repaired. Come. We have much to do to prepare for them."

And just like that, the abbey was converted into an orphanage.

The next day it rained, dampening the still-burning fires,

bringing much-needed relief. Martine couldn't help but believe that their prayers had been answered. The orphans were all alive. Gabriel was alive. The abbey was safe. And the vineyard was still intact.

She now believed in the power of prayer.

CHAPTER FORTY

COINCIDENCE OR FATE?

CHARLOTTE

1990

I BLINKED. I WAS CONFUSED. IT WASN'T THE SAME GIRL. SHE had a different name. I knew that, but Julien continued to stare at the picture, as if he was seeing something that I couldn't.

"That's not your mother," I said, wanting him to understand. "Maybe she had a stuffed rabbit too." It wasn't that unlikely.

"Look at her curly hair," he said. "And her age. My mother would have been that same age."

"Lots of little French girls have curly dark hair, Julien. Especially French Jewish girls. And of course, she's the same age. Thousands of little girls were. I would love for it to be her, but I know for a fact that this little girl died in the war." The gruesome way she died was something I didn't like to think about.

"It's the eyes," Julien said, handing me the picture. "Don't you see the resemblance? And her expression. I've seen it a million times. No one has eyes like that except my mother."

"She has a completely different name," I said, a bit too firmly.

"What if you're wrong about the name?" He sounded very sure of himself now.

"I'm not wrong. This girl's name was Martine. Her last name

was Viner. Your mother's maiden name was Élisabeth Katz. Not even remotely close."

"I hear what you are saying, but I swear it's her. And that rabbit belongs to her. I think she still has it." His voice held conviction, as if he'd already made up his mind. What was the matter with him? No wonder his winery was failing if he made rash decisions like this.

"I know it may resemble your mother, but it can't be her, Julien. It's not possible."

"You don't know that for sure. Many strange things happened during the war."

"Not this strange."

"Why are you being so stubborn about this? How can you ignore all the coincidences?"

"That's all it is. Coincidence."

He looked at me, his eyes wide. "Why can't you admit it might be more than a coincidence? Perhaps it is fate!"

And out of nowhere, it made sense. How he wined and dined me after I told him about the bottle of wine that belonged to a "friend." How he made love to me and spoke of a future together. I remembered how Henri had made a toast to "l'amour." Was this any different? But in this case, Julien was more interested in a rare bottle of wine than seducing me.

Instead, he got both.

I took a step back. Suddenly, the air in the apartment felt too warm, too thick. "You're trying to steal the bottle of wine. Just like everyone else. Just like . . ." And I stopped and spat out the last words. "You're no different than Henri."

Julien put a hand on his brow. "For someone you say wasn't important, he seems to be in your head a lot. Don't compare me to your former boyfriend."

It was hard not to. Both of them were laying claim to a bottle of wine that neither had a right to.

"You say you don't care about the wine. But if that were your mother in the picture, it would belong to her. And you know that."

"I was the one who offered to represent you. For free."

"Yes, so you could get the bottle and give it to your mother," I snapped.

He put his hands up. "Look, I'm just saying that there are many coincidences between the Martine you were looking for, and my mother, who rarely speaks of her childhood. I do know she lost all her family, she has a stuffed rabbit just like this one, and this girl resembles her a great deal. Plus, her father owned a winery and vineyard. If you could look beyond your insecurities, you would see it."

"Pilots don't have insecurities. We're analytical. We act according to facts and gut instincts. And we look for warning signs." I glared at him, letting the force of my words take hold.

Julien shook his head. "I never asked for the wine. You're acting defensively, and I don't know why, but I assume it was because of your previous relationship."

"You don't know anything about my previous relationship."

He put on his coat. "You are right. You haven't shared that information. Another way you are like my mother."

He stopped at the door. "I'm sorry. I don't want to leave this way."

"I think this way is just fine. I want you to leave." My voice was cool.

"You are mistaken, Charlotte. Please."

He reached for me, but I pulled back. "You're the one who is mistaken. I was just a fool to believe you."

He sighed. "If you would like to discuss this further, bring the picture with you to the winery. Just think it over."

"I don't have to think it over," I said.

He looked hurt but nodded. "Bonne journée, Charlotte."

And then he was gone.

CHAPTER FORTY-ONE

SÉRENDIPITÉ

I WAS ANGRY, BUT THE ANGER SOON DISSIPATED AND ALL I was left with was sadness. I stood in front of the door, half expecting him to come back, to say it had been a big mistake, and apologize for scaring me into thinking this was the end of us when we were just getting started. How had things gone so sideways in just a few minutes?

It had been different this time. Julien had been different. I hadn't expected too much. And, of course, he still left.

I wiped a tear from my cheek. No matter how many times I tried, I couldn't make it work. I ruined every relationship.

I grabbed my coat and went for a walk, letting the cold air sink into the spaces of skin that weren't covered up; walking just to keep moving, to keep away the fear that I was right about Julien just as I was right about Henri. Julien was correct in saying I gave too much space in my head to Henri. I had given him too many passes, all in the name of love. And he had cheated on me from the start. And now, looking back, I had known about Henri. My gut instinct about him had been right, even as I fought against it.

But Julien? My intuition hadn't led me to the same conclusion, which is why I felt so blindsided by his betrayal.

I still didn't believe Julien. A coincidence of this magnitude didn't happen in real life. That I would find the real Martine and fall in love with her son? It was the stuff of fairy tales, the type of drivel my mother read in romance novels. It wasn't rational, and I couldn't believe that Julien could be so irrational. He was an attorney, who dealt with laws and facts. He had to know that the odds of such a thing happening were astronomical.

Was it a difference in culture? The art of romance was ingrained in French culture. Everywhere I went I saw it: men buying bouquets of flowers for their wives and lovers, couples holding hands and sharing passionate glances at sidewalk cafés. There was even a magazine article that listed the most romantic places to kiss in Paris.

I was walking fast, puffs of cold air coming out of my mouth and wafting above. I had no idea where I was going, but it didn't matter. What it all came down to was trust. Was Julien really like Henri? Had he seduced me all in an attempt to cheat me out of that bottle of wine? Or was it my own insecurity that kept me from seeing what he saw in the picture? He was Élisabeth's son, after all. Perhaps he just wanted to see a resemblance. Or perhaps he really did notice one.

My one defense was what Madame Moreau had told me, that Martine had been killed by the Nazi's bayonet. But how reliable was her statement? I had to admit there were many similarities between Martine and Élisabeth.

Julien had extended an olive branch, an invitation to talk it over. But I was reluctant to accept. How would this affect Élisabeth? Would it cause her more pain? What if she didn't remember her youth and blindly accepted Julien's version of the truth? What if she ended up suing me too? I'd end up with two lawsuits instead of one.

Julien was right. It was a mistake to become romantically involved. It had ruined our friendship, and would ruin my friendship with Élisabeth too.

I stopped, unaware of where I was. My hair was a mess, and I was wearing a long jacket over a dressy top and my underwear. I was so frazzled I hadn't even put on my skirt.

I didn't know what to do. I didn't know what to believe. All I knew was that just an hour ago I had been sharing a shower with the man I was in love with, and now I was alone again. All because of a bottle of wine. Or because I was too insecure to trust Julien.

I hadn't meant for any of this to happen. I hadn't meant for Julien to even see the picture. But I had to admit that if I hadn't found the note, if I hadn't searched for the little girl, I wouldn't have met Élisabeth or Julien. And I wouldn't have opened myself up to fall in love again.

The smell of strong coffee made me look up. I was in front of a small restaurant. My stomach growled, and I opened the door to go inside when I noticed the name on the door, which made me blink several times. SÉRENDIPITÉ.

"Coincidence," I said, trying to convince myself. "There's no such thing as serendipity."

Then I remembered Élisabeth.

CHAPTER FORTY-TWO

FAITH AND HOPE

MARTINE

1944

ON JUNE 6, MOTHER SUPERIOR ANNOUNCED THAT THE ALlies had landed at Normandy. The few remaining Germans left their devastated village, abandoning it to head to the coast as reinforcements. As the Allies moved inland, the Resistance soon came out of hiding and took control of the public buildings, causing the leftover German sympathizers to flee. They were simply gone one morning without any fanfare.

French flags decorated window fronts, along with British and American flags. The maquisards boldly marched through the streets singing "La Marseillaise." But André was not among them.

There was worry that the Germans would return. But their small village was already ruined, the train tracks and roads blown up, and too much out of the way to interest either the Germans or the Allies.

The abbey's biggest concern was food. There wasn't enough to feed the orphans, and the Germans had sacked every pantry on their way to the coast. The delivery truck that was supposed to bring provisions for the orphans often didn't show up. The nuns had planted hearty root vegetables: rutabagas and Jerusalem artichokes, which had been grown to feed livestock before the war. Martine hated eating them, but it was all they had some days.

She wasn't used to sharing her room with four orphan girls, but she didn't mind the laughter that filled the abbey, or the sounds of other children. At least she had her own bed, in contrast to the orphans, who lay on straw-filled mattresses that were stacked during the day like plates in the corners.

And even though she had plenty of playmates now, Martine still spent her free time at the vineyard. It was her sanctuary, the place she found refuge and hope, and a kindred spirit in Gabriel.

Ever since his barn burned down, Gabriel had been less talkative about the war. He no longer counted the airplanes flying overhead. He no longer cared about how many panzers the enemy had, or where the Allies were advancing.

He was more worried about the vineyard. "The Yanks don't give a damn," he said. "They'll smash everything in their way. What do they care about a bunch of vines? They drink beer, anyway."

No Frenchman would ever think of trampling a vineyard. The war had been fought around the vineyards, but never through them. It was an unwritten rule. Now that the Allies were winning, would Gabriel lose the one thing that mattered most to him?

Martine was afraid to say it out loud, that the war might be over soon. But what if Papa didn't come back? What would happen to her then? She hadn't seen Papa in two years, and it had been more than six months since they had seen André. She went to find Sister Ada to ask her about it.

She found her in the garden by herself, kneeling over a tomato plant that had failed to produce more than a single fruit. The heat of the day was waning, but it was still steaming in the sun, especially in a long black habit. It was only when she got closer that she realized Sister Ada was crying.

"What is wrong?" she asked, touching Sister Ada's shaking shoulder.

She spoke between sobs. "Resistance fighters were held in Caen Prison. When the Allies landed at Normandy, the Caen Gestapo executed all eighty-seven of them."

Martine gasped. "Was André . . . ?"

Sister Ada shook her head. "I don't know. I have no idea where he is, or if he is even alive. But what if . . ." She buried her face in her hands and sobbed again.

Martine had never seen Sister Ada like this, except for that one moment in the forest. It was as if she had lost all hope, as if she had given up now that help was on the way.

She needed to bring Sister Ada back from despair. This woman had saved her two years ago. It was her turn now to rescue Sister Ada.

She squeezed Annabella for courage. "He's alive," Martine said. "He'll come back."

As she said those words, for the first time she now realized they might not be true. Not for André or for Papa. She was older now, had seen what war did to people, had seen what evil lurked beyond the abbey. What would her life be like if they didn't return?

"I know it's true," she said with conviction, because that is what Sister Ada needed to hear. It's what Martine believed for the two years that Papa had been gone, and she couldn't give up hope now that the war might be ending.

Sister Ada wiped her eyes with her sleeve. She slowly stood up and put her arms around Martine.

"You are the best thing that came into my life," she said. "I'm so grateful I found you at the Hôtel Drouot."

The Hôtel Drouot. It seemed a lifetime ago. The nightmares had disappeared, and all that was left was sorrow. Martine took Sister Ada's hand and brought her back inside the abbey. They didn't mention André or Papa again.

CHAPTER FORTY-THREE

A HERO'S PARADE

TWO MONTHS LATER THE ALLIES ARRIVED. SOME WERE British and some were American. They didn't trample the vineyard. They barely blinked as they sped through the small village, not bothering to stop for more than a minute as they raced toward Paris. As the trucks drove past, the village cheered them on and the nuns brought out bread and baskets of tomatoes to give them, as if they needed the support of starving orphans and nuns.

Less than a week later, Paris was liberated. That was more cause for celebration, a feeling of elation that was felt by everyone. Paris was the center of the world; the Champs-Élysées, the Cathedral of Notre-Dame, the Arc de Triomphe. The dignity of all France was restored in that moment when the Vichy Regime ended.

"This will be the best crop of all," Gabriel said, and not because the weather had been great and the grapes were fat and bulging. The air was sweet with freedom, and it affected them all.

"Is the war over now?" Martine asked him.

"It may as well be, now that Paris is liberated," Gabriel replied. "The Allies are pushing the Germans out of France, and soon they will push them all the way to Berlin."

Did that mean she would see Papa soon? Martine had stopped asking Sister Ada about Papa. Her life with him seemed so long ago, and even though she still felt close to him at the vineyard, she had forgotten so much of her former self.

A week later, Gabriel walked Martine home from the vineyard, with Oscar running ahead, when the dog froze for an instant and stared straight ahead at a distant figure. Then he barked and ran toward what they now could distinguish as a man limping on the dirt road. A rifle was slung over his shoulder. Martine stiffened. Surely it couldn't be a German soldier?

Gabriel stepped in front, as if to protect her. The man stopped by the barking dog. Gabriel took in a breath. But then the man bent down and rubbed Oscar's ears, as if greeting an old friend.

Martine pushed her way in front of Gabriel. There was something about the man. He was wearing a beret, not a German uniform. The way he stood seemed familiar. He didn't look the same as before. He was thinner, and his clothes hung off his slight body. A ragged beard covered his chin. But when he looked up, she recognized his bright blue eyes.

"André?"

He opened his arms. "Martine!"

She ran to him and flung herself into his arms.

"You're alive," she said, amazed and grateful at the same time.

"I am, thanks to a German guard. I was in a prison in Paris. He knew what they were planning to do with us before the Allies showed up, and he let me go."

"You were saved by a German?" Gabriel asked, his voice disbelieving.

André nodded. "Yes. I know it sounds unimaginable. But he was a new conscript, barely more than sixteen years of age. He said he had seen too many things he wished he could forget, and he refused to see any more, and the war was over anyway. So, he let us all out. I don't know what happened to him afterward. I told him to go home and if anyone asked, to say we escaped."

Martine hugged him again. All the guilt and regret she had felt since he disappeared melted into the warm air. He was alive. "Sister Ada! Have you seen her yet?"

"I was making my way there," he said.

"We'll come with you!"

She held his hand, while Gabriel and Oscar followed behind, a hero's parade of three. They strolled up to the abbey, and Martine opened the door and led them inside.

It was late afternoon, just before dinner. It was a muddle of activity in the great hall: Sister Jeanette was reading to the orphans, Sister Thérèse was knitting in a chair, others were busy in the kitchen preparing the meal.

"What is all this?" André asked.

"We run an orphanage now," Martine responded.

Sister Thérèse glanced up and raised her eyebrows when she saw André.

At the sight of this strange man, a silence settled in the large kitchen except for the kettle bubbling on the stove.

"Where is Sister Ada?" Martine asked.

"She should be . . ." But Sister Thérèse didn't finish because Sister Ada had entered the room, carrying a load of laundry.

Sister Ada froze. She stared at André as if he were a ghost.

"It is me," he said, reassuring her. "André."

Sister Ada dropped the basket. Her legs began to give way and she sat down on one of the benches.

André knelt before her. "All will be well now, ma chérie."

She started crying then and threw herself into his arms. He kissed her on the cheeks and the mouth.

"Mon Dieu!" Sister Thérèse set down her knitting and made the sign of the cross. Sister Jeanette dropped her book, and her mouth flew open. Several other nuns gasped and asked for the Lord's intercession on this sacrilegious occasion.

Mother Superior just nodded and smiled.

"What is happening?" asked Gabriel, looking confused. "Why is he kissing Sister Ada?"

"Because she is his amoureuse," Martine told him. "I think the other nuns just learned that Sister Ada isn't who they thought she was. That she isn't a nun at all."

CHAPTER FORTY-FOUR

A NEW LIFE

IN FRONT OF ALL THE NUNS AND ORPHANS, ANDRÉ GOT DOWN on one knee and took Sister Ada's hand in his. A gasp was followed by a hushing sound that came from Mother Superior.

André looked at Mother Superior, who nodded her approval. "I spent every day in prison with one promise on my lips," he said. "It is all that kept me alive, and I will waste no time in keeping this promise."

Sister Ada removed her hand from his. "Just one moment longer." She removed the headdress and let her long red hair flow around her shoulders. She was striking, so beautiful. Martine wondered that she had not noticed how beautiful Sister Ada was before this.

Sister Ada put her hand back in André's. "You are not asking Sister Ada, a nun, for her hand in marriage. Now you are asking Adelaide Levinson, daughter of Anne and Bernard Levinson."

She nodded. "You may proceed."

"My dear Ada," he began, "you know how much I love you. Now I ask you, before God and these kind sisters who kept you and these children in their care, to be my wife."

Ada smiled down at André. "I accept your proposal. I would not marry anyone but you, André."

He stood and kissed her again, and this time everyone cheered, even Sister Jeanette.

It took another month to find a rabbi to marry them. Ada still lived at the abbey, and still helped to care for the orphans. André stayed in the village to be near Ada, even though in Paris the best apartments of former collaborators were given to the Resistance leaders, and he said they could have a flat on the Champ de Mars with a direct view of the Eiffel Tower.

But Ada didn't want to leave. "I belong here, now, in this village," she said. She no longer wore the habit of the nuns. Martine had difficulty referring to her as simply Ada even though she'd known all along that Sister Ada wasn't really a nun.

Ada was so happy now that she barely noticed how Martine skulked around her until one day when Martine threw a dish down on the hard stone floor while Ada was describing where she and André would live in the village.

"That was terribly clumsy of you," Sister Jeanette scolded her.

"I don't care," Martine said and ran to her room.

A few minutes later Ada came to her room and sat on the edge of Martine's bed. "I have something to tell you. I should have told you before, but I needed to make arrangements."

"You're not here to punish me?"

"No. You are clearly upset, Martine. And rightly so. Things have changed a great deal in the last few weeks."

Things had changed for Ada, not for Martine. Soon Ada would marry André and leave her behind. Martine would be left to wait for Papa, if he ever showed up. Why would she be any different than all the other orphans here who had lost their parents? The hope she'd kept alive for so long had dwindled this year, even though people were being released from the French camps. But to admit this to anyone, even Ada, would mean she had given up on Papa. She couldn't do that, not when she'd lost the bottle he'd entrusted to her, the only thing he'd asked of her.

"The war still rages on. We may not have news of your father or other relatives for some time," Ada said. "But until that time comes, André and I would like you to live with us. If you want to, that is. We're staying in the village, at least until the end of the war."

Martine looked at her now. "You want me to live with you?"

Ada nodded. "I must warn you that our place will be much smaller than the abbey. It won't be as close to the vineyard, either. But André insisted that you come with us."

"You really want me to live with you?" Martine asked again, as if she had misheard Ada the first time.

"Of course," Ada said. "You are like a daughter to me, Martine."

"And you are like a mother to me," Martine admitted for the first time out loud. She hugged Ada, overcome with gratefulness and love.

The Jewish wedding was held near the garden behind the abbey, and attended by thirty-four orphans, nineteen nuns, and almost the entire village. An American serviceman, who was also a rabbi, performed the service, then left shortly afterward to travel to the front.

Germany surrendered seven months later, in May of 1945. Martine waited for Papa, but he never came. Then, one cold fall day, Ada and André told Martine that they had news of her father. Martine knew it was bad by the way they looked at each other.

Ada knelt down in front of Martine. "I am sorry, Martine. Your father died at a concentration camp. Your aunt has survived, but she is in poor health and cannot care for you."

Martine had no tears. She was ready to accept Papa's death by then.

"Your aunt said there are no other relatives left alive who can take you."

Martine shook her head. She was truly an orphan now.

"André and I would feel blessed to adopt you," Ada said, "if you want us as your parents."

"Yes. I want that very much!" Martine nodded and hugged them both. She felt grateful that she had found a home in the midst of the war, and she had Gabriel and the vineyard. She had two people who loved her and cared for her, unlike most of the other orphans.

A few weeks later, Martine sat down in front of her new parents. "I need a new name," Martine told them.

"But Martine is a beautiful name," André objected.

"It is who I was before. But that girl is an orphan, a girl who is no longer me. I am different now, with a new family, and I want a new name to reflect who I am."

"What name would you prefer?" Ada asked.

Martine thought of her mother, who had given birth to her in the vineyard and died shortly afterward. She now had a new mother, but she wanted to honor the one who had given her birth, so she would always remember her connection to the vineyard. She said, "I want to be Élisabeth."

Ada looked at André, who shrugged. "If Martine can call me Ada instead of Sister Ada, then I can call her Élisabeth instead of Martine. It is a new beginning for us both."

Many of the orphans were Jewish, although some had come to the orphanage at an age too young to remember their faith. After the war was over, a rabbi came to collect the Jewish children who had been sent away by their parents. Mother Superior asked how he would know which children were Jewish.

He asked for the children to be assembled and cried out the words of the Shema prayer. *Sh'ma Yisrael Adonai Eloheinu Adonai Eḥad!* Hear, O Israel, the Lord is our God, the Lord is One. At the sound of the prayer, many children rushed to him, crying for their parents, as this brought back the memory of them reciting this every night at bedtime.

The number of orphans was much smaller after that. Some were adopted by villagers. Others were taken in by the nuns even after a new orphanage was built. A few of the older ones took vows and became nuns.

Martine, aka Élisabeth, had Ada and André as her parents now. They recited the same prayer her papa had done every night. She kept Papa in her heart, and still felt him in the vineyard, as though the veins of the plants held his energy and infused the silken fruit that called her to remember her home.

She understood now that the wine bottle she had lost had not been her birthright. She remembered what drew her to the Hôtel Drouot, the picture of wine she'd seen in the window. If things had gone differently, if she'd gone another way, she would not have seen the picture, and Sister Ada would not have found her on the doorstep. She could have died, or been caught and sent to the camps like so many other children.

It was the vineyard that had saved her, the rolling ground of green plants where her heart would always be. Papa had encouraged her gift, and that was what saved her life.

Her birthright was not a bottle of wine, but the vineyard, where she would always belong.

CHAPTER FORTY-FIVE

DESTINY

CHARLOTTE

1990

I HAD REHEARSED IT IN MY MIND, IN FRENCH, SO THERE would be no misunderstanding. Everything I wanted to say to Élisabeth. But mostly I wanted Élisabeth to understand that, although the bunny was a coincidence, and she wasn't the same girl as the one in the picture, I was thankful to have gotten to know them both. And especially grateful for her friendship.

I had meant to keep the little French girl's memory alive. No one had remembered her except for a mean teacher and disgruntled neighbor who spoke of her with harsh words. I owed it to her, and through the bottle of wine and a donation in Martine Viner's name, I meant to do just that. I was certain Élisabeth would understand that, even if Julien didn't.

I found Élisabeth alone in her office. A stack of bills formed a mound in one corner of her desk, some unopened. Several had the words RETARD DE PAIEMENT stamped on them. Payment overdue.

I thought of the dinner cruise Julien had taken me on just last night and immediately felt guilty, knowing he couldn't afford it.

Élisabeth seemed unconcerned with the bills as she sat writing a letter, the tip of a pen perched on her lips and a pensive look in her eyes. I studied her for a long moment, trying to see her as a little pig-tailed girl at age six, to embrace a resemblance to a photo that could represent any number of French girls. It had been so easy for Julien.

Her curly hair and dark eyes did bear some likeness. And there were coincidences in their backgrounds. But according to Madame Reza and Martine's neighbor, the little girl I had searched for had been killed before she could escape.

When Élisabeth looked up, her eyes brightened, and she stood and walked toward me to give me a kiss on the cheek. "Charlotte! Salut!"

"Comment ça va?"

"Très bien."

I was overcome with a sudden nervousness. Maybe I should come back later. "Did I interrupt you?"

"No. I was just writing to a friend."

I looked at the cluttered room, which held two file cabinets, a crate of wineglasses, plastic bins used to collect grapes, extra chairs, an assortment of boxes, and of course, several bottles of wine.

I let out a sigh. "May I speak with you?"

"Of course." She motioned me to a cushioned chair, and I sat down opposite her. "Is everything all right? You look worried."

How to start. Everything I'd planned to say, the whole speech, escaped my mind. I didn't want to hurt Élisabeth or get her hopes up. Now I struggled with the French words, hoping I could get my meaning across, hoping I didn't get things mixed up in translation.

"How much do you remember of your childhood, Élisabeth?"

Élisabeth tilted her head. "I did not expect this question. You know that I spent some time at the abbey."

"Yes. But before that. What do you remember?"

"Not much, I'm afraid. Bits and pieces of my life with my papa. He was sent to Auschwitz. He never returned."

"I'm sorry. But *you* never spent time at a camp?"

"No." She looked agitated, as though it was hard to speak about the past. "I escaped to Paris, and then was brought to the abbey. Why do you ask?"

I sighed. "I don't ask this to bring up painful memories. I just . . ."

How to say it? Finally, I took out the old photo from my bag.

"I wanted you to see this." I handed the photo to Élisabeth, who looked at it, first questioningly, then with a dawning reminiscence. She turned the photo over and ran her fingers across the words printed on the back, as though she was reaching back in time.

When she looked up, her eyes were wet.

"Where did you get this?"

"From a man who owns a winery near Dijon."

Élisabeth gave the photo back to me. Then she stood and went to her desk. Inside a deep drawer she took out a stuffed rabbit, similar to the one in the photo, but this one had seen more wear and tear. The black eye had been sewn back on in an awkward manner, making it appear almost cross-eyed. Other than that, it did indeed look like the same stuffed animal.

"Meet Annabella," Élisabeth said. "I keep her with me always."

"I don't understand," I said.

"I've never seen that picture before. My bunny was new then."

"Are you saying that the girl in the picture is you?"

"Oui."

"But your name is Élisabeth. And your maiden name was Katz."

"Oui. I was adopted by André and Ada Katz after the war. I took their last name, and when I found out my papa had died, I also changed my name to Élisabeth to reflect my new identity, to mark a new beginning. Before that, before I was saved by Sister Ada, my last name was Viner. Martine Viner."

Suddenly, the room was spinning, but I couldn't move. I felt as though my feet were stuck to the floor. It couldn't be true. She was

Martine? *The* Martine? All this time she was right in front of me. I wanted to laugh and cry at the same time.

"You're her? Martine Viner?"

"Oui."

I felt a shiver run up my spine. None of this should be happening. "How can that be?" I still didn't believe it.

Élisabeth said. "You have that picture. I have another one."

She went back to her desk and brought out another picture. In it, a little girl who looked very much like the girl in the other photo, but a few years older, was dressed in a white Communion dress. Her rabbit was at her side, looking newer than it did now.

My skin prickled. "It is a miracle! I mean, I felt something the day we met. We just had this connection. And in my wildest dreams I wanted to find her. But I never believed it could actually be you. That you were the little girl I was searching for."

Élisabeth put a hand on her chest. "You were searching for me?"

"Yes! I've been searching for you, and for your father."

"But how? Why?"

"It's a long story, but I have had this picture on my bedroom dresser for months. And it wasn't until Julien saw it that . . ." I stopped as I realized what I was saying, that Julien had been in my bedroom. I felt my cheeks grow hot.

Élisabeth dipped her head and flashed a knowing smile. "May I have that picture? I have none of me before the age of eight. It would mean a great deal to me."

"Of course. But how did you survive? Madame Moreau said you were bayoneted to death."

Élisabeth frowned. "Madame Moreau? That woman is still alive? Of course she is. She was too mean to die. She must be ancient by now. A soldier did thrust a bayonet in the hay wagon I was hiding in, but he missed me. Monsieur Moreau took me to the train station."

"Then why would she say that her husband told her you'd died?"

"Monsieur most likely told her I was dead so she wouldn't be able to reveal where I was. She was never sympathetic to my situation, and she was very nervous about him helping me. I believe she would have gleefully handed me over to the Germans."

That made sense to me. I remembered the nasty woman.

My eyes were wet. "I'm so happy you survived! I mean, I'm so, so happy!"

Élisabeth reached out and hugged me.

I had thought it was impossible, a fairy tale. But now it didn't seem such a stretch. France wasn't a large country. It was smaller than the state of Texas. And of course, the Martine I was searching for, a girl whose heart was more invested in grapes than her studies, would have found her way back to the vineyard.

But it still seemed like more than just a great coincidence. It was fate. Or was it serendipity? A magical destiny guided by a man who wanted to reconnect his daughter with that bottle of wine?

"Oh," I said. "There is something else. A note."

"A note?" Élisabeth's eyes widened.

"I found it on a bottle of wine that was sold at the Hôtel Drouot. It was under a fake label. That is what started this entire adventure."

"The bottle of wine." Élisabeth almost whispered the words, and closed her eyes, as if she was remembering another time.

I took out an envelope from my bag, removed the yellowed paper, and handed it to her. I watched as Élisabeth read it, as she silently wept and ran her fingers over the writing.

"Papa," she cried, when she finished.

I reached out to her. For someone who was averse to hugging, I was becoming quite the hugger. "I am so sorry, Élisabeth. I didn't mean to make you relive the horror."

Élisabeth wiped the corners of her eyes with her fingers. "No. It was not the horror I was reliving. It was my father's love. I waited for years, but I never received a letter from him after he was taken away. This note means more to me than anything. This is all I have of him. I see his handwriting, and I hear his voice in it for the first time in fifty years."

She closed her eyes as she recounted the story. "Papa hid me in the armoire and gave me a bottle of wine. He told me it was my inheritance, that I must never lose it. He said he would be back soon, that it was a misunderstanding. But after they took him away, after I waited for hours, I went looking for Damien to help me, and I dropped the bottle when I heard the Germans coming. I was so afraid, and so alone. I felt so much shame that I had lost the bottle of wine, that I'd let Papa down. For years I carried much guilt."

"You were just a child," I said. "There was no guilt to carry."

She looked at the note. "I know that now. And I couldn't read at the time, so I wouldn't have known what this said."

"And it was hidden," I reminded her. "As far as the bottle of wine . . ."

Her eyes brightened. "You have the wine? After all this time?"

"At the moment. But there are some complications. I will explain later." I didn't trust my French enough to handle that conversation.

"If all goes well, I will be happy to return the bottle of wine to you," I told Élisabeth. I would never be happier about anything in my life.

"There is one more thing I have to do before I leave," I said, standing.

"You have already done so much," Élisabeth said, caressing the note. "This is the best gift I have ever received. There is no word for the joy you have brought me. What is it you must do now?"

I wrung my hands together. "I have to talk to your son."

CHAPTER FORTY-SIX

LOVE IN ANY LANGUAGE

JULIEN WAS CHECKING INVENTORY. HE WAS IN THE DAMP cellar standing in front of a row of barrels, a clipboard in one hand and a pen in the other. A single bulb above dispensed inadequate light, and part of his face was in the shadows. The part I could see looked a bit sad, as if this was not where he wanted to be. Was it because of me? Or because he didn't love this occupation?

He squinted at the paper and rubbed his forehead. He looked disheveled, dressed in jeans and a T-shirt, covered by an open flannel shirt with the sleeves partly rolled up. Julien's hair was messy, and I felt myself attracted to him all the more because of it.

I watched him work, wondering what to say. *Je suis désolée. I'm sorry*? Perhaps if I said it in another ten languages it would be enough. Or would it be? Could he forgive me? I'd accused him of seducing me for a bottle of wine. I'd called him a liar.

Maybe I didn't deserve someone like Julien, who was open and honest, much like his mother. All this time I hadn't even told him about Martine, or the bottle of wine. And when I finally did, I accused him of trying to steal it from me.

And he was right. I didn't tell him about my past relationships either, fearing that, like moldy cheese, they'd spread to this one.

I had known him three months now. Julien was a surge of emotion and life, but someone I thought I had little in common with.

He'd given up his dreams at the drop of a hat, while I fought for mine with every breath inside me. We lived in such different worlds. But somehow we'd found each other. And now I worried that I had ruined it all with Julien, that there was no going back, that he would not ever trust me like he did before.

And I couldn't blame him for it.

My heart was beating fast, waiting for him to look over and see me. Wondering what he would do. If he would pretend I wasn't there, if he would acknowledge me with a cool nod, or if he would ask me to leave. Any number of possibilities, none of them what I hoped for, but all expected. All what I deserved.

And then he was looking up, and our eyes met. Before I could say anything, before I could apologize, tell him what he meant to me, or even say his name, he had crossed the room and had embraced me. And then he kissed me, and I kissed him back.

"Je t'aime," he whispered between kisses.

"I love you too."

But a moment later I pulled back, putting distance between us. "I need to say this, Julien. I've been horrible to you. Mistrusting, suspicious, downright mean . . ."

"Don't forget that you mocked my fear of flying," he added with a slight smirk.

"Oh, God! Yes, even that. I'm horrible!"

"No, you are not horrible. You are practical and analytical, and you don't like to admit when you are wrong."

"And dishonest," I added. "I wasn't honest with you, not about the wine or how I met Georges, or even about Henri. I thought Henri loved me, that we had a future together. I didn't want to admit what a fool I'd been, to admit my failure in relationships. And I was afraid I'd make the same mistake with you."

"That is understandable, but it's in the past," he said, taking a step toward me.

I put my hands up. "No. Wait. I'm not finished. I was wrong about your mother. She *is* the girl in the picture, just like you said. I didn't want to believe it! But it's true!"

"I knew it," he said, nodding. "She has always been so secretive about her past. There was a reason for it."

"Well, even when she told me, I needed proof. And she was able to give it to me. I'm afraid I don't have such faith as you have, such belief in miracles. I mean, look at the two of us. We're not really meant to be together. We're so different from each other, and . . ."

"And you overthink everything," he said, putting his arms around me. "You must embrace what makes you happy, no matter how many complications are involved."

"That's what your mother said too. I just don't want to fail again. But there are no guarantees in life. So, I need to be honest. Everything I need to tell you . . ."

"Is no longer necessary," he said, covering my mouth with his.

CHAPTER FORTY-SEVEN

A FORFEITURE

JULIEN CARRIED THE PIERRE CARDIN LEATHER BRIEFCASE I had bought him to the courthouse. He wore a dark gray suit and burgundy tie. Draped across his arm was a black robe, which he would put on once inside the Palais de Justice.

I met him in the courtyard that led from an arched gateway to the steps of the building. I was dressed in my pilot's uniform with my hair tucked into a bun under my cap, which I felt lent a certain authority and trust, and frankly, I needed the judge to believe my story.

"I'm a bit nervous," Julien confessed.

I straightened the matching burgundy handkerchief sticking out of his pocket. "You have nothing to worry about. It's only a one-hundred-and-twenty-five-thousand-dollar bottle of wine we're arguing about."

"You have a grim sense of humor," he remarked.

"I do my best," I said, taking his arm.

"Let us hope I don't get disbarred for what I am about to do."

"Could that happen?" I asked.

Julien raised his eyebrows and nodded. "It's possible. At least there isn't a jury, as this is a civil law system. So, there is only the judge to worry about."

"I'm not worried in the least," I lied. It was a bright, sunny day, and I took that as a good sign. But as we entered the domed hallways that had stood for centuries, our shoes echoing off the tiled floors, I had second thoughts. I was American, and Henri was French. And I was a woman. That might make a difference.

Perhaps I shouldn't have asked Julien to do this.

I waited while Julien went to put on his robe. Then we walked down the long corridors. Henri was waiting in the hall outside the chamber, and with him was a thin, model-like woman with long blond hair wearing a short dress. She held a cigarette between her fingers, the long kind that French women preferred.

Henri was trying to intimidate me. Of course he was.

I wouldn't sink to his level. I put on a fake smile. "Henri. This is my solicitor, Julien Pelletier."

"We met once before," Julien said, reaching out his hand. Henri reluctantly shook it, a guarded look on his face. "My solicitor will be here shortly."

"Oh. So, this isn't your lawyer? Or your *wife*?" I motioned to the blonde, a surprised look on my face.

The blonde turned to Henri. "Mais c'est quoi *wife*?"

Henri's cheeks reddened, and he shook his head. "Un malentendu."

I wanted to add that the only misunderstanding was the fact that he had lied about being married. But before I could say more, his lawyer had arrived and introductions were made, and I found out that the woman was named Mademoiselle Legrand. She was a "friend."

The chamber doors opened, and we were ushered into a beautiful room, one with white sculptured ceilings, ornate chandeliers, and tapestries on the walls. Only the French would have such beautiful courtrooms. French provincial furniture made it seem more like a conference room than a courtroom, although there was a long bench where the judges normally sat.

There was one judge there today, a distinguished-looking man whose dark hair was peppered with gray streaks. He wore a white fur piece over his black robe. He had a no-nonsense look on his face, and I wasn't sure if that would play out well for me. I was certain Henri would lie and say he accidentally left the bottle at my apartment after I seduced him into having sex. He'd make me out to be the wicked American, one who had accused him of breaking into her apartment.

I hoped he wouldn't have a chance to speak at all. The court clerk, who sat below the judge, also wore a black robe.

Henri's attorney spoke rapid French during the introduction, and I looked helplessly at Julien.

Julien raised his hand. "Monsieur le président, as Mademoiselle Montgomery is American and not fluent in French, I will be translating in English."

The judge nodded. "That is acceptable."

Henri's attorney clicked his tongue and shot me a condescending glance. "Of course, for the *American*, we must accommodate her."

I clenched my hands, feeling a tightness in my chest the way I did when a heavy line of thunderstorms popped up unexpectedly while flying.

This wasn't going well. I'd already been deemed the *American*, the outsider who couldn't speak the language. Of course, any misunderstanding about the wine bottle would be blamed on my lack of fluency.

I took a steadying breath and flashed him an appreciative smile.

As the judge proceeded to read a copy of the mise en demeure, Julien interrupted him.

"Monsieur le président, although the wine was a gift from the plaintiff, free and clear of any conditions, Mademoiselle Montgomery has decided to forfeit the bottle of wine."

The judge looked surprised. "Am I to understand that you are willingly giving up your rights to this bottle?"

I nodded. "Oui."

Henri let out a small cry of victory and patted his lawyer on the back.

"Is that acceptable to you?" the judge asked Henri.

"Absolutely! I am glad you have made this honorable decision, Charlotte." Henri suddenly was all smiles and graciousness.

"Then it is agreed," the judge said. "I wish all cases were this easy."

It was only when Julien opened his briefcase and produced the bottle of wine that Henri objected.

"What is that?" he asked, his smile now faltering.

"It is the bottle of wine you gave Mademoiselle Montgomery, is it not?" Julien asked, holding up the bottle that Georges Lapointe had given me during my visit to his winery, a bottle with the Viner wine label that he'd found in the cellar. An exact replica of the bottle Henri had left with me.

The color drained from Henri's face. "But that isn't . . . I thought . . ."

"I'm sorry I told you I drank it," I said, my voice dripping with honey. "I should have been honest with you from the start. But it was a gift, and I was angry. I was reluctant to let it go."

"That is not the right bottle," Henri objected.

"I have the list from the Hôtel Drouot that states the bottles he purchased," Julien said, producing the paper and handing it to the judge, along with another copy for Henri's attorney. "This was one of the bottles listed. He has two of the others, and two were opened and consumed. They are all accounted for."

"This is all correct," the judge affirmed. "What is it you object to?"

"I . . . I . . . but I thought it was a different bottle. It was supposed to be a rare bottle of wine." He peeled the label, as if there was something underneath. There was nothing, of course, and both the judge and his attorney stared at him as if he'd just lopped off his own ear.

"I don't understand," he said, looking up at me. "How did you—" but he didn't finish because his attorney cut him off.

"We accept the wine," he said, turning to his client. "And I hope you are prepared to pay me for my wasted time."

Henri's face turned a lighter shade of pale.

AFTERWARD, I TREATED MY SOLICITOR TO LUNCH AT LA PEtite Chaise, one of the oldest restaurants in Paris. We climbed the small wooden staircase to the romantic restaurant situated above the street in the most romantic city in the world. Accordion music played in the background, and we ordered the house special: onion soup and escargot.

"You were remarkable," I told Julien, smiling. "And Henri's expression was everything I'd hoped for."

He raised his glass of wine to mine. "It was your brilliant idea to switch the bottles. That wasn't entirely legal, you know."

"Maybe not, but he got what he deserved."

"Oui. We could have fought for my mother's right to the bottle, but honestly, I enjoyed this way better. But perhaps I should quit while I'm ahead. Before I'm disbarred."

He sighed. "I do miss it. Did I tell you that I'm now taking over the business side of the company, while my mother devotes more time to the plants? We just need to hire her an assistant."

"I happen to know someone who is looking for an internship in both aspects. I spoke with Georges Lapointe. His son is interested in exploring other wineries, seeing how they work, so that when he does take over his father's business, he'll have more experience. I also suspect he wouldn't mind time away from being under his father's constant scrutiny, and he'd love living closer to Paris. You could hire him to assist you and Élisabeth."

"Can we afford him?"

"You can if your mother sells that bottle of wine," I said. "I think it's time she traded in her inheritance. And with his help, you'd have more time to practice law."

"Wouldn't that look a bit suspicious? Your solicitor's mother selling an expensive bottle of wine?"

"If anyone asks why I got an appraisal, I'll simply say that I was checking on the price for her. She is the rightful owner, after all."

"You're very generous. You could have kept the wine, you know. It is legally yours. No one would have faulted you for it."

"Legally, yes. But not morally. Your grandfather hid that wine so that your mother would have a future. And now she has her birthright. After all she lost in the war, it was right that the bottle was returned to her."

"It is a story our family will never forget."

"Neither will I."

He reached across the table and took my right hand, fingering it between his. "So, you are planning two jobs for me while you're flying across the globe? Is this so I won't have time to look at other women?"

I reached over and ran my other hand along his cheekbones, thinking they weren't too soft and they held just the right amount of ruggedness. That unlike another Frenchman I knew, Julien's only mistress would be the vineyard, and I was grateful for that. And once again I was reminded of my grandfather, but in a good way this time. I remembered how he was a "wounded soul," as my dad would often say, and how I had wished I could ease his pain.

I couldn't buy Grandpa's vineyard. Dad had sold it to a young couple who had high hopes of making it successful. I hoped that easing Élisabeth's pain was enough reparation for whatever sins my grandfather carried back from the war. Because the memory of war was painful enough.

I had promised myself that from now on I would be who I was meant to be: a strong, kick-ass woman, one who wasn't afraid to tell Julien the truth. And it was time to start now.

"Actually, I thought that if you had an assistant, you could come with me to visit my parents in Texas."

His eyes widened in panic. "You're not suggesting I fly?"

I flashed him a teasing smile. "Sooner or later, I will have you on my flight. You may as well admit defeat."

He sighed. "I knew you were trouble the moment I saw you."

"I'm glad I haven't let you down," I said, and kissed him.

CHAPTER FORTY-EIGHT

WHERE IT ALL BEGAN

MARTINE/ÉLISABETH

1991

NEAR ALBERTINE, FRANCE

IT HAD BEEN ALMOST FIFTY YEARS SINCE SHE'D BEEN HERE. The lane leading from the road was shorter than she remembered, and the house seemed smaller. Had it always had that peak at the top? Memory had a way of playing tricks on a person. But the way the valley dipped and rolled, the manicured rows of vines that sculpted the land. They were the same.

Georges's oversized hand took hers and guided her inside, as if she were royalty, followed by her son and Charlotte. She had assured Mr. Lapointe that she wasn't interested in obtaining the land that once belonged to her father. She had her own vineyard and winery, and besides, she had received the reparation she felt entitled to: the bottle of wine. Along with that came relief from the guilt she had carried since she was a child, the guilt of losing her inheritance when she promised her papa she wouldn't let it go.

In the process of being reunited with it, she had also found a new friend, and perhaps a future daughter-in-law. Her only regret was that Gabriel wasn't alive to meet her, and to see this place where she was born and lived before the war. She hadn't even remembered where it was located; she'd only known it was somewhere south of Dijon, a place she'd long ago remembered visiting.

She had often felt that her father was looking out for her. She believed that Gabriel was sent to her as a gift, much like Sister Ada, who she learned to call her maman. And with Gabriel came the vineyard, where she found purpose and solace. And a life and a family.

She stopped in the parlor. A sharp ache, like she'd brushed up against the past, triggering those same feelings she'd long since put behind her. The room felt the same, even though it was decorated differently. She turned and took in the room, letting in a flood of memories. She could see her father standing over there by the table, praying over the bread, smiling down on her.

And off to the side of the kitchen was her bedroom. She walked toward it, feeling like a little girl again, the wooden floor creaking under her feet in a familiar way as if it remembered her too.

Her bed was gone. Of course, it was gone. But over in the corner something caught her eye. The armoire. The one she'd hidden in all those years ago, faded white and still decorated with pink swirls. It looked the same, as though the years hadn't touched it. She walked to it and ran her hand over the raised panel doors.

She remembered her father's last caress of her face. His reassuring smile. And her fear as the German searched for her, swiping his glove inches from her head.

"May I open this?" she asked.

"Of course," Georges replied.

She opened it up. It was filled with assorted jackets, boots, hats, and a lace tablecloth.

"My apologies for the mess," Georges said, looking embarrassed.

She knelt down and put her hands inside the armoire. "How did I fit in there?" she asked, incredulous that she hadn't been discovered by the Germans when they opened it. So many miracles that had kept her alive. Had she lived in a way that honored the life she'd been given?

She hoped so.

Next week the wine would go on sale at Hôtel Drouot. The starting bid would be $150,000, the highest opening bid ever for a bottle of wine.

It happened at just the right time, when they were in danger of losing their business.

Papa was still looking out for her. Just as he had when he hid her in the armoire. And when she was lost in Paris at the Hôtel Drouot and Sister Ada had rescued her. Just as he had in guiding her to Gabriel.

She closed her eyes and whispered her thanks, then stood and made her way outside.

AUTHOR'S NOTE

LIKE ALL AUTHORS, I READ A GREAT DEAL, AND MY FAVORITE read is historical fiction. Also, like other authors, I pick up bits and pieces of interesting information in my reading, and sometimes it ends up as a book idea in my head that sits for years until I finally pay attention to it. The story of Martine was such an idea, as well as the bottle of wine that was her inheritance. I originally wanted to title my book *On the Steps of Hôtel Drouot*, except that Hôtel Drouot has no steps outside, and *On the Doorstep of Hôtel Drouot* didn't sound right. Also, I'm not that great at titles.

Hôtel Drouot is the oldest and largest auction house in the world. It sits in the 9th arrondissement of Paris. Two thousand auctions take place there in a year, and two million items exchange hands. Rare finds are sometimes discovered among its garage sale–like atmosphere. The red Moroccan leather portfolio mentioned in the story was auctioned off for $500 and held the bill of sale for the Louisiana Purchase. It's worth at least $50,000 now.

During the Nazi Occupation, Hôtel Drouot sold works of art and other antiques stolen from the French Jews. Jewish auctioneers and buyers were barred from Hôtel Drouot during the Occupation. Although many valuable bottles of wine are now sold there, during the war they were simply stolen.

The book *Wine and War* describes how Germans looted wine cellars and requisitioned wineries and vineyards. German officers would drive their military trucks directly up to the vineyards and haul away massive amounts of wine. Even though Hitler didn't care for the taste of wine, he amassed one of the largest wine cellars and collections of alcohol in the world in his "Eagle's Nest" mountain villa, including a half million bottles of champagne.

Some winemakers hid their best wines behind fake walls. Others used false labels to disguise their most valuable wines:

> *When Göring ordered several cases of wine from Château Mouton-Rothschild, he was sent bottles of ordinary wine with the Mouton labels glued on. (Kladstrup, Don and Petie.* Wine and War: The French, the Nazis, and the Battle for France's Greatest Treasure. *New York: Crown, 2002.)*

Like others in the French Resistance, winemakers did their best to undermine the German army and save France's most treasured resource.

The Roberge wine from Burgundy is a fictional one that I created for this story. But for reference, in 2018 a bottle of 1945 Romanée-Conti, a red Burgundy wine from Côte de Nuits, sold for $558,000.

ACKNOWLEDGMENTS

FINE WINE IS ATTAINED THROUGH SKILL, DETERMINATION, and a bit of luck. The same is true with the creation of a book. And both pass through many hands in the process. My book owes much to the support of friends, family, fellow writers, and a committed publishing team.

My agent, Marly Rusoff, was not open to queries, but my story that takes place in a French vineyard, much like the one her beloved husband grew up in, touched her heart, and she championed my story to publication.

My editor, Sara Nelson, is a true connoisseur of books and words (read her book *So Many Books, So Little Time: A Year of Passionate Reading*). Her intuitive and knowledgeable guidance is a gift every writer would love. Thank you to everyone at HarperCollins, including Edie Astley, Suzette Lam, Joanne O'Neill, Rachel Molland, and Megan Looney. Thank you also to Kathleen Schmidt of KMS Public Relations.

I had to wait until after COVID-19 to visit France and do further research at the settings where my book takes place. My travel companions Amy O'Connell, Brea Ellsworth, Kasia Ellsworth, and Erin Brownell kept me on task and made sure I visited every location—without them I would have gotten lost on day one.

My friend Joyce Rosenbery connected me with Michelle Greer, a pilot and captain who has been flying since the 1980s. She kindly made recommendations about flying and women pilots that helped me immensely. Any errors are my own.

During the course of writing this book, I turned to two freelance editors: Alexandra Shelley and Anne Brewer. I know my book sold because of their thoughtful and detailed editing.

My writing groups not only support my writing, but they hold me to high standards and give excellent feedback. Thank you to Janet Graber, Nolan Zavoral, Eileen Beha, Pat Schroeder, Jane O'Reilly, Ricki Thompson, Susan Latta, Aimee Bissonette, and Carol Iverson. You make me a better writer and I'm so grateful to you all.

ABOUT THE AUTHOR

LORETTA ELLSWORTH IS THE AUTHOR OF FIVE NOVELS FOR younger readers: *The Shrouding Woman*; *In Search of Mockingbird*; *In a Heartbeat*; *Unforgettable*; and *Tangle-Knot*; as well as an adult historical novel, *Stars Over Clear Lake*. Her books have received many awards including Teen's Top Ten, Midwest Booksellers' Choice Award, *Kirkus Reviews* Critic's Pick, the International Reading Association Notable Book, the Cooperative Children's Book Center Choice Book, Northeastern Minnesota Book Award, and the Charlotte Award, to name a few.